Aimee and the
Bear

TOBY STONE

First published in Great Britain in 2013 by Hic Dragones
PO Box 377
Manchester M8 2DE
www.hic-dragones.co.uk

Cover design by Rob Shedwick

A CIP catalogue reference for this book is available from the British
Library.

ISBN 978-0-9570292-5-5

Designed and typeset by Hic Dragones
Printed and bound by CPI Group (UK) Ltd, Croydon, CR0 4YY

Part 1

Chapter 1

AMY TRIED TO TURN the pages of the photo album, but her olive fingers were as rigid as Pinocchio's, and she couldn't let go of the first page.

Pinocchio wasn't on the TV. Amy didn't go in for Disney. Instead, she was playing The Texas Chain Saw Massacre on DVD. Amy had seen it many times, over her eight years, and she put it on when she had to do something that frightened her, like sneaking a look at the picture of her mother. She wasn't supposed to pry, and the film's soundtrack comforted her fretting heart in the same way as cuddling a teddy bear would a normal child. Amy cuddled a teddy as well, but it wasn't a normal bear.

She was on her knees in front of the album and hidden in the shadow of the settee. The knees, as well as the rest of her body, were covered by bunched, over-big dungarees. The pictures the album contained were of Amy, enough to keep

Nan happy, but there were more blank spaces (empty flaps of plastic like pierced blisters) than filled slips.

Amy glanced at the lounge door, and back down to the page.

The first Polaroid photo had been scissored in half. Amy often stared at it, prodding the crescent-moon white edges where it had been halved, as though she could make it whole again. There were blank spaces in her memories, like the one where her father had stood, bending over the chair to kiss her baby-fatted cheek. After the scissoring, all that was left of him was a nose.

"Cut off his nose to spite his face," her mum would say, when her voice slurred. Then she would cackle, and have a good cry, and say, "Serves him right—going off with that witch."

Amy believed her, as much as she believed in witches, which was entirely.

On the white space at the base of the Polaroid was written the word **Amy** in the scratched-out, heavy hand of her mother. To its left was a scribbling of ink in the same black as the **Amy**. It'd taken a long time for Amy to connect the dots and the curves and the grey lines that were barely visible beneath this scribble.

Little Aimee, 1993, it had read, in pencil soft as a moonbeam in a make-believe wood.

"Bloody stupid bastard," Mum would say. "Couldn't even spell your name. Eh? Bloody, stupid, stupid bastard." Then she would say a whole lot more, particularly if she had been listening to Celine Dion again.

Her dad's nose was the colour of Amy's finger, off-white in the way dirt is. Her little brother, Aidan, was the spit of their mother—white in the way her spit was, in the way her skin was, in the way her hair was. Sometimes, Mum would wonder aloud how Amy could be hers. She never did this with Aidan; he was her little prince, clear as water, he was hers and always would be.

"Things happen hereabouts, they don't tell about," said Amy, along with the man on the TV. She knew all of the lines from Texas Chain Saw Massacre, including the screaming.

She was a doll, her mother. Here, in this photo, her blonde hair was in a perfect bob as though each strand had been sewn in, her alabaster skin a shock to the rough colours of the old Polaroid, her cheeks a spasm of rouge, her lips red, swollen, bee-stung, and quick as a wasp to sting. She looked less a mother with her firstborn than a favourite doll positioned so as to hold an unwanted wooden toy. A doll, like the one in that film Uncle Chris liked to watch... Bride of Chucky, that was it. For a long time that film had scared her, until Amy was old enough to realise the toy wasn't her mother.

In the Polaroid, there were tears in her mother's eyes. She said she had cried for three weeks after Amy's birth. She said she would have cried for longer, if she'd known what the child would cost her, and she *was* talking about the bloody money. The tears had given her eyes a glaze, and they were hard, in the picture, and staring away from Amy, past the paisley curtains and out of the window. In all of the photos, they stared the same way.

Amy didn't blame her for looking away. She avoided the mirror.

On the television, a chainsaw hacked into life, a woman screamed. Amy whispered, "Nooooooooo. Pleeeeeeeesssse—" to brace herself and placed a hand on the Polaroid.

She took care not to touch her own face. Amy didn't trust it. It had the look of a wooden mask pulled over a hole, with a scream that had gone digging for its tonsils and fat, frozen cheeks. The face didn't look real but more like how she imagined a golem would look, or a changeling.

Pinocchio, thought Amy.

She didn't like that story. It didn't seem very real, but something silly children would believe in. The toymaker should have been able to make his toys be real. It wasn't hard, it really wasn't, especially when it came to teddy bears.

Amy glanced up at the window above her, distracted by a car, the wind, a knock, her fear. She was unsure which. The teddy on her lap was named Barney, and she cuddled him to her chin. She waited, but there was nothing.

Staring, head still, she departed from the film's script, and mouthed, "Aimee," and looked back to the picture. "Aimee," she said again, out loud, making it last... tasting it. She tried it, as she would try the different flavours of Fruit Pastilles, rolling it around her tongue and teeth. "Ay-muh-eh," she said. Or, "Ah-muh-ee." She liked it best as, "Ay-m-ay." Though she didn't know the term 'symmetry' at this stage of her Maths education, she knew it when she saw it (or heard it, in this case), and it pleased her.

She couldn't leave this Polaroid alone.

"Mum," she whispered.

She took the teddy bear's paw and it gave her a pull so small it may not have happened at all.

"Mum," she said, louder.

There was a rush of air that had the sound of a sneeze, but backwards.

She was falling into the photo.

"Mummy," she said in the photograph, from beside the chair.

Of her father there was no sign, not even a nose. When she'd first found the nose in the frame, she'd travelled Here, to the photo, searching for the other end of its strong brown bridge. Searching for his cheeks, for his eyes, for him. But he was missing: a mangled hole in This Place, like those in the corridors of Alien. Her mother had said he was "long gone, like a fart in the bloody wind". But Amy couldn't smell him. He had never come back, neither Here nor There, and she didn't know why. The whole thing was incomprehensible to the little girl.

"Mummy," she repeated.

The picture wasn't unmoving anymore, not from the inside of it, and 'Mummy' jerked and twisted, her shoulders, neck and lips instinctive as any predator. Her mother had never liked being called this, at least not by Amy. This Mum was younger (and looked more fragile) than the mother Amy knew. Behind her, where her father used to stand, stood a large brown bear.

"Smile at me. Please Mum," said the little girl. "Tell me you think I'm pretty."

"What?" said the mother in the picture. "Who the bloody hell are you?"

In this Place, and Places like it, she wasn't called Amy: her name was Aimee. She didn't tell her mother this. Instead, she said, "Mum, tell me you think I'm pretty."

The bear made a face—a growl without a sound. It shushed Aimee with its longest claw, holding it before its snout, and backed away, shuffling behind the curtains, which were paisley and daisies. The bear pulled the thin fabric across as much of its body as it was able: a leg, an arm, a paw.

"I'm not your fucking mummy! What are you doing in my house?" Aimee's younger mum shouted at her.

The baby in her mother's lap began to cry. There was something listless in the posture of its head, like a lollipop that had been dropped down the side of a sofa.

"Tell me you think I'm beautiful," Aimee said, unheard beneath the wailing of her younger self.

The curtain caught on the bear's claws and ripped. Her mum turned, unseating the baby, who slid against the arm of the chair.

"Oh my God," said her mother, biting her bee-stung lips.

"Uh... hello," said the large brown bear. It extended a paw as if to shake the woman's hand, then seemed to think better of the action and withdrew it.

Her mother ignored the baby as it tried to right itself.

"Oh my God," said her mother again.

This was too much. Aimee walked to the bear, took his uncovered paw and came back out of the photograph.

Returned to stillness, her mother was no longer looking out of the window, but at the curtains. Her young, pretty, blonde face was turned away from the lens. Half a bear was visible in the background, failing to hide behind a daisy on a curtain. Amy blanched and shut the album. She would have to return and change the photograph back before Nan came round.

ONCE UPON A TIME, I was an average old teddy bear. I owned a little boy with blond hair and green eyes as big as my world. When he laughed, his dimples went deep into me. He would cuddle me, in secret, and I would cuddle him back. There was nothing he couldn't survive with me by his side. I'm a battered brown bear, and the adults didn't suspect me.

One day, they took him away, to the room next to ours. I couldn't reach out to him. I was only a teddy bear then, and had to listen as he screamed out my name. This time, they went too far to hide it from the teachers, from the social services, from the police. On that day, I stopped being a teddy bear and became a real bear.

AMY'S FINGERS recoiled as she lit the hob with the yellow lighter. Her mum tutted. It had taken seven clicks to light it, each taking her nearer to where the fire would bloom, with her mother tutting on every click. To Amy, her tuts had the sound of sparks.

The blue fire looped over the congealed hob like Mr Him's greasy comb-over. Seven of the seventeen flames were missing, Amy had counted them, and the fire tended sideways. Amy eclipsed it with the full round face of the frying pan, mooning the metal with an egg. She cracked in one more. Her mum watched her from behind a cigarette. The fridge hummed at her back to the tune of Yesterday, Amy thought. She had learnt it in music class in her Day School.

"Too hot," her mum said.

"Yes Mum," Amy said.

Amy didn't mind when her mother watched her, because when Mum was watching her, she wasn't watching *him*.

Amy turned the knob. Ten flames became seven, all the same colour blue as the dungarees she wore. Her mother looked pale, bleeding into her background. She was on her time of the month and, at these times, she seemed to fade from this world and into another. Amy knew how that felt.

The fridge was old and lined. Her mother's doll face was now the same. They couldn't possibly be laughter lines. Amy blamed the cigarettes. The one her mother smoked now went red at its end as she sucked, as if it were gaining energy, as if it were sucking the life from her, rather than her from it. The grill was turning the same colour as the end of the fag. Amy slid the bread in. The yolks were bubbling, but were still flat. They looked, to Amy's eyes, like her mother's breasts, at least from this distance. Up close, her mother's breasts were bigger. The plastic cups of the eggs' packaging had **Value** printed on them.

"Nearly done, Mum," Amy said.

"Suppose I'd better get ready, eh love?" Her mother sucked the cigarette, then stubbed it out, fingers curled as her lips had been. The cigarette sighed.

"Yes Mum," said Amy.

Amy fish-sliced the eggs onto the buttered toast, having already set the latter on the plate, and placed the whole thing on the square wooden table. Her mum sat, wearing a black top that got lower with every year she worked the floor at the bingo hall, wearing perfume that also intensified but could never hide the odour of tobacco. She smelt like the flowers at Grandad's cremation.

Amy was remembering her mother's hissed words, that day, "good riddance to the sick old bastard", and didn't notice that the knife-scraping had ceased. Her mother picked up the remaining second egg, staring at it. A line of uncooked white drooled onto the plate. Mum was still chewing what was left of the first egg, but her lips were stretching on one side—her right—as though, alongside the dinner, she were being force-fed a Snickers. If it was a sneer, it was a sneer that didn't know when to stop. Her mum spat white petals and yellow flecks onto the plate. It looked as if her daughter had been slipping her daisies.

"Bring the rubbish," she said, around a mouthful of disgust.

"What Mum?"

The words were muffled.

Quieter, but clearer, "*Bring the rubbish.*"

With an effort of her young frame, she hefted the bin and, scraping it only slightly on the lino, pitched it up beside the small wooden Argos table.

Her mother pulled open the front flap of her blue dungarees and deposited what remained of the meal into its pouch, saying, "Not the bin. I meant you."

Then, as Amy felt the second yolk break and ooze against her crotch, her mother began to yell.

BARNEY'S SCALP SMELT of other children's tears. Amy held the teddy bear about his abdomen. His pelt was coarse against her cheek—rough as the carpet at her bare feet. Both had the texture of the skin at the end of her nose.

She cried onto Barney in dribbles.

Her knees were covered by the blue pool of ill-fitting dungarees. Mum bought all Amy's clothes at car boot sales, or garage sales, or school fêtes, the last of which was the worst for Amy, because her classmates then knew what she wore when she wasn't in uniform. Mum didn't like to waste pennies on clothes when all Amy did was ruin them, as she had now, by cooking the eggs badly.

The smell of Barney's previous owners spiked her nostrils, skewering through the mucus and her thoughts only when she sobbed. The yolk was caked against the inside of her thighs and the lower reach of her belly, like dried wee but thicker.

"They're not cooked! Are you trying to poison me? Are you?" whispered Amy into the teddy's ear. Her lips traced out imprints of gunge. "Are you trying to give me Sam and Ella? Eh? You little witch." Amy had not misheard her mother here. For Mum, 'witch' was the worst thing she could call her daughter, and she did so regularly. "Awww—" Amy's lips widened on their right in a sneer. Her jaw ached and felt like it just might bite Barney's round, soft lobe. Instead, she hissed into it, "You're too special for cooking, aren't you? Too special to be my daughter by a long bloody mile."

Amy burrowed her head into Barney's, as though she were a rabbit going to ground. At her crossed knees, beneath the dark stain where she was soiled by eggs, a Winnie the Pooh book lay open, pinned to the carpet by her right palm. The skin of

Amy's olive arm looked like the bark of a root, gnarled and dirty.

Playing with the fairies, thought Amy, for no reason other than it had been drummed into her.

Her fingers were in the 100 Aker Wood. Tears fell on Eeyore's field, flooding it.

"Typical," said Eeyore, in her mind.

The tears slowed until they seemed to move back and up. If she could've seen it, there was a look of determination in the withdrawal of her chin, in the dwindling gaps between her teeth. She hugged Barney tight, snuggling her cheek against his. They would travel together. She could smell the other worlds again. They would travel together.

Amy closed her eyes. There was no more moisture to squeeze out, only everything that she could see: the white of her cupboard, the Michael Jackson picture over her bed, the books on flora and fauna and legends, the yellow wallpapered wall.

"Barnaby, Barnaby, take me away," she whispered, calling her bear by his real name.

She took him by the paw, and he seemed to pull in return. The action was so slight, so unlikely, that in all probability it didn't happen at all. Still, there was a sensation like being pulled through the carpet and through a crack in the floorboards below it.

She coughed, a singular cancer kind of hack, wet and threaded with threat. She opened her eyes.

THE BEDROOM HAD BEEN taken away and replaced. As had Amy. She felt fresh as the odour of green she could now smell. There was grass beneath her feet and it was dense, each leaf piled one over the other and overlapping to give the impression of richness even through the hardness of her red shoes. Trees clustered nearby and below one, which stood wide and proud and almost smug, sat a small wooden hut. The hut slouched in its sitting position and was slightly obscured by the sign before it. The sign said, in ramshackle writing: *Pooh Bears House*. As in the Other Places, here Amy was called Aimee.

"Oh, Aimee, isn't that cute?" said Barnaby, who stood beside her. "He forgot the apostrophe. Why, that means he's a bit silly, a bit forgetful, but a jolly nice old bear! It doesn't mean he's thick at all."

Aimee let go of his paw. "Don't be such a grumpy bear," she said.

"Are you saying I'm bloody well like him? A silly old grumpy bear? I could eat your head in one gulp. You know that, don't you girl?"

Aimee smiled. "Come on." She walked toward Pooh Bear's house. The sky above them was blue and unspecked. It made her think of Aidan's eyes.

"Oh God. Are we actually going to visit? He'll make me eat honey. No bloody raw meat for me, oh no. No fish. Just jars and jars of bloody honey. No wonder he's such a fat, boring—"

Aimee ignored him and started to skip. The lilac dress she wore in her dreams rustled as though the grass continued up to the straps at her slight, translucent shoulders. She couldn't smell eggs anymore.

Barnaby continued, "—and he never remembers anything you say. He's like a goldfish. Oh, there's a jar of honey!... I forgot it was there!... Oh, there's a jar of honey!... Idiot. I hope Piglet's there. Do you hear me, little girl? I hope Piglet's visiting. Do you have any apple sauce, little girl?"

I KNOW WHAT YOU'RE thinking.

I'm leading Amy on, taking her places that aren't real. Leading her up the garden path to play with fake fairies, round and round with teddy bears.

Giving her false hope.

But no hope is false, not in the dark of a child's room where there are fingers that can be felt but can't be seen. Besides, you're reading the words of a talking bear. What kind of state is your mind in? And does it have princesses, witches, those flying monkeys? I wouldn't answer these questions, if I were you. You'd be talking to a teddy bear, and what would that say?

CHRIS LAUGHED AND looked at Amy. Their eyes and smiles met then parted. Amy liked Uncle Chris when he was Christopher and not Step-Dad, which he changed into when

Mum was home, becoming as thin-skinned and dented as the aluminium can in his fingers. She had that effect on men, Mum. She was at the bingo hall, working. Earning, she would say to Uncle Chris, before saying a whole lot more about how he wasn't.

Amy shifted, but felt comfortable in the wide expanse of the peach settee, camouflaged like a mosquito on tepid water. Her pyjamas were little longer than a mini-skirt that carried on going up, and skin-coloured, plastered to Amy by the greasiness of both her body and her hair. Her mum had said she'd given up on making her clean, that she was naturally dirty. Most days, except Wednesdays, Amy went unbathed.

The house was warm. Christopher always turned the thermostat until it clicked when Mum was out, and allowed Amy to cuddle Barney in the lounge. He let Amy sit alone on the settee. Christopher never asked for a cuddle.

In the DVD player, Aliens played. All Christopher watched, when he wasn't watching Star Wars, were horror films: Dawn of The Dead, Day of the Dead, The Evil Dead, The Thing, The Omen, Labyrinth. Only the last gave her nightmares. Christopher hadn't warned her it was a true story. Amy imagined the infant Toby in the goblin's maze, and her thighs and neck goosebumped, going pale and cold as cuts of poultry. Her baby brother was upstairs sleeping. Bump by bump, her skin smoothed, calmed by Aidan's repose. He seemed safe— for now. It was in the night, when she was asleep, that Amy worried. Amy did a lot of worrying while she slept, and all she fretted about was how to stop what happened to her, happening to him.

"I love this bit. Ewww—" said Christopher, grinning at the girl. His eyes left her quickly, as they did whenever she wore her jammies.

Amy nodded and smiled briefly. Christopher loved everything, according to his mouth. He loved her mum to bits. He loved the kids to bits. He loved his life to bits. Occasionally, his eyes crumbled and washed away, all the more often when he'd been drinking.

Uncle Chris did not, according to Mum, watch his drink. Amy didn't understand why he would want to watch Stella, or stare at the rum he'd bought from Kwik Save. She guessed it was the same as Mum telling her to watch her mouth. Amy had tried and it made her dizzy. (Amy couldn't bear to look in the mirror, though that would have made the watching easier.) Still, those times were better than when Mum said she should wash her mouth out. Her mum bought cheap soap, and you could tell just by the taste.

Amy had seen Alien many times before, but not Aliens. The actors were in a room made of metal and glass jars in which were suspended the aliens. Christopher said something, and if Amy had heard she would've smiled, but her legs were jiggling like they did to make Mr Mann think she was desperate when she asked to go to the toilet.

She was distracted. The aliens were anaemic, misted by the saline in which they hung and vague like Amy's memories. They twitched in the same manner as her memories, from deep below the surface. An actor pushed his wide, cartoonish face towards the glass of the jar. The alien spurted towards him, quick as bodily fluids, liquid as intimacy, all folds of skin and pinks and beiges and plump ridges of flesh. It tried to graft onto his lips, greasing against the sheer glass.

"Gonna get a beer," said Uncle Chris, rising.

Left alone, Amy hugged her teddy bear tight enough to feel its innards pressing against hers. She didn't notice their feel, taking in nothing but the look of the alien's soft and pink flesh under its skinnish flaps. Instinctively, she reached for Barney's paw.

"WHAT THE HELL?" screamed Ripley.

She was bigger than Aimee remembered, and 3D. Lieutenant Ripley smelt of sweat and terror. There was a skittering sound.

Aimee had turned before she realised she was standing up and no longer sitting on a peach settee. Her shoed feet squeaked on the polished, saline-puddled floor.

Aimee looked down. A pair of red shoes stared back. The toes of them gleamed maliciously. The right one seemed to wink. She looked away, disconcerted. To the side of her, with all the awkwardness of an elephant in the room, stood a large brown bear.

"What the hell?" screamed Ripley. "A *bear?*" She looked like she wished she had a gun.

The skittering was closing in.

"Girl," said the bear. He extended a paw.

Aimee reached out. She turned her head, but left the shoes facing the way they had been. A pale form—the colour of mucus and looking like saliva on the move—sprang towards her head. A proboscis shot towards her open mouth, slicked even before it reached her small rose lips. In a spurt of terror and shock, her bladder opened.

Aimee's hand closed on the paw, and she was back on the settee in her pyjamas. She bit the insides of her cheeks until they bled. Her thighs were wet.

"EWWW... NASTY ALIENS, man." There was laughter—not on the film, but from Christopher. He returned to the room as Amy did from the film. The little girl's legs had stilled, as though she no longer needed the toilet. As he sat, Uncle Chris stopped laughing. "Jesus kid, why did you go and do *that?*" he said.

Amy stared at Uncle Chris. His lips were moving. They were less viscid than those of the alien, and they seemed unreal.

"Get up. Get up. Your mum'll be home soon." He was up, even if she wasn't. "Get some hot water on a bloody cloth and some washing-up liquid. For shit's sake, wake up and get a shift on girl." There was anger there or, perhaps, fear. "Put the bloody bear down!" He grabbed Barney and threw the teddy across the room. Barney rolled to a broken stop below the sweeping faux-brick fireplace, and lay staring at them with thick black eyes.

Christopher wrenched her up. She noticed the settee cushion was wet as she left it. It was darkened all over, a peach that had not so much been bruised as thoroughly beaten. Christopher's hand was rough on her wrist, but did not stay there. He left and returned, dripping blue cloth from his hand in a stalactite, and soap-whitened water from that.

"Bloody hell, child, I'll do it then." Christopher glared at her. He knelt and scrubbed at the urine on the cushion cover. "Go on and wash yourself off. Christ."

Amy walked away, legs stiff and apart like a stickman that had soiled itself. Her head was a round hollow. It was times like these that she wouldn't remember later. She grabbed Barney, walked to the door, and crabbed up the stairs to the bathroom. As she climbed, Amy heard Christopher's swearing and the exasperated spray of an air-freshener. Amy could hear it until she turned on the tap.

The bathroom was a cream colour that had mortified to grey, decorated with a wallpaper of small pale roses like the pages of a vast flower-pressing sketchbook. It smelt slightly of faeces and damp.

She stripped, ran the cold water not the hot, and washed between her legs, her lower belly, and her crotch. She soaked her pyjamas then wrung them like a line of rolled skin. Amy took them out of the bathroom and into her mother's room. She always tiptoed on this carpet. Amy hid her eyes with her palm as she walked past the single ceiling-high mirror that her mother used to dress herself and stare into. There used to be more mirrors on the wall. Now, there were only the bullet holes of sheared-off screws. The exposed wallpaper was yellow and paunchy, looking just as old as Nan's skin. At the top of the paper there was a large circular brown mark, a thumb-print that a giant might leave, if that giant loved shiny objects and had magpied the mirrors for its cave.

She stopped in front of a dresser. On its surface stood a wooden Russian doll. Inside that, Amy knew, stood another. She didn't like the Russian dolls. They were smiling but their eyes were blank, and that made the smiles seem false. She opened the dresser's top drawer, took her mum's hairdryer, plugged it in, blow-dried the pink cloth, put away the hairdryer, put the pyjamas back on and went to bed. They were still a little wet and she lay shivering, as if scared.

AMY'S LIFE WAS HER room at night. Her days felt vague, disembodied, the product of an overactive imagination. In the night, orange came in through the window, outlining the desk by the blinds, the cupboard, and the blinds themselves. Beyond the window, it outlined the city, the roofs and the tower blocks, as if the cityscape was trapped in the centre of a gigantic wine gum. Somebody in the street below was shouting, "Man U, Man U." Someone else shouted, "Not fucking here we're not. Try China." And another sang, "Blue Moon," even though it was cloudy.

At the foot of Amy's bed, Care Bears formed the edging of storm clouds, lit from the side by the colour of the landing light where it shafted into the room. Amy had left the door closed to discourage her mum. Her mum left it ajar when she came in and sat at the side of the bed, stroking Amy's head.

Her mother didn't say anything at times like these: no 'sweethearts', no 'loves', no stories. It was difficult to read in the dark, Amy supposed. Her mum stroked her hair, her cheek, her chest. There was a tension in her fingers. It was like being stroked by the dead. Amy tried to think about horror movies, about zombies, but it was difficult to think of anything but fingers.

She looked beyond her mother. On the wall above her bed was a picture of Michael Jackson, printed by the one printer at school, from the single PC. The ink must have been running out, because the skin you could see was yellow, rather than the black of the other pictures Amy had seen. His eyes, though, were kind, as though they knew exactly what she was going through. Her mother's face, bent over Amy, was all liquored breath like sweets sucked until gums rotted and black nothingness. Amy didn't stare. Her mum had told her not to stare. Amy turned her head left, towards the fuzzy, cosy corner of her bedroom, where her favourite teddy bear lay. Barney. Barnaby Bear. Barney looked at her as though he could barely stand to—askance—and rolled to one side.

He reached out his patched paw and placed it within Amy's outstretched hand. The teddy bear didn't smile. This was not a time for smiling.

Amy was glad her mum didn't spot the teddy bear move his arm and place it against her palm, but then, of course, her mum couldn't see, not through the linen and through Amy's chest and left shoulder. Besides, her mother was busy.

Barney winked at Amy, and the little girl thought as hard as she could about Another Place and felt herself falling.

THE NECK-LENGTH GRASS was grey, black where it crowded together. Indistinct, it webbed against her skin. There were insects below her—she could hear their carapaces chittering, their hard limbs chattering, their lips squeaking with pleas.

"Please, don't sit on me," they said.

Or just, "Please!"

She ignored their last wishes and sank back until she was sitting down. The sound the grass made was a sigh, like that of Aimee's soul when it upped and left her mum. The grubs crackled.

Aimee lay back, elbows behind her ears, hands gripping their joints. The stars above her hung in patterns that seemed to make sense, as if the bedroom ceiling was not still artexed to the corneas of Aimee's eyes or her mother's face sculpted into her brain. Aimee retrieved a hand and reached out, making shapes out of the stars with her forefinger. The stars and her finger distracted the girl from the moon that rose in the north. The Witch's Moon. It was as yellow as Chris's Stella.

Aimee had just finished pointing out the outline of a man's nose (the same nose she traced in the wallpaper beside her bed) when a roar batted the long grass. The slim waifs of the stems huddled together. The black of Aimee's pupils widened against the dark, pushing it back. Her breath made translucent speech bubbles of vapour that floated away. Her fear was nameless.

The roar came again. It sounded almost human and it shouldn't, Aimee couldn't help but think. Surely a creature that ate men shouldn't sound like them?

"Save me," whispered Aimee, sitting in a twitch.

At the edge of the swirling whirlpool circle of grass that was the Glade, there was a circumference of trees with a Witch's-Moon hue to them. Laburnum, thought Aimee. The thought registered but was quickly erased. A bear burst from the trees. Aimee stayed very still, and her lungs tried to join in. She closed her lips. You could never tell what kind of mood a man-eating bear might be in. It could be in a girl-eating mood. She shrank where she sat. The bear had an awkward way of moving, hunched on its right. Still, it came fast. The soil shivered at her rump. Then the bear was looming above her, its fur ruffled and annoyed, its teeth shredding the pattern of the stars.

"Come on, girl." The bear looked down at her, canyoning the moon with its snout. "It's time to go to school. We can't be here when the moon rises full."

IN THE DARKER hollows, Aimee could not see the wood but could feel the trees. Their fingers were all over her. Of anything, Aimee knew the touch of fingers. All rigid, unbending twigs. They ripped at her dress. Aimee loved her dress. She stumbled.

"Climb on my back, girl."

He lifted her up, pressing her face into the matted, warm fur at his back. It smelt like bark after a quick summer rain.

In Aimee's extensive experience, there were copses and there were forests. Then there were forests and there were woods. And then there were woods and there were real woods. This was the latter. The Latter Wood. It was vast and portentous, and it made the 100 Aker Wood seem as small—as thin—as a drawing on a page. In the Latter Wood, the podded tendrils of the laburnum trees were black and hollow and wraithlike, pawing at Aimee's face. In certain folds of land, the yellow moon poured down through the canopy. By its lunar light, Aimee could see faces in the trees. Most of these were ugly. During the day, the trees were dirty and yellow as, her mum would say, a Chinky's bum. Aimee didn't like yellow because Amy didn't like blondes. In Amy's class at the Day School, there was a girl called Lucy. Lucy was golden and their teacher, Mr Mann, loved her. Worse, her hair shone as if she were happy.

The trees were giving up their ghost, thinning out as the bear and Aimee approached the Night School.

"We're late for registration," said Barnaby, huffing in a you-should-have-got-dressed-quicker sort of way.

Aimee got down and stared up at Barnaby. In the diseased light he looked nothing like the teddy bear who slept in her bed.

"Thank you Barnaby. I'll tell the teachers it was my fault, I promise. You won't get into trouble."

Barnaby smiled wide enough, Aimee thought, to accidentally swallow a little girl.

"I'll go the rest of the way on my own," she said. "I'm safe here. The gates aren't far away."

"Yes." Barnaby cast his eyes at the heavens, and they caught a light Aimee couldn't see, glinting pure white in the black centre of their beads. In the south, beyond the growing moon and the canopy behind them, the Wishing, Wanting and Needing Stars would be twinkling at each other. "Have a good night."

Aimee didn't answer. She was walking away, her delicate, truncated stride (as though she dared not open her legs too wide) picking its way over snaggle-toothed thorns and splattering, secretive brooks.

Aimee stopped, looking up. She could see the Night School gates. They were thin, filigree, magical, iron and tall. She couldn't see their tops, nor the gargoyles who sat, discomforted, on their spikes. They had to be high, to keep out the Witch on her broomstick. Aimee stared beyond them to the moon, which seemed caught between their barbs. It bled moonshine and the lunar curve went on beyond sight, like a breast to a newborn's eye.

"Cold as a witch's tit," said Aimee, her breath floating away in a haze. It was the kind of thing her mother would say, which Aimee thought was strange, because her mum's breasts were not cold at all. What Aimee did not think strange, what both Aimee and Amy thought entirely natural, was that, in this world, her mother was the Witch. Glancing skyward, her skin bumping as if it had a thousand moons to rise, Aimee ran to the gates and, when they finally opened, through them.

AT THE END OF THE night, the bear took Aimee's hand, and Amy fell upwards into her bed. Facing the artexed ceiling, Amy opened her eyes and breathed, taking in the unwashed towel on the radiator, the odour of her mother on the linen, the smell of alcohol-slathered fingers on her chest and belly. The morning light made yellow yawns on the wall. She was plain eight-year-old Amy again, and the waking knowledge of it left her feeling ugly. Her pyjamas formed a second skin, sweated to her first as though she'd been running.

Now that Barney was no longer holding her hand, she recoiled her fingers, limbering them in, bringing them up to the bridge of her nose. She loved her nose. Mum said she didn't get it from her side of the family: too coloured, too obvious, and good for nothing other than smelling—just like, she said, Amy. It was her father's nose. Her cheeks beside it were sallow, deflated from any untoward expectation, and had none of the baby fat of Aimee's. The twilight-lilac dress and Dorothy-red shoes were gone, vanished into the thick air of the bedroom.

Amy rolled back to face Barney. Behind his head the thin skinnish wallpaper was scarred by the seventies floral design beneath it. The original lining made white and broken kiss marks on the paper's epidermis—the mouths of monsters trying to get through from another world. Of anyone, Amy knew other worlds were back there, clustered close, leaning in.

The breathing of them was audible when Amy pressed an ear to the wall. She hoped the monsters wouldn't get through.

In the shadowed corner of the bed where she had sequestered him, Barney sat, tilting, angled, it seemed, to fall. In this world, his face had expression but just one, and Amy could only tell what the teddy was feeling by cuddling him. Only by holding his paw could she travel to Other Places and ask him outright.

She cuddled him now, squirming out lines of her limbs through the bed linen, careful not to hold hands. It was nearly time for Day School, and no time for travelling to the places she had been. Amy rubbed her feet together, not so much massaging in warmth as making bodily contact. She made monkey hands at the back of Barney, gripping herself, pretending that one hand did not know the other, or why it cared enough to caress. In spasms, her skull filled with the sensation of fingers, tremors of delicious, gluttonous touch. She let the feeling twist under her scalp and careered her hair around the pillow, scratching itches that did not exist. Barney was happy, she could tell.

"What time do you call this, you lazy shite?"

Amy stilled. At the sound of her mother something in her froze, and some of her ran away. The teddy bear bunched with anger.

"How many times do I have to tell you to get up?"

Her mum was beside Amy's bed. She could move quickly, her mum, even when she was drunk. Faster, when she was hungover.

"Shit and shite, girl, have you looked at this room? How many times have I told you to clear this up? It's disgusting. I can't take it anymore. I'm going to go through this pigsty today and throw away everything." She clutched Amy by her wrist. "Even your smelly bear. Especially that bloody bear. Let go of it—*right now*—and get up!"

AMY STOOD AT THE front of the house in the tight, coffiny porch. The morning had been a series of Polaroid stills. Clothing herself. Dressing Aidan. Putting poison in Aidan's cereal. Cleaning his teeth. Stay still. Smile.

Please don't throw Barney away. Please don't throw my teddy bear away, Amy thought but didn't say. She smiled as her mum looked down.

"Have you got clean tissues, love? Are they clean?" Her mother said in the voice she used at school. Her mum put on its sound with her make-up.

"Yes Mum," Amy said. She didn't move as her mother reached down.

"Let's see, love." Her mum's fingers burrowed into her pockets. Amy's mind went walkabout. Once, on a field trip, she had seen a dead rabbit by the road. Beyond a pastry of flies, the end of a fat larva had winked, mucusy, from the ripped flesh, its segments like knuckles. If the rabbit had been able to feel, the grub would have felt like Mum's fingers did now.

Amy's mother pulled out a wrinkled line of white tissue, nettled with green.

"Why do you lie to me?" she asked. The words might have sounded hurt but not to Amy, who had blanked out the sound of the sentence and couldn't respond. She knew what was coming. Not words but actions, and all the clearer for it.

Her mother's hand whipped up and to the right, drawn to the corner of the porch. It stayed, perhaps sensing that this was a school day. The nails were red but tinged with pink, as the rabbit's bowels had been. In the light from the faux stained glass window, her mother's palm appeared to be green. She stared at Amy with icy, chipped-out eyes. Jerk by jerk, the hand climbed back down like a gecko.

"And have you got tissues, sweetheart?" her mum said, turning to Aidan.

Amy twisted down and round, her hand whisking into Aidan's pocket. She took out the tissue made of toilet paper that she had given him in the bathroom earlier. It was a folded square, a tiny flag. Amy waved it, not in surrender, but in a stand above the boy's head.

"Fine, let's go." Her mum held out a hand to the little boy.

Amy took it.

THEY HAD WALKED SOME way from Anstil Place, through the B roads, and were into the C roads and closing in on the school. C did not stand for Close, nor for having an ocean view, but was so named because the blocks across from the Old Road were ordered alphabetically. This helped the children to learn their ABCs, being by the school, though their education finished at F. The roads after F were private, and could afford their own capital letters.

The houses they passed were, like Amy's, the mottled grey of corpses that had dug themselves out of the grave. The inhabitants were a paler shade. Their front windows were lidded and suspicious. In the late summer afternoons, the occasional barbecue would be struck up and celebrated long into the night. The occasion would be apropos of nothing more than there being sunshine and, of course, Stella. Now that the summer had turned Indian, like (she supposed) her at number 41, the drinking was always hidden indoors.

Children emerged from alleys like small, silent ghosts, passing the green electricity boxes on which they would usually sit and swear and spit. The pavements were landmined by chewing gum. Apart from the odd gobbing, the sporadic catcall, the children were now too sleepy to be anything other than social. After a day of school they would up the ante. It wasn't uncommon for twelve-year-olds to joyride these streets. Behind the houses were garages. There were holes in the garage walls. In the holes, plastic bags. In the bags, marijuana. Amy had seen teenagers take out Wilkinson carriers, their hoods up, shoulders closed in. She saw them from her bedroom window, like that time a flat was arsoned. She had watched it burn, flames licking around the edges of its brick wall, smoke hungrily lapping around the edges of the blaze. She didn't know who called the fire brigade.

The Day School gates emerged from the C roads and they, Amy and Aidan and Mum, walked towards their green metal across a broken concrete patch. The weeds had been ground down underfoot. Mum's walk was as brisk as ever, demanding adult motions from Amy's legs. The girl stumbled, eyeing the faded white and yellow lines of the common land. Mum stopped abruptly. She didn't like to wait at the gates but had little choice, as a family pushed in before them. Amy had seen the family's mother in a front garden in the F roads, all slapped-pink flesh, short hair and a waist that went on forever. Fishwife, Mum had called her. She looked more like a whalewife, thought Amy, not altogether maliciously. She liked whales.

"Get a move on, love," her mum said, twisting Amy's fingers. Forced to move, the girl was buffeted by another family. "Say excuse me!" Mum said to Amy, smiling at the adult. "Kids, eh?" She laughed, but the smile didn't reach the top half of her face. Her eyes killed it as it crossed her cheeks.

"Bye then, sweetheart," said her mum in the Day School voice when they were through. She bent and kissed Amy's cheek. Amy felt herself receding, as she did when Barney squeezed her hand, but there was no world to slip into and she returned as her mum petted Aidan, hands on his small, shaven head, on his bare elbows. Amy knew the raggedly bitten tips of those fingers, and the little girl's toes rubbed against each other, itching to run into the school reception. She was rooted though, like the laburnum tree at the bottom of the Rileys' garden. She couldn't break free. To move would have taken a Herculean Feat, as her Night School teachers would say. Amy had seen a picture of Hercules and she didn't have one foot that was as strong as his, let alone two. Not in this world. Not without red shoes. Her mum let go of Aidan, and Amy finally walked into the Day School. She didn't take the boy's hand, but he followed as though there was something between them, something invisible, something secret.

A BLACK BIN BAG HAD been through Amy's room and taken the one thing she cared about. The Care Bears were also gone, as were several books and three coloured-in drawings.

Barney was a hole in the duvet that the little girl sank her head into. To Amy, this was when she was at her best-looking. Small children have a way of lying: head down, arms gated, bottom in the air. Amy did not lie this way, but lay on her side, back against the wallpaper, head twisted and forced into the duvet cover. Her fingers held her ribcage as though restraining the ache within it. Before, she had wondered how they felt in Alien when the creature came out of their chest. She wrapped her palms around the outside of her arms and felt the fine blonde hairs there. They were insubstantial, ghosts rubbed up the wrong way but unable to take revenge. Unlike them, Amy felt entirely present and no longer able to leave. Her chest and throat burnt and her hands twisted, becoming rigid, grasping an outline that had gone. Amy did not cry, but gunge collected in her nostrils and ran down onto her upper lip. The spume collected like rain in the mossed gutter at the back of the house. It overflowed.

Crack.

Her head righted itself, and the crack of her neck—as loud in her skull as a house torn off its foundations—brought Amy back to herself. Pain swirled around her nape, clawing at her scalp and seeming to scratch up the bedroom wall, the Argos cupboard, the discoloured Michael Jackson. Momentarily, Amy wished she hadn't moved. She liked being vacant. When her mum wasn't watching Corrie or Neighbours or EastEnders, Amy would watch BBC2. She liked programmes about outer space. The motion of the stars, constellation playing hide-and-seek with constellation, out through the coldness of time, never getting close enough to tig each other.

Amy blinked and wiped her nose on her forearm. The hairs plastered to her skin. She turned, opened her door and tipped forward onto her toes to stare down over the banister at the bottom of the stairs. She could hear conversation. As always, in her house, it was the TV. In his room, she could hear Aidan playing with something unidentified and plastic. He was growling. Amy descended the steps singly, toes curled around the blunt edges of the carpet, nails pressed into the forest-floor colouring of its weave. She moved like they did in The Evil Dead, careful not to snap any twigs in case a tree snapped them back.

She stood at the door to the lounge.

"Oh my God," her mother said. "Why did you do that?... You little bastard."

Amy stilled. Her mum didn't move, facing the television screen. Its glow embalmed her features. She seemed stiller than normal. More still, even, than just before she threw things.

"Oh my God."

The television made a slow, crashing sound, and Amy couldn't help but look.

"Oh my God," said someone on the TV, but in an accent that sounded like Jerry Springer. On the screen, a tower block collapsed to the ground in puff of white smoke, as though hit by a spell.

The Witch is dead, thought Amy. The Witch is dead. She was rooted by hope to the carpet. The Witch's tower had been brought low. By the look of the TV's screen, someone had driven a plane into it. Amy could even see the Witch's monkeys, taking flight from the windows. Amy had a feeling between flying and falling, between dancing and passing out. Her insides expanded as if made of the dust that flooded from the falling tower block. No more picture. No more walk. No more Witch. Why isn't Mum smiling? she thought. It was all she could do to stop herself running to the settee, leaning over its peach back and cuddling her mother's white shoulders beneath her blonde bob.

She would realise the Witch lived that evening when she visited her tower and found it still existed.

A man appeared on the television. He was the same colour as the woman and her children who had recently moved into number 41.

"Now the Asian face is the face of evil," said the man. He looked appalled.

"Damn fucking right it is," said Amy's mother and picked up the phone.

It was all Amy could do to keep moving. Her mother was dialling in thick clicking actions, like the sound her spiky shoes made on the kitchen lino before she went to work at the bingo hall.

Amy walked by, behind the settee. She tiptoed, careful to look like she wasn't creeping. Her mum didn't turn round, and Amy's toes touched lino as she made it to the kitchen. She turned right, past the square faux-pine table. The patio door key was secreted in a white drawer to the right of the cooker. She lifted it slightly as she rolled it out and touted the key on the end of her swearing finger.

"Where have you been?" said her mother, to the phone. "Haven't you been watching the TV?" A pause. The tinny excited tone of a voice at the other end of the line. "Yeah, right. I was just like watching Crossroads, you know? To see if that Jake was going to get caught getting his end away... yeah... yeah—" Giggle. "—he's a proper man, isn't he?... and then *it* came on. Nothing in the sky, then the planes were like flying in. Jesus. No more Crossroads. Been watching it all afternoon, apart from getting the kids. Them towers just went down. It's so sad. I was like *no* when the first one went, and I couldn't even like think when the second one went, you know?"

Amy walked to the patio door, inserted the keys, turned the lock, slid it open, and eased out. The patio slabs were cold and tugged at the skin of her feet. At the bottom of next door's garden, hanging over the fence, stood a laburnum tree, wizened by too many summers. The chains of its pods were burnished, rusted by spots of rot, and drifts of its seeds had been swept by the wind to strangle the weeds.

The Rileys lived next door with their dog Jack.

"Jack! Jack!" Mr Riley would hiss late at night, when he let Jack out and the dog barked. Mr Riley didn't seem to want to get Mum's attention. Once, Amy had seen him step out of his front door and step directly back in when he saw her mother coming, a look on his face like the fear Amy often felt in her gut, pale and cold. Mrs Riley would also shout at Jack: "Jack! Jack!" she would say. "Get away from those seeds! They're poison!" And she would hurry over and shoe at the dog with her feet whenever Jack drew close to the tree with its laconic leaves.

As with many things, Amy had looked it up:

Symptoms of laburnum poisoning may include intense sleepiness, vomiting, convulsive movements, coma, slight frothing at the mouth and unequally dilated pupils, it said in her Flora and Fauna book.

It'll be saying that to a bin bag now, thought Amy.

At the corner of the house was the bin, its lid tilted open, an arm of creamy brown hanging out like when Mum had a bath. She couldn't see Barney's face. For the first time, Amy felt anxious. She could tell because her feet twitched, her heels coming together in a jittery clicking action.

Got to be quick, she thought. Or, hurry up you useless little brat. It was difficult to tell who was speaking inside her head. Sometimes her own voice, on the inside, sounded like her mum's.

She stretched, reaching for and past the bear's brown patch of paw. Her finger bushed his bumpy, rough, eczemic skin. She couldn't grasp its blunt width, or she would leave this world and this body behind, and she couldn't physically reach beyond it, nor just jump and pull. The bin would fall with a corrugated metallic crash that would carry into the fragile, egg-like air of her home. Tears pulled down the corners of Amy's eyes, curtaining her sight. She jiggled back and forth and stubbed her shin on a bin bag. She hissed. The black, inscrutable plastic was hard, full of books and their sharp spines. (It couldn't be Winnie the Pooh: Barnaby said he didn't have a spine. Besides which, Winnie was one of the few reference books left in her bookcase. Maybe because it was a gift from Nan.) Grasping and bent to her hips, she pulled the bag close to the bin, climbed on top of the Flora and Fauna cover she could see through a noose of bag, opened the bin lid, and pulled Barney out by his right shoulder. He had a piece of cotton on his nose. It was damp and going mouldy and looked like a bogey. Amy didn't care and didn't move, holding Barney for several seconds, pressing his scalp to her chin and up to the peak of her nose, taking him in. He still smelt of her.

Amy retraced her footsteps to the patio doors. In reverse, she slid through the glass panes, closed and locked them, and replaced the keys. She walked behind the settee. Her mother was saying, "Yeah, one of them on the TV was like "we're the face of evil", and I was like yeah, I've never trusted you lot. One them's moved into number 41, you know when old Mrs Fryers died, yeah?"

Aidan's door was open a crack, and the little girl let her sight fall into it. On the wall, lit by the diminishing light, was a monster in shadows—eight-armed and hunchbacked. Aidan had changed from his school uniform into his spider costume. It had six felt arms and, as two moved, all of them clawed. Aidan was hidden behind the door.

"Buzz, buzz," said her baby brother. "I'm gonna eat you up, Fly-bot-tron. I'm Manspider and I'm gonna eat eat eat you up, yum, yum, yah." The velvet limbs raised a plastic-etched shadow across the Spider-Man wallpaper.

Amy shifted so she could watch him.

Surrounded as it was by the thick hairy face of his spider costume, his mouth was a storm cloud within cut-outs of darkness. "Fly in my spider belly. The mummy eats me. Spider

in the mummy's belly, fly in the spider's belly. Mum... mum...
me."

Amy walked towards him. The carpet crinkled under her
tread. Barney was limp in her arms.

Aidan scissored the spider toy in his hand. She could see it
now: a Woolworths bin-gift, tattooed with stickers, moulded in
gaudy purple and tawdry grey. Aidan bit the air. His voice
changed. "Buzz, buzz, you can't eat me. I'm Fly-bot-tron. I
knew you were going to be-a-tray me. But you can't be a tray!
You're a spider!"

"Aidan?" said Amy. She held Barney towards him. It wasn't
the first time she had done so, and Aidan ignored her. She
always took the bear back at night while he slept. "Aidan," she
repeated.

"Yum. Yar."

"You need him," Amy said, "to stop her doing it to you."

She pushed Barney against the skin of his spider arm.

"Take him to bed. It'll stop her," she said, pushing the
teddy.

Aidan shied back and away. "Silly bear," said the little boy.
"Silly stinking bear."

"SHUT THE FUCK UP YOU STUPID LITTLE SHIT."
The words had left Amy before she realised they were behind
her lips. For a moment, she thought someone else had shouted
them.

Aidan crinkled. He opened his human mouth, surrounded
by silhouettes of spider-black felt, and wailed. "Muuummm—"

"I'm sorry," said Amy. She wrapped Barney back up against
her chest.

"Muuuuummmmmmmm—"

"Shut up. Both of you. Or I'll knock your stupid heads together," yelled their mother. The yell, like Amy's, came from below.

Amy ran along the landing to her bedroom. She shut the door and crawled under her bed, into the shadows in the far corner, depositing Barney. She wiggled back out, then tugged the bed by degrees away from the wallpapered wall. Amy rolled over the linen, reached down between bed and wall, grasped Barney's paw and wedged it into the gap. She rolled back and pushed the bed flush to the wallpaper. Barney's paw protruded unseen beneath the duvet, in the corner in which she curled when she slept.

SHE LIKED THE WALK but not where it led, through the Jewish quarter, which was no more than artery with loops of roads like veins on an old person's legs, some going nowhere, others disappearing into the flesh of the city. Amy put great faith in the Jews. She had once read The Hobbit and remembered it, if not word for word, then image for image. The Jews in the quarter dressed in black with hats and, as often as the rains, plastic bags over their hats. More importantly, they wore beards—extensive and fantastical to the girl—that made her think of an army of Gandalfs. Even the little boys had beards growing down the sides of their faces, from their wispish hair and stolid round-caps, as though they would not make do with one beard but wanted two, one on either side. They, the Jews, made Amy feel safe in a way that few things did. She reckoned that, if anything had a power over the Witch, if anyone could protect her, it was not one Gandalf but many.

But it was still there. Past the church, past the school, past the park, and there it was—the tower block where the Witch lived. She lived, Amy had known as long as she had known her memories and the sound of her mother's voice, on the top floor. This seemed fitting for a Witch—all the better, thought Amy, as she grew past five, through six, and eventually to her current age of eight, to get to the roof. There, there would be the broomstick and the flying. Witches were as made to live in high places as they were to eat small children.

They'd walked that way (church, school, park) and now stood before the block. It was night, as it always was when they came here. Some of the lights were off, some on, more than two winked between the two states, like someone wrinkling tinfoil below a light. Shadow, then glamour. Either way, they seemed to draw Amy in like a spell. She didn't like to walk to the tower block, which was visible first behind the swings at the top of a short but sapping rise where dog shit went to meet shoes. Uncle Chris liked to watch Star Wars, despite its bland lack of gore and nudity, and the block reminded Amy of the Death Star (with its tractor beam), the place where evil would live and do its work.

Though it was grey dusk when she first spied it, and glowering night when they stood before it, Amy knew the building itself was always black, as she should have known it would always be here. It was worse this time—the tower—more solid because she had dared think it had fallen into dust.

She had been wrong; the planes hadn't got it.

Abruptly the skin of the building flashed as white as stripped bones. There was a whine as the old Polaroid motored out its slip of black that would become a picture.

"Ding, dong," said her mother.

The photo flicked in her hand in the dark, sounding like the wings of a trapped moth. She blew on it, if not for luck then for bad luck for its recipient, as she always did. They came here every year. The pilgrimage was better observed than Amy's birthday. The day he'd left mum for *her*.

"Here, witchy witchy, see what you make of this."

Amy wondered if the Witch ever paid any attention. They'd been doing this for… what? This was the fourth year, she figured. The same photo of the tower block, the same message scribbled on the white slip at the base of the picture. Amy walking, when she was old enough to slip it in the correct letterbox, through the gate to the lattice-worked glass doors and the serried numbers on the postboxes. The same greedy click as the box tried to take her fingers, and Amy would recoil her hand as the Polaroid slipped down into darkness. The first time she had cut her hand, and her mother had been too ecstatic at her revenge to notice until… well, she hadn't noticed, and the bleeding had ceased on its own.

"Revenge, love," Mum said—in the same mangled, teeth-constricted voice she used when she said "cut his nose off to spite his face, didn't I, eh?"—"is a dish best served cold, ain't it? There, take it." She stared up at the tower block and looked as though she were imagining planes being driven into it.

This year, as every other, Amy's feet crept nearer as if they expected to be caught in a tractor beam all of a sudden. Her eyes were planted flat on the door. She didn't look up, even as the block loomed above her, even as it swallowed the stars or (being Manchester) the clouds cushioned by street-light.

What if the Witch was watching her?

What if her eyes were the tractor beam?

Amy consumed books as other children did strings of cola flavoured sweets, and one of her favourites had been Unwin's Greek Mythology. She raised the Polaroid like, she recalled, Perseus to the eyes of the gorgon. On it was written, as ever it was: **Ding dong the Witch lives here**.

The photo shook, but the words remained stark and sure and deep.

Amy slipped the photo into the top letterbox (number 37). Through the glass of the door, webbed by thin dark lines like the web of a spider that had gone OCD, she saw the floor of the foyer. Black and white chessboard squares. Amy didn't know how to play chess, only draughts (and that badly), but she knew the squares were waiting for her and that she would step on them one day. The lift on the left of the foyer was tight and gleaming metal, a coffin that went above the ground instead of into it. In there, in Amy's imagination, everything was upside-down and the wrong way around. She turned and, without actually doing anything other than a walk, came as close to running away from the dark tower block as she could.

Chapter 2

THEY WALKED TO SCHOOL in silence, a human hand in a bear's paw. Around them could be heard the pitter-patter of little laburnum pods. The Latter Wood was a random eco-system, weather-wise, and tonight it was doing autumn. To the north, it was forever winter. Aimee did not go there, and nor did any school trips. Risk assessments would have sections on Abduction and Death. Health and Safety would never have allowed it. That was the realm of the Witch.

Aimee and the bear trudged past a tree she knew well, even in the shadows. On the other side of its bough was a carving of a large heart, in which had been etched the name *Aimee*, with a smaller heart to dot the head of the *i*, and an accent over the final *e*. At its end was the kiss of an *x*. On her first trip here, Amy had carved it and had transformed, from the cleaned curl of her hair to the toes of her red shoes.

Abruptly, there was a whispered sound different from that of the falling seeds only in that it went on for longer. There was no wind. The bear stopped, and the skin at the back of its right paw bristled against her arm. Aimee turned, staring behind and through their connection into a gloom seeded by yellow pods bleached to white by the lack of light. The scene had switched to the look of a blizzard, a snow globe upturned and returned.

At first, her eyes refused to see it as they did from time to time, but soon its pale form wisped between two trees. She'd seen it before. The form was half a head taller than Aimee, with skin pallid as a child's teeth.

"Is that a boy?" she said.

The bear muttered in reply, almost to himself, "Nothing is what it looks like it appears to be and fewer things are what they seem."

"Eh?"

Barnaby pulled her forward, his muscles bristling as his pelt had above them. "I've told you not to stare, girl," he said.

Aimee, however, continued to do so, having as little control of her eyes as she had over the motion of her feet.

"IT'S ANOTHER CHILD," said the gargoyle.

"Really? Dear Witch, what is a child doing here?" said the gargoyle perched on the other end of the gates.

"This is a school."

"Oh, that's why they keep coming." The second gargoyle attempted to turn. He winced, the scales around his lizardine eyes narrowing. "I can't look. It hurts."

The two gargoyles sat on spikes at the apex of the school gates. The bars of the entrance were thin, blue and curved wickedly—at least as far as their anal passages were concerned.

"I know exactly what you mean," said the first. "I wish I was a grotesque."

"Mmmm, hmmm, what's she doing?"

"Waving, I think."

"Pretty little thing… It's the one with the bear." The gargoyle raised a claw and waved five talons in return. "What a bonny dress she's wearing," it said.

"I wouldn't look so happy. She's opening the gates."

"Little bitch," said the gargoyle, before yowling in pain as the blue metal bars swung outward. His bottom leaked red lava. "That hurts like buggery."

The other gargoyle wasn't listening. It scrabbled at its buttocks with its slate-grey wings and tried to hide the blood. "I hate school," it growled.

"I hate children," said the second.

"MR HIM," SAID BARNABY, extending his paw.

Mr Him shook hands as one would shake the face of a snake.

"Good day?" said Barnaby.

By this, Aimee knew he meant: did you have a good day? Bears and men always talked the same way, in their own company, as though a word was better than a sentence, and a grunt best of all.

Mr Him nodded and grunted, "Uh-huh." His chest was pressed out against his lemon coloured shirt. His hands, however, skirmished with a tissue in his pocket, and he chewed the whiskers around his thin damp lips. The single long hair on the top of his head appeared to be crawling away from the bear, or looking for an ear behind which to hide. "You?" he said.

Barnaby looked down and to the right, his paws opening and closing as though on a fresh corpse. Aimee wondered what he had been up to. "Yep. Field Trip?"

"Ah, yes." Mr Him smoothed the moustache that lay on his top lip. He slipped comfortably into teacher-mode. "Well, yes, we will be taking the class on a Field Trip into the Latter Wood," he said. "Completely safe, of course—it will take place in the middle of the night, and should give the children ample opportunity to develop their oligochaetological skills... ah, I mean... the study of invertebrates—" Mr Him's eyes flicked between the bear and the air off its right shoulder. "Lots of opportunities to develop—" he said. "—the chance to experience—" he added. "I'm sorry. One of my children is trying to lick the hamster's head. Excuse me, Mr Pooh." He swished past the bear with the sound of soft linen and loose hair.

Barnaby's eyes narrowed. "I'm not—" he said.

"Time to go," Aimee said.

"Do all bears look the same to you humans, girl?"

"No. *It's time to go*," said Aimee.

"Give me a hug," said the bear.

"Arggghhh," said Aimee, part of which was muffled by the bear's pelt as he leant in. "Go," she managed as he rose.

He smiled in a way that made Aimee think of trolls under bridges. "Bye little girl. Be good," he said, and left.

"AND, OF COURSE, I... uh... I still need to decide who gets to carry the lanterns and the buckets," said Mr Him. Momentarily, the lantern he carried flickered, and Mr Him disappeared from Class 7. He often seemed to wish he could disappear. The light then threw itself back out, yellow over the sallow pods of the laburnum trees, and Aimee could see the class again. Mr Him was wearing the kind of smile only adults owned, put on like a spy's facial hair. Tower, who stood directly before it, tremored.

Tower raised his hand. "Please sir, me sir," he said.

"What?" said Mr Him. Behind his thick round-rimmed glasses, his eyes made Aimee think of horror films. Psycho, perhaps. The face around them was wooden, and carved into an expression of patience.

"Lantern, sir?" said Tower. Tower, of course, was his nickname. Like most of the nicknaming in This Place, Aimee was unsure how it was applied. The only tower Tower resembled was a minaret of soup. Despite his angularity, he seemed always to be wobbling and about to fall.

"No. No. No," said Mr Him, possibly stuttering as he sometimes did or disagreeing vehemently, which he did whenever Aimee answered a question.

"Bucket?"

"No!" Mr Him's finger rose to the grey whiskers around his mouth, modulating them. "No Tower."

"When are we going to see the nymphs?" asked a child.

He hadn't put his hand up and Mr Him ignored him. Mr Him often said, "With these children consistency is the key and inconsistency the burglar. Especially with these children." He often said this in front of Class 7. Aimee had no idea what this meant.

Angel's hand went up.

"Angel?"

"When are we going to see the nymphs?" Angel said.

In the dark, children could be heard sniggering. It was a mixed age group, and some of the class were ten and eleven. Sometimes, they talked about kissing each other but Aimee ignored this. She was too young to have any interest in kissing or boys.

"We are not, as you well know, in the wood to chase nymphs, no matter what your burgeoning hormones are telling you Angel. We are here to talk to insects." Angel didn't reply, but somehow made a sighing sound with the rolling of his eyes. Angel was as far from an angel as Aimee could reckon from her readings of the bible. Except, of course, a fallen one.

Aimee put her hand up.

"Aimee," said Mr Him after a pause.

"Are we going to talk to butterflies?" she asked. As with many girls of her age, she was obsessed with butterflies. And flowers. And love hearts.

"No," said Mr Him. "We are going to talk to worms."

Aimee couldn't decide if he was being sarcastic and smiled, in case he was making a joke.

"Right," said Mr Him, "the buckets go to Earnest, Sunshine and Peter. Well done for standing so well. The lanterns go to whoever can listen best to these instructions. Now—" Mr Him paused—not for emphasis but as if, for a moment, he didn't know if he could go on. As usual, though, he did. "Worms come out when it's raining. All of you have buckets with water in them. Dribble these on the forest floor and, when the worms come up, ask them the questions we wrote down in class. Please apologise to the worms for disturbing them. We are representing the Night School, remember."

"But they're only worms," said Angel, more to Peter than to Mr Him.

"Many say the same about children. Especially in the staffroom," said Mr Him. "Watch me, though, when I put my hair up." He demonstrated this by running fingers through his remaining follicle. It stood to attention. Mr Him didn't need to lick his fingers to achieve this. His skin moisturised itself. "You are all to come back when you see this. Okay children—" He paused. "—off you go. Get into groups."

Aimee shifted as, around her, children looked at each other and nodded and ran together like socially aware iron filings. Eventually, Aimee was added to a group of three boys—Angel, Peter and Tower. They didn't look pleased to be with her, despite her smiling at them, and Tower looked scared. He was gripping the lantern, the light of which fluttered. Peter held the bucket Angel had pressed on him. Angel was holding out his hand.

"Welcome to our group," he said to Aimee.

She shook it like her uncles had taught her, and, looking down, found herself holding a long line of snot.

The boys laughed together and scampered behind a rise of trees. As they showered her with moss (and shouted "the Witch is coming"), Aimee followed. She crested the silhouette of earth to where the lantern light flapped like a moth's wings. There, she saw Angel had placed the bucket, upturned, on Tower's head. Tower appeared to be crying, though with all the spilt liquid it was difficult to tell.

"We need that," said Peter.

"Cry baby," said Angel. "We don't need that. Look." He began to unbutton his pants.

"You can't do that," said Peter. He looked at Aimee. "Not in front of a girl."

Angel shrugged, the action freeing his top button. "She's seen it all before. Why do you think she comes to this school?"

Peter had no reply and Tower was saying nothing, bar what sounded like a soft mewling.

Angel urinated with some vigour on the wood's floor. "It's pissing down," he shouted.

Aimee glanced at Tower. He had tilted the bucket so that it now resembled a helmet. It still hid his eyes.

"Here, here, little wormy," said Angel.

"You're the little bloody wormy," said Aimee. She didn't know why she said this. She did know she felt angry and was staring at his penis.

Abruptly, with a splutter of indignant shock, he ceased urinating. "Shut up," he said.

"Little worm," she said. She kept staring. She had never seen a penis before.

"Shut up," he said.

"What—" said a small, acerbic voice. A pink curling finger of insect writhed up in the puddle of mud. "—kind of bloody rain is this?" The worm made a hacking sound. "Oh my Witch, that is vile," it said.

"Little worm," said Aimee again.

"Yes?" said the worm. "Who are you?" He looked first to the girl, then to Angel. "Why are your pants around your ankles? What is that smell?"

"Shut up," said Angel to Aimee.

"What?" said the worm. "How dare you? Impertinent youth! If you knew how many offspring I have produced. How many times I have divided. Do you know division, young man? Or are you still on one add one?"

"You're just a dirty, little worm," said Angel, who didn't take kindly to being talked to in this way, especially with words he didn't understand.

"Oh, when you die, please don't be cremated," said the worm. "I would so like to swallow your tongue. I really do doubt you could do it."

"Eat my tongue? Why would I do that? You eat poo, and I'm going to stamp on you." Angel pulled up his trousers and his underwear and rocked backwards and forwards from heels to toes. He raised his fists, though Aimee was unsure why.

Peter, meanwhile, was backing away. "Uh, Angel, I think we should—"

"I'm going to stamp you to itty bitty pieces," said Angel.

"I'm going to eat your ears," said the worm. "You mark my words. You won't be able to when you're dead, *partly because I'm going to eat your ears*. Where's your teacher?" the worm added as an afterthought.

"Teacher has put his hair up," said Tower. Aimee didn't know how he could tell, with a bucket over his eyes and through a line of laburnum trees and a hillock of dirt. She

~56~

didn't move, watching the boy and the worm circling each other.

Peter and Tower were running, their feet as heavy and fast as the sound Angel's urine had made on the earth. Tower ran into a tree, rebounded, and continued away along the ridge-line.

Angel looked up, blinking in the abrupt lack of light. He sprinted up the hillock in a spurt. Before the lantern's light died away over the ridge, Aimee raised her right hand and the tattered oblong of paper within it.

"How do worms multiply by dividing?" She read her own slightly underdeveloped script. "Mr Him says I'm wrong when I do this."

AMY STARED AT THE photo of her younger brother, closed her eyes and remembered when it was she had decided to poison him. It wasn't the first time she saw her mother cuddle Aidan. It wasn't the way Mum left her lips on his forehead as she kissed him goodnight, or let him breastfeed until he was four. No. It was the moment of the accident.

Clear as a summer sky by the coast, she saw her little brother, as she often did from behind her eyelids, with his cheeks plumped by retriever-puppy fat, his shaven head glittering golden under the sun, his Man City shirt blue as his eyes. (They hadn't been able to afford enough letters, so it read only **A**, as if a football team had twenty-six players.) There was a reason for the sunshine; in her memory he had been playing in the garden—by the laburnum tree—and Amy was colouring in her colouring-pad and so hadn't noticed him eating its pods until he had started to choke. She may have been a 'stupid girl', but Amy knew her books, having read them from the age of three and a quarter, and knew what Flora and Fauna had to say about the seeds of a laburnum.

She'd run to him, her temples pulsing. The summer heat was rising and shivering as though the garden were made of tarmac. Every step jarred.

"Spit it out, spit it out, it's poison," she'd shouted but he already had, splattering the trunk of the tree where it met the dirt. She could see his saliva looped around the yellow lumps, like dog paw prints on the bark.

Amy opened her eyes and looked at the photograph of her brother. He was in the garden. He didn't look real. The picture was blurred, not so much by the motion of his body and his laughter, but by his happiness. His eyes, even greyed by a bad focus, had the bright blueness of a boy who hadn't seen life for what it was. Amy had. The album was thick with him… him… as was her mind. She flicked back through time, to a space in the book before he'd been born and began to turn the pages from its front cover. It was best to start at the beginning, she thought, or so Nan said.

LATER, THE YELLOW IN her pocket weighed her down. Its vegetative colour was as fecund, as thick, as the air in the deepest jungle in stories about singing animals that wanted to be man cubs and stroll into suburban areas. Amy found it difficult to breathe, fingering her pocket as her mum put on foundation in the small elliptical mirror on its stand on the workbench. Amy's fingers came away stained, like the times she had stolen her mother's cigarettes.

"Get a move on, love," said her mum, distracted by her own reflection. It really was quite beautiful, and not only in her daughter's eyes. "I want him fed before I go to work."

"Yes, Mum," Amy nodded and added milk. The egg went white where it had been yellow. Mum applied fake tan to her pallid forearms, neck and ankles. Her daughter drew out a fistful of laburnum pods, trying to watch her mum without looking at her. The girl scattered them in the places where the milk was mixing with the egg. She whisked with a fork. The yellow became luminous. From her readings of Flora and Fauna, Amy mentally added 'and poisonous'.

She had a plan for Aidan.

A smell of blackened toast rose. Amy didn't recognise it, staring at what she had done with eyes that did their best to encompass the frying pan.

In the mirror and on her face, red lipstick slipped onto the slight puppy fat of Mum's upper chin. "Jesus, girl, watch what you're bloody doing."

In a spurt of forearms, Amy grabbed the handle of the grill pan, drawing it out from under the branding of the grill. Luckily, only the edges of the white slices had curled, dark as fungus around the roots of a laburnum tree. Amy expertly trimmed them, buttered them, and scraped them from brown to beige.

"Aidan," she shouted. Her throat caught on his name, scarring it, weakening it, and he ignored her.

Her mum twisted around the alcove to the lounge, shoulders and head snaking out of sight. "Get down here now," said her mum, in a scream.

There was a scamper of feet and the wooden retort of steps. The girl put the bowl of scrambled egg on the table, between the knife and fork she had placed there earlier. Aidan clambered onto his cushion before them.

"I'll get you a drink," she said quietly and his eyes caught hers. She looked away, but not before he had passed her a silent question. What's wrong with you? He knew his sister.

She went to the fridge and poured a cola Panda Pop into a glass decorated by fading butterflies. She put it on the table, to the side of the empty fruit bowl. Aidan was eating, his cheeks working around the meal, bunching, slowing. He spat with an 'eugh' onto the toast.

Mum turned, her body following her neck in segments, her neck following her face as if scared of what it might say. "What did you just do?" she asked.

"Don't like it," said Aidan. "Tastes funny."

"Eat it," said Mum. The command was repeated in her eyes and again in her posture. Amy saw her hands tightening around the lipstick, as though it were one of the knives she threw at Uncle Chris. The steak ones.

Aidan didn't see, or the taste in his mouth misled his lips. "Tastes funny," he said.

The breath had left Amy's body. Her urine wanted to follow by the feel of it.

~60~

Mum walked to the table.

"Eat it."

"No."

The lipstick dropped to the floor, not so much a knife now as a round from a rifle. Things were escalating. By the time it had finished clattering and rolling, Mum was behind the boy, her fingers in his hair, the others in the egg. She rammed this at his small mouth. Though his lips twisted and curled into a point, she found gaps.

"Eat it," the words were breaths.

Aidan didn't reply and ate, and Amy watched him, feeling diseased right down to where her feet were rooted to the kitchen lino.

When she'd finished, Mum said, in a mutter, "Now I've got to wash my bloody hands," and did so.

*IT WAS AT TIMES LIKE these, between 10.00 and 11.00 at night, that P.I. **Jennifer** put on her disguise and fought crime.*

Jennifer was underscored by ellipses and typed in a different font. The book—Crocodile Monster—was one of the Your Own Adventure range that parents ordered specially for their own children. Amy's mum hadn't but somebody's had, and so the book was a stolen hand-me-down, and thus well-handled. Amy etched out **Jennifer** with a biro and wrote **Aimee**, a little larger.

*Holding her teddy bear ~~**Jennifer**~~ **Aimee** walked down the stairs. She had to find clues to where the Crocodile Monster was. Her teddy, ~~**Droopy**~~ **Barney** ~~was scared and hid his head behind~~ **Jennifer**'s legs* *was **ANGRY** and wanted to eat the bloody monster's head IN ONE GULP, girl.*

The private detective was child-sized and had a grey wig and a cloak that had seen brighter days so, Amy supposed, the reader could imagine themselves underneath both.

Amy pulled open her bedroom door. Its planes hissed on the thin carpet. She crept out onto the landing, careful not to break the twigs in the foliage on the carpet, or to step on the creaks in the floorboards beneath it. Her mother was singing Celine Dion downstairs: My Heart Will Go On. Book in her left hand, bear in her right, Amy stood on the tips of her toes and walked to the end of the landing. Aidan's door was open, as it always was. The girl slid between the door and the jamb, both chipped by the passage of people and yellowed by the cigarette smoke of previous owners. Against his Spider-Man pillow cover, Aidan's head was a circle of grey lit at its chin by orange where the streetlights peered through the papery curtains. One of his hands, tight and small and balled, gripped the top of his duvet, misshaping Peter Parker's skull beneath its disguise. Amy could hear the boy breathing. It sounded like a whisper: "you, you, you". She stopped, the skin of her arms blushing about her elbow joints, down to her wrists where she had wrapped them around Barney.

What can I do? she found herself thinking.

She couldn't let go of the bear.

I can't, she thought, can't. Not Barnaby.

She prised her arms apart. The bear felt reluctant at her chest, like a child on the first day of Day School. She unpeeled the end of the duvet and Aidan's fingers and burrowed Barney gracelessly in. The little boy sighed and he laid his arms around the teddy. Biting her bottom lip and her teeth below it, Amy trembled away, feeling like a leaf. An autumnal leaf, withered and bled of its green shoots. She returned the way she had come, back to her own bedroom, the book chill and waxy and dead in her spare hand.

HER MUM HAD FINISHED with My Heart Will Go On and was singing I Will Survive—the explicit version—and throwing things at Uncle Chris. Soon she would be going to bed. Possibly hers. Amy held Crocodile Monster still in her hand. It felt insubstantial, unweighty. Amy had torn out all the pages and had eaten some of them, before spitting them onto her window ledge, masticated and bubbled by drool. Her eyes felt hollow and she wondered where her tears had gone. Her guts were as fisted as her hands. She'd been staring at the outlines on the wallpaper for an hour, waiting for the monsters to come out and take her. They hadn't, and she felt as worn out as ~~Jennifer's~~ Aimee's grey cloak. Amy rose and walked to the bedroom door and stepped out onto the landing. The lights of it hurt her scalp, shafts of yellowed white running nails through her hair and down to her eyes. Stumbling, she walked to Aidan's room. She hitched inside, accidentally ramming the door against the whitewashed inbuilt cupboard behind its arc. Her mum didn't hear. Too busy Surviving. Neither did Chris. Too busy surviving the knives. Amy reached down and grasped Barney's head, lifting him out of Aidan's grasp by the ear. In his slumber, Aidan mumbled. A crack of a frown subsided down his pale forehead. It had the look of thin ice. There was a dark stain on his cheeks that might have been shadows.

My shadow, Amy realised and quickly left, running to her room.

Amy closed the door and slid into the soft gloom of her linen. In the bed, the sheets made themselves a secret place. It might keep her safe, keep her whole. It might even keep *her* away. Beneath the grey of the sheet, the colours seeping in from the landing and via her blinds separated into the crumbs of the rainbow. Amy gripped the head of her teddy bear. She held Barney close. She reached for his paw, but didn't take it, though she could hear the loaded click of lights turning off downstairs, the stumble of steps on the stairs. Mum was coming. The footsteps rose to the landing, and Amy squeezed her eyes tight but couldn't do the same with her hands on a teddy bear's paws. Not yet.

The feet sawed on their edges across the carpet, and seesawed at her door before turning away. There was a flutter of sounds, the wing beats of skin on carpet, and then her mum—Amy could hear her—passed into Aidan's small room. She closed his door. It shut lightly, as though it had no idea of what it was doing. Silence, bar downstairs. Then, up the well of the landing came the sound of The Exorcist, of crucifixes stabbing into skin. Amy had watched this scene with Uncle Chris time and again.

AIMEE BREATHED AND opened her eyes. Her hair had grown and rested in tresses on her shoulders. Her pyjamas were no longer pink on her shoulders, but hanging there now was a dress instead. The fabric was the colour of twilight when there was magic in the air. The colour of Yeats's poetry, in bee-loud glades. They were taught Yeats at Night School from the age of five. The older children read Plath, as a warning. There were no bees in this Glade, though there were insects and they were complaining:

"Please, you're sitting on my head."

And, "Oh God! Somebody just went pop! Was it Bob? Please tell me it wasn't Bob. Bob can you hear me?"

Aimee wasn't listening, though she sat quietly.

She didn't need to raise her finger to feel that her cheeks had taken on a round of puppy flesh. She didn't need a mirror to see that the hue of her hair had gone from dirt-brown to tawny. She didn't need to do anything. She was happy and she waited for the feeling to pass.

The sound of the bear was at her shoulder, and his paw gently pressed her upper arm.

"You came early, Aimee."

She ignored this. "Are you okay?" she said. She couldn't look at him, at his dirtied pelt. She could smell the aftereffects of the bin on him.

"Don't worry about me. Let me worry about me. You should be going back before she comes out of your brother's room and comes into yours. You need to be awake when she comes in. Sometimes, Aimee, it isn't as dangerous being Here as it is not being There."

"Okay." She sighed softly, with the sound of a stone that didn't want to sink. "Okay. I will, Barnaby. I will."

He nodded and hunkered down, wrapping his fur-hung arms around her body. She didn't like to go again, not from this Glade. He cuddled her and, when she was ready, he took her by the hand and squeezed.

SWEAT LINED HER CHEST and dampened her pyjama top. As the top was all she had—and it did little by the way of covering her lower body—her shame moistened the connecting skin between her lower legs, beneath her knees, and the pressed flesh between her inner thighs. She was unable to reach out to Barney. She couldn't be There if her mum came Here. She didn't dare squirm or slough off the sweat against the duvet. She didn't want the linen to begin its monthly stink and for Mum to have to change it more often than she did, besides which she didn't dare move.

The bear stared at her, eyes somehow visible in the darkness as would-be rabbit holes down which she wished to flee.

Nothing happened. Nothing came, and certainly not her mum who, some time later, could be heard leaving Aidan's room, walking past Amy's door, entering the bathroom and dry retching into the toilet bowl.

AIMEE WAS BACK BEFORE either world could waggle its eyelids and was sitting in her Night School classroom. The Night School was a new-build built in the oldest of places. She'd walked from the Glade, through the gates, along the corridors, to her classroom like a gallstone being passed. Compacted, hard yet falling apart, and bloodied from passing through the crap of it all.

Her mum had grown tired of Aidan's bedroom.

On the interactive whiteboard at the front of the Night School classroom was a timetable. Tonight, there was no assembly; the evening began instead, as it did on Tuesdays and Wednesdays, with Show and Tell.

Mr Him had explained that this was to help the transition from home to school. A transition they understood wasn't easy, he had said, what with all the multi-dimensional travel. Aimee, like the rest of the class, had stared at him with eyes as boggled as his. A central plank of the Night School's curriculum was to treat the pupils, as much as possible, as adults in order to empower them. Aimee remembered Barnaby explaining to her at Guardian Evening that this didn't mean treating her like an adult in the way her mum did. Over time, Aimee had learnt the Night School was as much to be trusted as Barnaby was. To her, it was as safe, as solid, as the world in which it was hidden.

"Okay Brains," said Mr Him. When he spoke, his comb-over lifted indistinctly, as though conducting his lips. "You first."

Brains stared at the teacher, crossing his eyes. He had teeth the same orientation as his eyes, but only when he did this.

"Well Brains?" said Mr Him, smiling in what he seemed to believe was a not-sociopathic way.

Brains struck himself on the right temple and, like marbles, his eyes corrected. Brains proffered a stick. It had a lump of green on the end of it. He tried to speak and swallowed. His knees jittered as though of the belief that they were running, his fingers as if they were catching up. His tongue seemed to be the only inactive part of him.

"That's lovely, Brains. What is it?"

The boy breathed. "It's not," he managed. "Stick," he added.

"Sorry Brains. Please speak up. The whole circle needs to hear you."

Sunshine leant forward. She had the face of a baby that had died and become an angel: pale and cherubic. She was the most grown-up child in the class, and acted it. "He said it's *not* a fucking stick. The mad little twat," she said.

Mr Him stared at the girl. "What are the school rules on swearing Sunshine?"

"Don't say fuck, twat, shit, bugger—"

"*Thank you* Sunshine," said Mr Him who turned to look hopefully at Brains. The boy demonstrated his stick's use, using it to prospect his right nostril. He came out with nuggets of green. "A snot stick," he said.

~68~

"Ah, I see," said Mr Him. "Very useful. Kind on the hands, I would suppose." Mr Him turned where he sat. "And what did you want to show us, Master Tower?"

"Um," said Tower.

The circle shifted to look at what Tower had put on. They looked like knee-high leather boots which, on him, came up to his hips, where he was wearing something frilly and pink.

"And these are boots and... ladies' underthings," said Mr Him, whose expression seemed stretched as though the mind behind it were close to snapping.

"These are my muh-muh-muh—" said Tower, who was not a natural at public-speaking and nearly as bad at one-on-one.

"He's dying on his arse," said Sunshine.

"Mum's," growled Mr Him.

Tower recoiled then realised he should be agreeing and nodded. "Ay-ay-ay-I'm bad walker," he breathed, "and these huh-huh-help me practise." He smiled.

"Excellent, Tow—" began Mr Him.

"These are your mum's?" asked Sunshine.

"Ye-ye-ye—"

She didn't wait for the boy to finish. "You wear your mum's knickers?"

The circle began to giggle, laughter passed from one to the next.

"Nah-no, shhhhh-she doesn't wuh-wear nah-nah-knickers when shhhhhhe goes out."

"Jesus, Tower," said Sunshine. "Your mum's a ho!"

"*Sunshine!*" said Mr Him.

"What? I only said 'Jesus'!"

"What's a ho?" asked Tower quietly, and no one seemed to hear him.

"Thank you for bringing those in Master Tower," Mr Him said. "And Aimee—" the words fluttered out on a sigh.

Aimee reached behind her and drew out a model of a house.

"You're-you're-you're—" Tower breathed, "—you're ho—"

The heads of the circle turned to stare at him.

"Your home," shouted Tower.

Aimee nodded and Mr Him's hair lowered.

"This is my bedroom," said Aimee, turning around the model and pointing at the rear, the second storey. She lifted the roof off. It was made out of corrugated cardboard. She tilted the model, so that the other children could see. On a matchbox bed, there was a cut-out of a paper girl wearing a dress that had been inked in purple and red shoes as big as her legs.

"That's me," added Aimee unnecessarily.

"Well, that's really well-made," Mr Him paused, as though forgetting something, or remembering it. "Does the class recall our lesson on homes? On the power of homes?"

"No," said Samantha.

"Was it the one ending in 'full stop'?"

"No, that was sentence construction, Brains. The lesson on homes was about how powerful they are. The one when I showed you The Wizard Of Oz?" Mr Him's voice took a hopeful turn upward.

"Was that the film with Alice in it? And the rabbit? Was the rabbit a wizard... in a green room?" asked Brains.

The lenses of Mr Him's glasses misted. He suddenly scurried backwards to the wall, writing on the board in chalk.

He wrote:

Air keeps the power of the things that has happened in it.

And, attached by a line:

In This Place, magic is in the air and you can use emotion to cast it.

With a squeak of chalk, he finished a final line:

Like Dorothy squashing the witch.

This he underlined several times.

Then he stared at them.

"No," said Brains. "Don't remember it." He shrugged.

"Ye-Ye-Ye-Ye—" said Tower, "—no."

Mr Him slumped on the wall, smearing the skin of his cheek against it. All soft yellow and beige and moistened lips, he looked like a swatted moth. Eventually, he raised his head and said, "Yes, brilliant. Look, Aimee; concentrate all your hurt and all your anger on the house you made. If you put all your anger there, you will see the power you have in This Place that you don't in The Other."

"What do you mean?" said Aimee.

"Just... try."

Aimee stared at the house, trying to feel angry. It was difficult. She never felt angry. She couldn't remember what it felt like.

She slumped.

"Okay," Mr Him climbed down. "What makes you livid?"

"Live where?" said Sunshine.

Mr Him ignored her. "What your mother does to you?"

Aimee stared at the model then shrugged.

"That your Uncle Chris just ignores it?" He was leaning forward now and peering, as though at a specimen of a disease.

His slight nostrils twitched. His lips drew back into his moustache.

The model home stood in her hands, seemingly more solid than the paper and cardboard and pen it was made out of.

"That the teachers ignore what's wrong with you?" Mr Him's tone had taken a strange turn. He licked his lips.

The girl in the purple dress on her matchbox bed appeared to be asleep.

"What's happening to your baby brother?"

Several books fell off the library shelving. A4 paper drifted into the air and danced up the wall beside Mr Him's desk. The windows rippled as though they were ponds with pebbles being dropped into them. Wind filled Aimee's ears, but she didn't hear it. The classroom reverberated as though it had been slapped. There was a crack. The circle of children stared at the house. It didn't seem to have moved. Aimee couldn't see. Her vision was covered in nameless shapes, like shadows on the wall at night, or like what the mind made of them. The model appeared to be unblemished.

"Dear God," said Sunshine, as though shocked enough to follow the school rules.

The board on the classroom wall had a large fissure running through its centre, crossing out *witch*.

"Stop! Stop!" shouted Mr Him, eyes shying as though waking from a dream.

Aimee couldn't hear him. Her ears were filled with screaming, and it sounded like her voice. Unseen through the shade that had shoaled in her corneas, the model house flew out of her palm and impacted in the light above the Show and Tell circle. Sparks floated down like magical dust.

Aimee leant forward and coughed, cupping her mouth as her mum had trained her. She stared at the lump of blood on her palm.

"Children just don't understand—" It was Mr Him. He stood nearby. Aimee looked up and saw that he was smiling his adult's smile. "—there are consequences to every action."

"WHY CAN'T I BRING my baby here? Why can't I bring him with me?" said Aimee.

"Not here," said Barnaby, meaning the argument not her younger brother.

Other guardians waited close by to pick up their pupils from the classrooms. It was early morning and time for the children to go home and get out of bed. A giant plastic baby crouched behind a cluster of yellow tables; a Rainbow Brite flickered in and out of existence, tapping her right foot impatiently as she waited for Sunshine and glancing at the clock on the wall. The face had one hand, and it read quarter to Get Up! Time was getting short, not to mention blunt. A dragon's throat filled the corridor to the hall, and other guardians pushed their way past her scales, muttering apologies. The dragon said sporadically, "sorry… sorry—" huffing out ashes that had been caught between her teeth (one of which looked like a sheep). The Christian (the Night School caretaker) wiped soot from the floor around her snout.

Aimee's voice fell to a whisper. Her eyes were red around the edges of the irises and as veined as the classroom board.

"She's going to touch him. I have to save him," she said.

Barnaby sighed. The smell of red meat emanated from his maw. "I can only rescue one child at a time. The child has to hold my hand. You know that… I don't have any spare hands Aimee."

The girl's shoulders sagged, disappearing into the ruff of her lilac dress.

"Don't worry about the board," he said, thinking she felt guilty for her emotions. "It'll heal."

"She's going to get him," she whispered. "She's going to get him."

THE NIGHT SCHOOL STAFF often said that the Christian put the 'taking care' into 'caretaker'. Now the guardians were gone, he fastidiously picked his way across the tiles, careful not to stand on the lines between each. Small dark cracks were anathematic to him. Softly, he whistled hymns from Mission Praise. He ritually recited number seven, beginning:

"All creatures of our God and King,

Lift up your voice and with us sing."

Not because the lines bought him closer to God, but because he considered the number seven lucky. So were, as far as the Christian reckoned, nine, three and one. He didn't really think any numbers were unlucky, but then he would have to think of unlucky numbers to regard them as such, and he refused to think about certain numbers at all.

The Christian entered the disabled toilet on the way to the hall. 'The Christian', as a name, was both a misnomer and completely accurate. Accurate because he was a piously observant Christian. A misnomer because he also worshipped false idols. He spotted a mosaic of a magpie on the wall to the Infant classrooms and saluted it. He didn't only salute fake magpies, however, but also sparrows, finches, swallows and any other bird. Birds were sacred to the Christian because they flew in the air and because, in This Place, that was where the magic was. He carried salt in his pocket and threw it over his shoulder whenever he entered a new room. This didn't aid his cleaning of the disabled toilet. Neither did the sand.

"Dear God, Allah, Vishnu—" The Christian continued for a few moments before saying, "—this is a mess."

It was always the disabled toilet, and it was always sand, and when it wasn't sand it was blood. Children! he thought with some vexation. How do they make such a mess? He also thought, I'd better clean this before the Headmistress sees it, but these words didn't register consciously. Only the tension did. He began to scrub, using his bucketful of brushes and water, and was particularly careful to clean each tile three times in an anti-clockwise direction.

"THIS IS YOUR break-time you're wasting," said Mr Mann. He was going red, as he did whenever he shouted. Mrs Skinner stood at the back of the class, washing paint pots with the kind of clunking, satisfied sound that suggested she was smiling at the wall.

"*This is your break-time you're wasting,*" said Adam.

"Right. Detention for you, Adam. Anyone else want to join him?"

Adam looked as if he might say, "not me," but Mr Mann's eyes did their best to grow until they had swallowed his glasses, so Adam didn't. Mr Mann was losing more hair each night, unveiling a scalp that had begun to resemble a no entry sign with a series of hairs as its horizontal bar. The follicles were already going white.

The line stood quietly.

The palettes in the sink clunked against the water-pots, and Mrs Skinner began to hum to herself.

"Right," said Mr Mann, not for the first time. "Out you go. And no running."

The corridor to Class 7 ran alongside its wall and Amy, who stood near the back of the line, could hear the pitter-patter of tiny sprinting feet as they passed by.

She also heard Mr Mann as he walked to the pile of dark green books on his desk. "Where's my pen? Why do pens always go missing?" His voice was breathless, the syllables of a man who had been strangled for some time. Amy passed out of hearing him as she left the classroom and entered the corridor.

She skipped, somewhere in the world of the passageway and the Junior playground at the end of it and somewhat outside both. As ever, her mind bridged the divide between This Place and The Other and, if adults said she was in the Land of Nod, they were always at least half right.

It took some time for the little girl to notice that Catherine, her classmate, was speaking to her.

"—do you want to play with us?" Catherine repeated.

Amy considered the question from the pigtailed brunette as if it were a question being asked by a pig that was flying. She didn't play with anybody at break-time, or lunchtime for that matter, and hadn't been asked before.

"Yes," she said after a moment. During that moment, she'd looked down at a quartered square painted on the ground, each quarter numbered one through to four, and then up at the sky, which was cloudy. She hadn't looked around her, at the gathering group of girls—each clinging to the arm of another (and giggling)—until they surrounded her. Attached to more gigglers than any other girl was the blonde-haired Lucy.

"Do you want to play a game? It's called tig," said Lucy. "Spit-tig."

"What's spit-tig?" said Amy.

"*Weeell* it's like tig, but you make the person it by spitting on them." Lucy's diction was as flawless as her hair, which managed to catch the sun and glimmer even though it was now beginning to rain. "Do you want us to show you?"

Amy shrugged. "Yes," she said. Used to being alone, she felt confused by the number of children and her brain was having a hard time keeping an eye on them all, as well as listening to Lucy.

"It's like this… Catherine… show her."

Catherine's jowls, already widened by the passing of a large amount of Walkers crisps, Coca-Cola and McDonald's, wiggled as she hawked then spat a line of gunge. It laced out like spaghetti—hanging between her lips and Amy's tights—but see-through and not entirely yellow.

"You see? You're it," said Lucy. "Probably the best bath you've had in weeks, isn't it?"

The crowd of girls laughed and a red blush, shiny as Mr Mann's scalp, spread up from Amy's legs to her face.

Another girl (she couldn't see who, not because the girl was behind Amy but because Amy's vision was wavering with heat and compressed rage) spat on her neck.

"Dirty girl," the girl said. "Get her clean."

The rest of the crowd began to spit, except Lucy—who had wandered away, smiling.

Ms Lydia, the teacher on duty, caught Amy five minutes later, crimson-faced and punching Catherine in the cheek until her jowls vibrated on their own. Amy spent her next break in the foyer outside the headmistress's room. She stood alone, having not told Ms Lydia about spit-tig. Amy didn't like to talk to adults.

IT HAD BEEN RAINING and the wheels of the bus, as it drew to the stop, were silky black like rolls of liquorice. They kicked up a frond of water which soaked Christopher's jeans and missed hers. An inopportune wind blew him off-balance, plastering a bag with **Yams From Uganda** on it to his wet shins. The writing was thick and dark. If it was a sign, Christopher had no idea as to its meaning. He felt abruptly on edge, aware of all of the foreigners about him in the bus stop, of their languages, their foreign looks. Often, they were bigger and balder than him, especially the ones with tattoos. He wouldn't have admitted it but he feared them and whatever they meant when they whispered, and the fear threatened to make a racist out of him if only from sheer desperation. Prejudice was fast becoming his last shred of self-respect.

"Why haven't you got the change ready?" she said with a hiss. She wasn't at her happiest in the drizzle.

The bus doors opened to the same sound as her lips. Christopher loved those lips. There was nothing remarkable about his face. His features were the kind that no woman would recall, unless he had saved her from beneath the wheels of a bus. And nothing could save Amy's mother. More than once a day, he wished he didn't love her.

"For fuck's sake, get a hurry on. You're worse than my kids. Get the money out!" She smiled at the driver as she mounted the steps, cocking her left thumb. "He's got more bloody money than sense—" she said, before adding loudly, as she walked into the gangway, "—and we're bloody broke."

Along the bus, laughter spread quick and nervous as coughing.

Blushing the kind of colour you get from bending over, Christopher dug in his jeans and placed a tenner on the driver's dashboard, saying, "Family DaySaver". The driver printed it off, stared unpleasantly at the note and gave Christopher the change.

Aidan was already sitting on his mother's lap. Amy was doing her best to work herself into a smudge on the wall beneath the window of the seat in front. Christopher tried to work out which pocket was best for the ticket. She would murder him if he lost it. They didn't have the money to just chuck it away. Money didn't just grow on trees. He should just go and get a fucking job. She was looking out of the window and playing with Aidan's hair, her nails on his scalp. The toddler shifted and whined and the nails dug in. Christopher went for his right front pocket, stuffing the ticket in and down.

"Hurry yourself up and sit. You look like an idiot just standing there."

The bus began to move and Christopher staggered, making a prophecy of her words. He sat.

"I hate buses," she added loudly. "Bloody poverty wagons. If you could afford to fix the car, we wouldn't have to be sat here."

There was no laughter now, only stares. She could start a punch-up in a nunnery, Christopher thought but didn't say aloud. The stares pricked his skin as the bus stopped again and filled quickly. There must be something going on in Bury, Christopher thought but didn't say. He didn't like to talk on buses, not because he didn't like the sound of his own voice (which he didn't, in public), but because he knew the looks he would get when she replied. Why do you put up with that? the stares would say, but would keep schtum. When the staring said that, Christopher would think of Tommy and what she had done with him at the local on New Year's Eve.

An old man, wearing a blue cap and with skin that looked like it had been sketched on ancient canvas, shuffled slowly past. The driver watched in the rear view mirror, waiting for him to sit. The old man didn't say anything, but the slowness of his gait was enough for Christopher to know there were no other seats available. Christopher knew the sign hidden by Amy's mum said *Please give these seats to people who need them.*

He should get up.

He rose. Her hand taloned onto his right thigh. Christopher thought of a dragon. It was the most physical contact they'd shared that day.

"Don't you bloody move," she said. "I don't want to sit next to some weirdo."

The bus driver sighed above the sound of the engine as he gunned it. The old man was forced to grab at the grey plastic of the post beside Christopher's ear and to lean against his side as the bus moved off.

Mutters spread along the aisle and to the seats, as the giggles had before. The prickles of stares on his back became a rash that blistered up from Christopher's nape and to his face. He began to feel like that hitchhiker in Texas Chain Saw Massacre; he blushed so frequently, its red stain had become permanent. He wondered if he was going a little crazy and wished he had the hitchhiker's flick knife in his pocket next to the DaySaver.

"God, can you smell that?" she said, glancing at the old man.

Christopher thought he could. Despite the slick that had formed on his own skin, the smell wasn't sweat—it was deeper, older, sourer than that, and had long ago sunk into him.

"HOLD UP, LOVE," said Uncle Chris.

Mum dragged Aidan all the quicker. The toddler squalled as the rain did, before she threatened him with a stare and the shower fell back into a laconic drizzle. Amy's forehead had quickly gained a sheen of wet. She drew her arm across it and greased her fringe, which made absolutely no difference.

Amy swung her arms and the sketchpad at the end of her right hand. She was smiling. She liked to go to Nan's. Her cream-coated, cosy-centred house was another world to the little girl. Though it was separated from her own by only a bus ride, this seemed like an extraordinary length to go to in order to travel to an Other Place, especially as she was used to travelling by teddy bear. But Uncle Tommy would be there, and Amy liked Uncle Tommy; he was good-looking and funny. She thought Mum liked him too. She thought Chris knew.

She skipped, and puddles splashed around her feet. "Can we race you through the park, Mum?" Amy asked. "Can we?" Mum didn't like parks. They contained children and so she would go the longer, pavemented way around. "Please, Mum?"

Her mother looked down at her, eyes darkening as though deciding what emotion to be. She glanced slyly back at Uncle Chris, who was starting to catch them, and said, "Go on then, love."

Amy's heart swelled with joy and adrenaline.

"Ready—" said Mum.

Amy bit her lip, and it bunched and reddened like a sting.

"—Steady—"

With that, Mum let go of Aidan and ran down the street.

"Hang—" Uncle Chris started to say. Amy ignored him, laughed, grabbed Aidan and ran, tugging him left past the swings. His short legs peddled on—and half the time off—the path. The slide whooshed by. They ran between a dog and its man. Amy jumped, and wrenched Aidan as his trainer got caught in the lead. The dog tried to bark but found itself out of breath.

"Oi!" shouted the man on the dog's behalf.

"Sorry," said Amy over her shoulder, as she pulled Aidan away and they ran.

"She's going to beat us. Faster! Faster! Faster!" Amy yelled into the rain.

Aidan said, "Weeeeeeeeee—"

She could see the park gate. The old lady before it. Her nan's road beyond.

Giggling, she yelled, "Quicker!"

Giggling also, Aidan shouted, "Quicker!"

They ran quicker. The air coming out of her lips was as much a blur as the path.

Amy, though, could see the road clearly as they closed on the gate and, at the end of it, her mother appeared, sprinting.

"No!" she shouted, laughing.

"No!" laughed Aidan.

Mum was smiling.

The old lady on the path said, "Aidan?... Little Amy?" She had a purple duffle coat slightly darker than her rinsed hair. Nan's next-door neighbour, Amy thought. Her tongue ran away with itself, Nan said. Amy was the one who needed to be running, so she didn't stop.

"Amy, is that you love?"

The old lady turned on her cloggish black shoes as the children passed and Amy shouted, "No, I'm Bob. This is Jackie!"

"Bob—?" the old lady said, but they were through the gate now, and up the road, and right into the drive, and squeezing past the black BMW that shimmered in the rain like a mirage

for the wet weather. Mum was giggling as they reached her—
and the porch. She was knocking. Her cheeks were as high as
when she was throwing things and swearing at home, but her
eyes were different. Amy couldn't figure out how but would
have willingly spent a lifetime studying them to find out.

"Hah, losers," Mum said, as the door opened and she went
in.

Flushed, Amy skipped into the doorway. Before she could
even take off her shoes (because this was the only house in
which she had to) she was lifted off her feet.

"Put that girl down, for God's sake. Have some bloody
manners at your age," said Nan.

"Oh, come on, she loves it. Don't you, Little Fart?" said
Uncle Tommy.

He pushed her head into his lustrous hair. He was dark-
skinned, but not in the way Amy was a black sheep with her
clay coloured face and awkwardly melded features. He had the
look of Hercules, and Amy should know, having traced him by
forefinger in her Unwin Book of Greek Legends. She often
tried to sneak a look at his feet to see if they were Herculean,
but he always wore trainers (like Lucy's—with the tick—but
blue not pink), even at Nan's. Nan only let him wear shoes. He
looked utterly unlike Mum, but that was because they weren't
really brother and sister, Nan said. Amy had often wondered
what an uncle was.

Tommy was good-looking and muscled with white teeth,
which were, right now, laughing as he perched Amy on the
polo shirt that covered his wide shoulders. Her head, as he
spun her, hit an intricate crystal lampshade that shivered and

tinkled with the same delicacy as her innards did when Uncle Tommy was near.

"Put the child down," said Nan. From above, her shoulder pads were wide and floral. Her glasses glinted like his eyes. "That fitting cost a bloody fortune."

"Okay, okay, keep your fake teeth in Mum," said Uncle Tommy, lowering Amy.

He always called her Mum, even though she wasn't really, and she swiped his arm as if he was her son. "Got a hug in there for your old Grandma, have you love?" she said.

"Oh, you're a Grandma, are you now *Nan*?" said Mum. Her mouth always sounded like it was in her nose when she came to Nan's. "Why not 'Ma'am'?" Mum gave a little curtsy.

Nan ignored her and buried Amy into the width under her armpits. She smelt, as she always did, of perfume as flowery as her dresses but thick like week-old flowers clumping brown in their vase.

Behind her, Amy heard Uncle Tommy say, "Oh, who's this? He's so big, I'm scared. Are you a boxer?"

Aidan giggled.

"Oh, don't hurt me, Mr Little Man," said Uncle Tommy. Amy could feel him cowering into her back as Nan released her. "Please, please don't hurt me or I'll have to—" Uncle Tommy whisked out towards the toddler. He lifted Aidan off his tiny trainered feet. "—I'll have to cuddle you. Give your old uncle a cuddle, Little Man." He laughed, his teeth flashing white in his tanned face.

Aidan always got Little Man.

Uncle Tommy was closing the front door with his free hand when a muddy old trainer poked below it. Uncle Chris's leg followed.

"Oh, sorry mate. Didn't know you were coming," said Uncle Tommy.

"Aye, I did," said Uncle Chris. He sounded sarcastic but only by accident. "I mean, yeah, I came... mate."

Amy could hear the slight linen hiss of Chris and Uncle Tommy shaking hands. She knew Tommy would tower over him, and Uncle Chris would crumble and try not to show it.

"How you doing, mate?" Chris said in a squeak. Uncle Chris's voice heightened when he was crumbling.

"Can't complain, bruv. And you?" said Uncle Tommy.

"Yeah, the same, yeah."

There was no animosity between the two men, and no love lost. It was clear who Mum looked at most when they spoke, and the knowing of this hung around Uncle Chris like an unidentified smell. Either that or it was his trainers, or maybe his stained jeans.

"Do you want a brew, young man?" Nan asked Uncle Chris. She always called him 'a nice young man' and, when he wasn't there, 'you could do worse, love'.

"John's in the lounge," she added.

"Hello," said Uncle John from his seat in the lounge in front of a large black TV. He looked how Amy remembered him and was in the same position, with his flushed bald head limned by the football playing beyond it and wearing the kind of casual sportswear that was in Mum's Grattan catalogue. Uncle John had the look of an orange goblin in soft cotton. Uncle John was not an uncle, but Nan's new husband. He couldn't be one of Mum's brothers, Amy recalled thinking, because that wouldn't be allowed. "Hello Amy, sweetheart," he said.

"Hello Uncle John."

"Stop sweethearting the child and turn that bloody nonsense off. You have guests," said Nan, before saying, "Come and help me in the kitchen, sweetheart."

Amy nodded, walked into the kitchen, put her sketchpad on a surface that looked like it was trying to copy the marble in the Roman history book she had stolen from the school library, and boiled the kettle. She poured the water over the tea bags, spooned sugar, added milk, and cautiously carried the cups into the lounge.

"Careful," said Mum, "don't stain the perfect house."

Amy blushed as she stared at the beige circles of tea. Tea swilled toward the thin lips of china with each of her steps. Not for the first time, she felt like she was made out of wood. As quickly as she could, with her chunky feet and clunking limbs, she put the cups on the dwarven wooden tables positioned around the lounge. They were the same dark colour as the giant-sized one in the dining room. In Nan's house, everything was matching—except that there were lots more pictures of Auntie Cat than of Amy's Mum, and Cat's had frames.

Amy sat on a slip of sofa beside her mother. She felt swollen, with a second skin made of blush and incipient sweat, and tried to disappear into the soft, wide, white settee. She wasn't doing as good a job as Uncle Chris, who was still standing. Despite her house-pride, Nan hadn't noticed this.

Uncle Tommy walked in and all eyes went to him instead. He had come from the kitchen.

"Hang on, hang on, Little Fart, I've got a present for you," he said. His right arm was bent up behind his wide polo-shirted back. On the front of the shirt there was a horse and a rider, which bent out over his muscle as it bunched.

"Oh no, not this," said Nan. The right side of her lips turned out, like her daughter's did, into a sneer.

Mum grinned and shifted slightly on her soft cushion. She lowered her head, blew on her tea and stared up at Uncle Tommy. Uncle Chris looked at anywhere but them. There were too many people in the room and his eyes seemed hemmed in. He was even more pale than normal and bled into the neutral lounge walls.

"Aye, now where was it, this wonderful present?" said Uncle Tommy as he spun around searching. There was a jar in the hand behind his back. Amy couldn't help but giggle, even as the blush re-emerged to choke her throat and then her cheeks. "It's such a special present, and it was around here somewhere, I'm sure. I *do* hope it hasn't been stolen."

"It's behind you," shouted Uncle John grinning, his cheeks glistening as they bulged.

"Idiot," said Nan again, though this time to Uncle John.

"Oh, yeah, here it is, yeah," said Uncle Tommy, pulling the jar out in front of him. It was one Nan used in her cooking for her bowling dos.

Mum laughed, her lips and cheeks moving when her eyes would not leave Tommy.

"Thank goodness," said Uncle Tommy. "Oh my days, that was close." He smiled at Amy.

"Uncle Tommy!" said Amy, her feet twisting at the end of her legs. The red on her face was hot as spilt tea.

"I told you not to take that," said Nan. "I use it for my chutney."

"Chutney! No... this—" said Uncle Tommy, "—is a very special jar. A magical jar. Because this magical jar is the Magical Jar Of Invisible Water!"

"All water's invisible!" shouted Uncle John.

"Idiots," Nan said to them both.

Uncle Chris didn't say anything.

"But—" said Uncle Tommy, "—this water's so invisible, you won't even see it when you drink it. And I can prove it! I can prove it, Little Fart. Just you open up this jar and take a big swig, and it'll be inside you before you can say Jiminy Cricket, and *your lips won't even feel a thing!*"

Amy stared at him as he pushed the jar into her grip. The room had quietened.

"Ready to drink, Little Fart?" His fingertips were around the lid. "Down the hatch, as they say."

Amy nodded. She thought she might accidentally cry. She stared at the jar and its contents may well have been wavering, like little waves of water. Or that could have been the tears forming in her eyes.

"Ready—" He unscrewed. "—Steady... Drink!"

The lid came off, and Amy opened her mouth and gagged and dropped the jar. It clunked on the thick-pile carpet. Her cheeks writhed around her lips. Her nostrils drew back in an instinctive snarl.

The living room exploded into laughter.

"A fart for Little Fart," roared Uncle Tommy. He was gripping the back of Nan's chair as he laughed, as if to stop himself falling. "A big fat fart."

The flowers on Nan's dress shook like a garden in a gale. From beneath her laughter, Amy could hear, "Bloody idiot… Bloody idiot—"

"That's disgusting, mate." Uncle John slapped Tommy's back. "When did you lay that?"

"Just now in the kitchen."

"Sick, son."

"That was for my chutney," managed Nan again.

Uncle Tommy grasped back the jar and, staring at it, said, "I think I started it off for you, Mum. The fart was like a bit wet."

"That's my bloody brother," Mum said. Her eyes were labelling him in a different way, and she was wiping at their sides. "Farting in a bloody jar. Go on, love, get a real drink. You look like you need one."

Amy's eyes were weeping, perhaps from the stink. A picture in the stolen Roman history book was captioned *The Fall of Rome—Vandals in the Senate*. Her family reminded her of this: their stretched, laughing faces, the white settee, the white carpet, the magnolia walls, the sharpness of their teeth and eyes. The walls echoed as though they were clapping hands.

Auntie Cat walked into the lounge.

"What's this racket about then?" she asked.

Mum's eyes slid off Uncle Tommy, her laughter hanging awkwardly on her gums. Her sight flicked away to the mantelpiece and its pictures of Auntie Cat getting married, Auntie Cat graduating, Auntie Cat in her bank uniform. The last of Mum's grin was road-kill plastered to the grill of her teeth. Her alabaster face tightened as though it would split, going so pale it may as well have been see-through. There were no photos of Mum in this room. They were in the kitchen on the corkboard.

Uncle Tommy distracted Amy by moving smoothly (too smoothly—he made Amy think of spittle in a sink) to hug his wife by the shoulder and kiss her cheek. "Nothing but me acting the idiot," he said.

She shrugged him away. Like everything else in the room, he seemed overly close. "No surprise there then," said Cat, and the laughter returned for longer than Amy thought it should do. "Alright sis?" Auntie Cat said to Amy's mum.

"Aye, fine. You?" said Mum.

"Still looking for a beach to get stuck on," said Auntie Cat, rubbing her belly.

Laughter.

Her mother thrust Amy away from her and towards the kitchen.

"Go on," said her mum. "Get your brother a drink as well. Adult time now. Go on, find little Aidan."

"He's in front of the telly in the dining room," said Uncle Tommy. "I put some cartoons on for him."

"Thanks," said Mum, smiling at him.

"No problem love," he said, smiling back.

In the kitchen, Amy filled two cups with squash, walked through to the dining room, and put one to the side of Aidan, who was sitting on one of the dark wooden chairs and watching a mouse skinning a cat.

"There's more than one way to skin a cat," the mouse said.

Aidan stared at it, unmoving. There were TVs in three of Nan's rooms. You aren't doing well, Amy thought, if you haven't got at least three TVs.

Amy put down her drink on one of the short tables. Also on the table-top was a Russian doll, like the one in her mum's bedroom but skinnier, as though the bigger one around it had gone for a snack. Like her mum's, Amy didn't like its blank eyes or hungry smile, and she placed her drink as far away from it as she could then went and got her sketchpad, which she'd left on the kitchen surface. She returned to the dining room, sat on the chair, and opened the pad. It said, over the sketched Latter Wood (the top of which was coloured in anaemically in white crayon), *The Witch is Beautiful and has been Asleep for many years. Only one who loves her, and one she loves, can wake her...* Ignoring this, Amy began to colour the opposite corner of the Latter Wood in yellow.

"I GOT THE DUCK FROM Tesco," said Nan. "It's as good as Marks and Spencer, you know, these days."

Amy nodded, in lieu of the fact that her mum didn't. Mum's icy eyes were firing up. Amy could have told Nan that was a bad sign, but then again, Nan should have known.

"Cat's done such a good job helping me cook it. She's going to be a great mum, aren't you love?"

Cat nodded, her head long in a way that could have been described as horsey, her belly wide in way that could only have been described as pregnant. Amy glanced at the nectarine curve of her belly then at her mum's, and couldn't quite believe she had ever been in *there*. Amy couldn't shake this disbelief, which was unusual for a girl who believed in talking bears. She was sure, though, that Auntie Cat's stomach was nectarine, because the rest of her skin was so tanned it was orange.

"Yes Mum," Cat said, interrupting Amy's thoughts and doing nothing to defrost the colour of Mum's eyes.

Cat had been in the bathroom when they'd arrived. "I'm *always* in the bathroom these days," she'd said when they'd 'retired to the dining room' (as Nan had put it).

"I thought you retired when you married John," Amy's mum had said.

Cat and Mum had hugged, as stiff as the fine china the tea was served in and nowhere near as warm as its contents. There was something between them, and it wasn't the unborn, hidden child. It was a secret, and Amy intuitively didn't like secrets that involved her mother.

"Stop hanging around the bloody plonk and get in here," said Nan to Tommy, slapping his bottom with a tea-towel.

Uncle Tommy laughed, deep and bubbling as the gravy that had been on the hob.

They went into the dining room and sat around the dark-wood table on the dark-wood chairs. In cabinets of the same wood sat delicately white figurines ('Lad Row' Nan had called them—one of the models was of a boy rowing a boat, which explained that) and Russian-sounding crystal pieces of cats and mice and things Amy didn't recognise, but which made her think of the northern reaches of the Latter Wood and the Witch's kingdom. Had she been old enough to know it, Amy would have realised that her nan had married into the nouveau middle class. Certainly, her mum used to mutter on the nights after days like these, "She made right sure she married up, didn't she? After my dad. And me? I got you, didn't I? The only thing that went up for me was my belly. The only thing I got was a bloody bastard." And Amy would fall silent and pensive and try to go away in her mind, because she thought Mum was talking about her dad. She wouldn't have been upset if she'd realised the bastard was her.

"Help yourself to the vegetables," said Cat, as she waddled in. She had, apparently, cooked this dish. "No need to stand on ceremony, it'll go cold." She had a tiny, tight, feminine voice, each word precise and defined as a pin shoved into Amy's mum's skin.

"Stop making that bloody racket," Mum said to Aidan, who'd been sitting silently. He stared at her.

"Well," said Uncle John, glancing at Mum, "did you see the Twin Towers, love?"

Mum's lips untwisted around her mouth. "Aye, it came on during Crossroads. Horrible wasn't it? I was saying to Tracey from work, what if they fly into the Arndale? They've not finished rebuilding after the last time. And she was like, every time I see a plane in the sky, I think it's going to fly into my house."

"Oh, the jihadists aren't after any old building, you know. They're not like the IRA," said Cat, who was now sitting.

"They're after financial institutions." She pronounced the last two words carefully, as though they were learnt from a French dictionary and she gripped Uncle Tommy's hand, who quickly did the same with hers before picking up his knife.

"Are they now?" said Mum, her lips doing the chewing thing though they hadn't started eating yet.

"Oh yes," said Cat. "Try the duck. It's best hot, you know. Yes, the Twin Towers were full of financial traders and financial companies. That's what al-Qaeda wanted to hit. Our bank's on high alert, you know. They're looking for suspicious packages, but we haven't been told why."

"Just as long as you're protected sweetheart," said Uncle Tommy. "In your condition."

"They're not only after *bankers*," said Mum. She always pronounced the last word as if it rhymed with another favourite of hers. "Loads of firemen died as well, you know. It said so on the news, you know, and they wouldn't be lying now, would they?"

Nan stirred. "Of course dear, they died because they were trying to save the bankers, weren't they?"

Mum's cheeks clotted red, her jaw muscles tensing. About now, she would normally be throwing something. Amy was finding it difficult to swallow.

"Well it's that lot, isn't it?" said Mum, through teeth she didn't seem able to ungrit. "They're everywhere these days. One's moved in to number 41, down my street."

"Weeeell—" said Cat. "It isn't all people from ethnic groups, you know. We have to be careful not to have a knee-jerk, reaction, I think." She served herself carrots, delicately.

Amy didn't know who the 'we' was, but her mum's knee wasn't the part Amy worried would jerk. Her mother's hands were fists clenched around Nan's cutlery, which was all metal with no plastic handles.

"So Chris, pal," said Uncle John nimbly, his skin glistening as it always did. "How's the car? How'd you get here today, mate?"

"Broke," managed Uncle Chris, hacking on a gobbet of breast. He went as red as Mum's cheek-spots but all over, and had to, after several heaves, spit it into his serviette. The redness went to crimson, like the DEFCONs in American war films.

Into the breach, Uncle John continued, "I'll pop round. You should've said. I'll have to check it over, get it up and running."

Uncle Chris nodded. By the look of things, he had no choice but to do so. He still couldn't speak.

"And how's business love?" said Nan to Uncle Tommy.

"Never better. It's a boom time in retail. We were fitting in Bristol last night, and Sheffield tomorrow. Putting them up all over the fucking shop," he laughed at his own joke, and his shining teeth laughed with him.

"Language," said Nan, glowering over a pea.

"Sorry, mother dear," he replied, laughing.

"Got any jobs for this one?" Mum jacked a knife at Uncle Chris. "He's been looking for a year."

Still bloated by the choking, Uncle Chris stared up the table with big watery eyes like those of dead frog at the bottom of a pond, slowly being eroded. "Ten months," he managed.

"Sorry sweetheart. Got a tight crew." Uncle Tommy seemed to abruptly realise that he should be addressing Uncle Chris and that Cat was watching him. "Sorry bruv. If I could, I would."

"Thanks anyway, mate. Don't worry about it." The way Uncle Chris said the last, it sounded like he was saying, "stop talking about it".

The conversation wandered into the safer territory of Corrie and Crossroads, and the dinner was finished and the plates cleared away. Mum managed to say "thank you for that", once to her sister, then quickly said to Amy, "Say thank you. Where's your bloody manners?" And then to Cat again, "Kids, eh?"

After dessert, they decided to play Monopoly. Mum had wanted to play cards like when they were younger, before Nan married John and, in hindsight, it would have been safer to have done what she said. Amy could have told them that, but she was doing as much speaking as Uncle Chris.

"Well, then, you should be the *banker*," said Mum.

Cat's eyes flicked up as Mum said it, as though her mind were catching a ball. She gripped her stomach.

Mum continued, "It's what you do all the time, after all love. How about some more wine down this end?"

"Haven't you had enough?" said Nan.

"Why nooo. Not like we're driving, is it eh? You should have some more wine, eh fella?" she said, not even looking at Chris. "Not like you're driving either, is it?"

Uncle Chris went to the toilet.

"Is his bladder alright?" hissed Uncle Tommy. Mum laughed harder than the rest and stared sideways at him through the narrowest part of her eyelids. Uncle Chris had been more times than the number of plates Auntie Cat had brought to the table. Amy eyed the cheese. It didn't look like the Dairylea triangles in her lunchbox.

"Can I watch TV with Aidan?" asked Amy.

Mum shrugged, and Amy got out of the room while the going was good.

Mum's going, not long after, wouldn't be good.

Amy didn't watch TV but continued penning a thumbnail of the Christian instead, and only heard the argument as it reached shouting.

"Oh that's how you're all so bloody successful, isn't it?" Mum was shouting, "—well have your bloody money then, if you have to cheat and swindle to get it."

There was the murmured sound of Nan.

"And you can shut up, an' all. Who do you think you bloody are? Lladró this and Portugal golfing holiday bloody that. Like you're the bloody bees' knees. You married a bloody garage owner not the bloody king, with your BMW on the drive, all buffed and bloody shining—"

"That's enough," yelled Nan. The bang of mug on wood. Amy's pulse jolted the way Pinocchio's would have done.

"Oh is it now? BMW? Bloody Muppet Wagon! And I'm sorry Tommy, but your wife is a stuck-up cow!"

Yells.

Auntie Cat: "How dare you? I don't know what's up with you, and I don't know what's up between you two." Her voice muffled as it changed direction. "Tommy, tell me what's going on."

"I'll tell you what's going on," shouted Amy's mum. The magnolia walls seemed to draw back, aghast. "You think you've made it. You think you're better than me. Well, I ain't staying nowhere where I'm not wanted. Yeah?"

By the time Amy had worked out that meant they were leaving, Mum was already in the lounge.

"Get your stuff," said her mother. She scuffed her shoes across the clean carpet as she put them on. She didn't look at her children. Uncle Chris followed behind her at a distance. Amy had seen old dogs in the park doing the same, with a similar expression on their faces. Nan came after them, and her face was a mixed bag of rage, bloating and gelatine, moving as she shouted, "Don't you dare turn your back on me, young lady!"

"Young lady?" This was too much. "Young lady? When was I ever a fucking lady? I'm too much like you, you old sod. Don't think just because you've dyed your hair and got your bloody Joan Collins shoulders and your hoity-toity house, that I've forgotten the way it used to be in that flat with him. Don't you go pretending you were a bloody angel. What did you ever do for me? New husband, new life is it? Well I remember, and it never goes away. Never!"

There was jeopardy in her nan's voice, like that in the teachers' when they told Amy to stay on the pavement on school trips, as she said, "Don't you go there. I've had enough of that! Don't you go there."

But go her mum did, barging through the front door. Amy was unsure if she and Aidan should follow, but she did anyway, with a quick hug from her Nan who said, "you best go love," and who was crying tears as thick as the lenses of her glasses.

Amy didn't ask if she wanted to race her again. Mum was still shouting as they walked into the street. Though nobody was at the window of Nan's house, neighbours were gathering at theirs. Mum wasn't shouting at them either though. At times like these, Amy would have sworn on the Witch's Moon that her mother was talking to voices that weren't there. Well, not talking to, as Amy doubted the voices would be stupid enough to speak back. At these moments, it seemed Mum was off with the fairies, and Amy would envy her and fade out somewhat to somewhere else, and her world would become all whiny like Aidan when she was feeding him laburnum seeds. Inevitably, her mother would turn on Amy and the right side of her lips would turn out, but Amy wouldn't hear her at all. And then the This Place would become an awful lot louder and more real.

By the time they'd stepped onto the bus, and travelled down the Old Road, and stepped off the bus, and allowed the houses of the F roads then the E roads to close in—with these streets narrowing like an asthma attack—Amy was more than ready to go travelling again, but this time by bear.

THE SHOUTING GOT under his skin, particularly that of his head, and crawled around his bones, particularly his skull. They—the pupils—gave Mr Him, even after several decades in the job, a headache. Mr Him had never got used to children, no matter how old and withered and parasitic he became (both in skin-tone and tastes). It may have been noted that teaching was not the perfect career for the likes of him, but there weren't many employers in the Latter Wood, and just as few teachers (especially ones that didn't defecate on the carpet).

The Night School had implemented a Play Curriculum. The Head felt that these children needed a forum in which to play securely, to experiment, to create. That they would benefit from talking to their peers, sharing, and from socialisation. Mr Him could not have felt any more differently. He thought that these children, particularly Angel and Aimee, could do with discipline. That they needed what they got at home, only more of it—the rod, the cane, the slipper, or anything else that came to hand, preferably metallic. However, he wasn't the Head and, no matter how hard he yearned to be the Iron Fist or the Foot Up The Backside, he couldn't be and he had to suffer as they shouted and ripped up his resources.

It came to a head, as it did at least once a week, that night.

While Mr Him was trying to stop Brains eating sand, Tower rushed up. "Miss… Miss—" he said to Mr Him. Mr Him didn't notice this transgendering anymore and did his best to ignore Tower, until Tower began to poke him in his back. Mr Him swung around, the back of his hand itching to be used.

"*What?*" he said, fearing the worst as Tower opened his mouth to answer. Mr Him swore he could see the boy's tonsils stuttering.

Oh crap, he thought.

He was to be pleasantly shocked. "Sunshine stabbed me with a pencil!" Tower said.

"Sunshine... really?" said Mr Him. Sunshine was his favourite, but then, he realised, she could well have done it. He liked his favourites to have a little fight, though not too much.

There was something of the teacher, though, in Mr Him, and an idea went off in the back of his mind like an alarm clock he had forgotten he owned, hidden at the bottom of a cupboard. It irritated Mr Him that he still had pedagogical leanings.

"Sunshine!" he shouted. He clapped his hands three times, and then again and, belatedly, the class did the same. "Sunshine," he said as they quietened. The sound of this was a balm on his head, and—most of all—on his ears, like the eye of a hurricane. "Come here!"

She did so, her sour lips turning down, her eyes black, her cheeks an opposite sort of white.

"Did you stab Tower?" Mr Him's voice raised as he asked this, not because he wanted to frighten her this time, but because Downbeat had begun speaking to Angel. Downbeat stopped, with a smile on his face that Mr Him would have described as 'silly'.

"Yes," Sunshine said.

"On purpose?"

"Yes."

"Why?"

"His stammering annoys me."

Mr Him stared at her. Good point, his mind offered but his mouth rejected out of hand. Instead he said, "Sit down on this chair."

He pointed, and she sat. This was going as he had imagined. His veins buzzed in his arms, making his wrists feel light. His arms felt as though they might be able to fly. The palms of his hands became sweaty at the thought of what came next.

"Take off your shoes," he said.

"What?" said Sunshine.

"Take off your shoes and your socks."

She stared at him. It was like being stared at by a witch. Her eyes are just as deep, he found himself thinking, though not blue. She took off her shoes, then her socks.

"Tower," said Mr Him. "Go into my desk. In the top drawer you will find a feather."

The class was silent. Mr Him was whispering now. He had no need to yell. He barely needed to speak.

Tower returned with the feather, which rustled in his grip. Tower's hands were just as sweaty as Mr Him's had become. Mr Him lent down until his cheek was proximate to Sunshine and grasped her by the upper arms. She didn't even struggle. That was one thing about these children—they were so well trained.

"Tickle her feet and tell her you're tickling her feet," said Mr Him.

"Wh-wh—" started Tower.

"You heard," interrupted Mr Him.

Tower blinked and, shaking all over, bent over so that he could reach the soles of her feet with the ruff of the feather. He began to tickle.

"I-I-I-I'm tut-tut-tut-tut—" said Tower, as he worked his way up to 'tickling'.

Sunshine squirmed. She began to giggle. "Stop it," she said, as Tower kept going.

"—tut-tut-tut-tit-tit-tit-ick—" said Tower.

Sunshine was going red, the blush diffusing like the colouring in an ice-pop. "Stop it, I said," she said, nearly in a shout.

Still Tower tickled, and still he couldn't say it. By now, he had reached, "—ick-ick-ick—"

Mr Him pressed his arms around her shoulders and turned his fingers into her flesh as her motions became more wayward. He was holding her too tightly, strictly speaking, for her safety, but he could as little stop as Tower could. His eyes bulged behind the lenses of his glasses, the veins in his temple throbbing as if they were gulping.

"—ing," finished Tower before starting again. "I-i-i-i—"

"STOP IT," screamed Sunshine.

The feather flew out of Tower's fingers. It hit the ceiling tiles, its spine snapped, and it didn't so much float as plummet back to earth as though it had been shot, landing with a soft *thwapp* on the carpet.

"I?" said Tower, seemingly as a question.

Mr Him didn't let go of Sunshine's arms. Not yet. Not until he had to. For now, he said, "Remember that for your next lesson tonight, children. That's what anger can do in This Place."

It was tempting to keep hold of Sunshine, but he let her go and stood up straight.

THE GLADE APPEARED to be as wide as it was tall—which was to say infinite—going straight up until it met the Witch's Moon and straight sideways to where it touched the silhouetted horizon. The long grass that stretched about them was a sickly sort of green.

"Some of you, in This Place, will be able to do magic," said Mr Him. There was no breeze and his hair was lulled. As were, by the looks of them, his class. "But you are not magical. Peter, stop doing that please. You are not magical; it is this world that is magical. You are simply riding on its magical coat-tails." Mr Him exhibited the hem of his jacket and smiled a smile that approximated sincerity. "You have no power of your own, children, but the environment does and you can capture this."

In between the hatchings of the long grass, visible here and there, were tents. The class had spent the early hours of the night pitching camp with Class 8. This, Class 8's teacher (Mrs Her) had told them, was a Field Trip. As such, they would be spending the night in a field.

"Quiet, Angel," said Mrs Her. She told off children from Class 7 more often than children from Class 8, even though they were always talking to each other. Mrs Her looked pointedly at Mr Him. Mr Him continued speaking, seeming to make a point of ignoring her.

"There are spirits in the air," he said. "We have covered this in class. Try to remember, Tower. These spirits are called our most extreme emotions. Ecstasy and joy... Why are you smiling Angel? Can you tell the class what's so funny? No?... Rage and despair. And all these spirits are in the air, like the bellows of a tempest or like puffs of wind. *Bottom, Sunshine*! Tonight you will try to control these spirits. To excite them. In short, children, you won't be sleeping in these tents, you will be trying to blow them down! And, if you are really good, you will be trying to blow them up." He pointed at the sky.

The boys looked at each other with eyes momentarily brighter (and seemingly wider) than the Witch's Moon and with gaping black smiles.

Mrs Her stepped in front of Mr Him. His comb-over, visible behind her head, appeared to bristle.

"Who here has seen The Wizard of Oz?" asked Mrs Her.

There was a pause in which the wind grew and the canvas of the tents slapped at themselves like self-harmers. Aimee wondered if Mr Him was feeling anger. His face looked like he was.

Tower put up his hand, which trembled before falling back on his head.

"Well—" Mrs Her sighed as much as said, "—in The Wizard of Oz, Dorothy—the character Dorothy—had a house that was picked up by a tornado... Does anyone here know what a tornado is?"

A hand.

"Yes?"

"It's a plane, miss."

"Ah, well it is, Downbeat, yes. Maybe if I said hurricane—?"
The same hand.

"Yes?"

"It's an old plane, Mrs Her."

"Quite the enthusiast, aren't you Downbeat?" said Mr Him.

Downbeat smiled and nodded enthusiastically, as he often did.

"No, ah—" said Mrs Her.

Mr Him interrupted, crabbing in front of her. "What Mrs Her is trying to say," he said (as Mrs Her glowered at him), "is that when we're finished tonight, you will be able to pick tents off the ground with your minds… whole tents clean off the ground."

A different hand.

"Yes, Peter?"

"We're going to clean the ground with tents?"

"Don't be obtuse, child," said Mr Him.

Peter frowned.

Angel leaned across to him and, out of Mr Him's earshot but within Aimee's, said, "He called you fat. Obtuse means really really fat."

Peter's frown deepened, canyoning his head in the dark. He was a slight child and only nibbled his food at midnight-snack-break.

"Stop!" shouted Mrs Her as several children rose. "We haven't told you to go. Did we tell you to go, Sunshine? Why do you find it so hard to find your bottom? Sit down! Now—" Mrs Her breathed and the wisps of her beard rose skyward which, now that the Witch's Moon had risen utterly, was moonward. "—who can tell me why we are trying to pick up tents instead of houses?" She paused, glaring at the two classes. Her eyes began to bulge, waxing in her face. "Well?" she grasped her beard in frustration. Mrs Her, as far as Aimee could tell, was always pulling her hair out. The girl wondered how she had managed to accumulate a beard. "Have you ever tried picking up a house? Well? Have you? *Have you?*"

None of the children answered.

Shaking, Mrs Her walked away. "I give up," she could be heard to say.

Smiling as real a grin as Aimee had seen from him, Mr Him said, "Well done for listening so well children. Do you have any questions before we start?"

Angel's hand rose.

"Angel?"

"Are you and Mrs Her married?" Angel said.

Mr Him shook his head. Nothing, though, was going to dislodge his grin. "I've told you before, young man, our names are a coincidence."

Angel didn't reply.

"So… off you go Class 7 and Class 8. Don't forget to think about things you hate," he added, glancing at the back of Mrs Her. With a flick of his fingers, he gestured at the nearest tent. It rocketed moonward.

AIMEE MADE HER WAY up the line to walk beside Mr Him, as the Field Trip returned via the Latter Wood to the Night School. She put her hand up, which he didn't seem to see in the dark. After a while it began to ache, even though she had been lifting tents with her emotions not her hands.

"Mr Him," she said eventually. "I think there were children watching us from the side of the Glade. I keep seeing children in the forest. Is the Latter Wood haunted?"

As they were at the head of the line and the lanterns were behind them, Aimee couldn't see the flinch in Mr Him's cheek or the tightening of skin around his eye sockets. If they weren't already darkened, a shadow would've passed over his eyes.

"N-no," he said. Before adding, "Put your hand up, Aimee. I can't pick you if you don't put your hand up."

"But I did," she said.

Mr Him, though, appeared not to hear her, increasing his stride until her legs could not keep up.

HAVING LET GO OF Barnaby's paw, she stared up at the artexed ceiling. Even in the dark, it had the look of shark fins circling. It was still night. She lay unmoving, perhaps hoping the predators wouldn't notice her. The duvet was drawn up to her chin, so they probably hadn't. Her legs were pressed together and that sealed it—her body was untouched. Her heart caught in her throat, her breath found it difficult to bypass it and reach her lungs, and her eyelids snapped open in panic. Adrenaline crinkled into her limbs, making them hard to move when she needed to get up and see her baby brother's door.

At some point, and later she wouldn't remember when, her bare feet made the carpet. She became aware of its tight grooved lines only as she left the bedroom and stepped onto the flattened, dejected texture of the landing carpet. The door to her left—the bathroom—was closed. Inside, the light was on and there was the sound of urine falling, which did nothing to elide the sound of tears joining it. Her mum was sobbing.

Aidan's door was open. She was as unable to enter her baby brother's room as she was to stop shaking her head. She didn't want to spot the way his Spider-Man duvet had been drawn back. She couldn't look at the way he squeezed his eyes shut while he pretended to sleep.

Amy retreated.

I'm too late to save him, she thought, and the words sounded like an adult whispering into her brain. When she returned to bed, she couldn't bring herself to hold her teddy bear's hand even though he looked scared.

AMY HAD COME TO school alone that day, without the flotsam that was her brother bobbing behind her. She was olive-skinned and wet-haired from grease. Mr Mann wondered, later that evening as he drank his nightly red wine, if that was why it had happened. She was never the same, he thought, on the days when her brother was ill. There was a special bond between them.

Mr Andrew Mann was, and had been since eighteen, a rattish looking man, having finished being a mouse of a boy, whose whiskery facial hair had failed to inform his scalp that he was hirsute. He was prematurely balding. He wore thick-rimmed, round glasses, as though in an attempt to capture his manic eyes, which always seemed to be looking for a way out. For one year (his first in teaching), Mr Mann's brain had joined them and had ceased remembering where he had come into this profession, or why.

His teaching assistant, Mrs Joan Skinner, was his height. Her hair was short and sprayed into a conformist helmet of tight blonde curls. She had the air of a butch lesbian embittered by years of denial. She was married, went out with the girls every Friday night, and had a face that lit up only when she saw a baby. It did no such thing when she saw seven-to-nine-year-olds, who formed the classes she taught. One of her favourite phrases was, "I'll be doing no such thing". Most of the time, in Mr Mann's experience, she didn't.

On the day Mr Mann would later refer to as 'Worms In Their Pants Day', Mrs Skinner stood in the forest walk taking the afternoon register. This—registering outside where they would take the lesson—had been her idea. Not that Mr Mann didn't have plenty of ideas; he did, but they rarely acted upon them.

"Amy," said Mr Mann.

The little girl didn't reply, staring off to the side and into a bush, her face looking every inch the Special Educational Needs child she was.

"*Amy,*" said Mr Mann.

"Good afternoon," said Amy.

"Good afternoon, *Mr Mann,*" said the adult.

The child stared back, and the June air wove tight and curled as Mrs Skinner's hair. Blond sunlight shone down between the trees.

"Good afternoon, Mr Mann," said Amy.

"Adam."

"Good afternoon," said Adam.

"*Mr Mann*," Mr Mann could tell this register was going to take most of the afternoon.

"Good afternoon, Mr Happy," said Adam.

Mr Mann flushed red. "I will not—" he said, "—you will not—" He was unsure how the sentence was going to end. He was pretty sure Adam had already done it. He had, already that year, done most things.

"You will not talk to your teacher like that," said Mrs Skinner before adding, "Should I finish the register, Andy?"

Mr Mann went several shades darker than Mr Strong. He had imagined screaming at the teaching assistant on many occasions and on some of them for calling him by his forename in front of the children, but could never so much as raise his voice. It was often the same with the pupils.

"Andy Pandy?" said Adam.

"Adam, we've talked about this before," said Mr Mann, his enlarged eyes finding Mrs Skinner. "Now," he continued, if only to stop Adam doing so, "we are going on a Worm Hunt."

They were studying We're Going on a Bear Hunt by Michael Rosen.

"Now worms don't like—Simon stop doing that—to come out when it's sunny. Michaela, are you listening? So, we're going to trick them." It was nine in the morning, and his cheeks were aching. His lips longed for a drink and he licked them and, accidentally, the moustache on top of them. "We're going to trick the worms under your feet—"

"Urghh," said Adam.

Nathan giggled.

Mr Mann had taken an instant dislike to the two children, an instant dislike that had lasted for several weeks. "—into thinking it's raining." Mr Mann's voice lowered to an elaborate whisper. "But don't tell them. Because there's nothing worms like more than the rain, and we're going to trick them into thinking it's raining."

"What did he say?" said Nathan to Adam. "I can't hear him."

Mr Mann looked over to Mrs Skinner, who was smiling fondly at the boys. She liked, Andy knew from previous experience, boys who were trouble-makers, as long as they didn't cause her any trouble. "Boys will be boys," she would say, somehow managing to imply that primary school teaching was no job for a man. Andy had no idea how she managed this.

"You each have a bucket of water and a trowel," said Mr Mann.

"Why do we need a towel?" said Adam. "Are we sunbathing?"

"Now Adam," said Mrs Skinner, smiling at the boy.

"So—" said Mr Mann, pinching his palm to stop it slapping a seven-year-old, "—what you need to do is pour the water on the earth—in drips—to pretend it's raining, and then dig out the worms that come up." He smiled down at Lucy, a golden, perfect, dollish girl who always sat close to him. She smiled back. It helped to pitch all his lessons at Lucy. She was the kind of good little girl that made teaching, if not bearable, then easier. "Okay, off you go children."

And they did. Mr Mann was so busy refereeing the ensuing scrum and chasing around after the boys that he didn't watch what Amy did with the worms and the pockets of her skirt. Later, he would wish that he had.

The next lesson of the day was PE. The boys changed in one corner of the classroom, the girls in the other. Mr Mann sat facing the boys, staring down their attempts to look at the girls and steadfastly refusing to turn around, no matter what sounds came from the girls' side of the room. Halfway through PE, Amy asked to go to the toilet. As a good teaching practitioner, Mr Mann later reflected on this moment and couldn't remember what he had said in reply. No doubt it was a hurried acquiescence. Mr Mann was a very reflective teacher, according to his observations (of which there had been many). This didn't seem to help him though. The more he thought, the more his thoughts turned to red wine—and to worse in the night.

When the class returned from PE, the change back into uniform passed without incident. This should have been a bad sign, but Mr Mann ignored it. PE was the last lesson of the day and parents were pressed to the window of the classroom like zombies that would soon work out how to get in, when Lucy suddenly screamed. She rose into a crouch and started to pull down her navy-blue tights.

"Lucy!" Mr Mann might have screamed. Instead he squeaked.

The little girl was now pulling frantically at her underwear. A large, bulbous, pale worm hung from the front of her knickers.

"Lucy's got a willy," said Adam.

The class laughed as one entity: the Ho Ho Ho of a giant. The sound boomed in the cavities of Mr Mann's mind. The parents seemed closer, despite the door.

Lucy pulled down her knickers, exposing herself. Mr Mann put his hands over his eyes. On reflection, he couldn't believe he had done this. As ever on occasions when he needed her, Mrs Skinner was somewhere else, pretending to be photocopying.

There was the wet sound of a clump of worms flopping onto the floor.

"Lucy's got *lots* of willies," said Nathan.

Their laughter crawled across Mr Mann's face. Lucy, no doubt, knew that kind of crawling. Oddly, Andy wanted to bury his face in dirt.

It didn't take long for him to ascertain what had happened, that Amy had excavated worms and then kept them, crawling, in her skirt pockets, before hiding them in the undergarments of Lucy. It took him considerably longer to talk his headmistress down from suspending him. On reflection, Mr Mann was unsure why he had.

AMY'S BODY HAD TRAINED itself for the walk home from her school as a marathon runner would—in stages. Steady-paced on the roads named from F to B, her gait slowed as she reached the As. She went through the wall when she approached her front door. As a runner would, she visualised the end of the course. She imagined the raised hand, the falling fist, the pain where she was struck. It was hard not to visualise it. It had been in Mum's eyes from the moment Mr Mann had said, "Can I have a word, *please?*"

Her mother held Amy's hand throughout the route, dragging Amy as the child's feet dragged.

As it was, the house was quiet when they returned— haunted by a sickly silence—and her mum left Amy at the porch and rushed upstairs to check on Aidan, her lips twisted as much as her fingers had been.

Amy took off her school shoes and walked to the kitchen, across the lino, and unlocked the back door. She went into the garden, not because it was safer, but because the laburnum tree overhung there and because her skirt pockets had one more duty to fulfil today. She was still gathering the seedpods when her mother returned. Mum had brought her fists.

Chapter 3

"Eat it or I'll tell Mum," Amy's whisper curled into the air like her mum's lips.

Aidan glowered up at her from the settee. In front of them was CBBC. It was early in the evening and Mum—after, she had said, "all the bother with Amy"—had taken to bed with a headache. Uncle Chris was out, having gone for a, "quick walk for some air, yeah," by which he meant a 'long drink at the local'. The speed of his exit was very nearly a run.

"Bits in it," Aidan said but he ate, the milk slipping down his chin as his mouth ground around the cereal.

Though she was upstairs, their mum was present in the creeping of the children's feet on the carpet, in the down-turned volume, in the threat in Amy's eyes. Aidan finished his bowl, swallowing the lumps of Frosties seasoned with laburnum seeds.

"Hate it," he said.

"I'll get you some coke," she said.

He nodded and stared at the TV. He was getting paler. Before she left, Amy swayed on the blades of her feet. It wasn't the first time she had stared at him and worried. The other occasions, though, were when Mum was around. Thinking back, she didn't remember her first ice-cream, her first stolen smoke of her mum's cigarettes. Her earliest memories were of Aidan being changed, and of watching as Mum's fingers efficiently pulled, wiped, tied. Watching the fingertips.

Amy walked to the kitchen and to the fridge. It shuddered as the light came on, and she removed the plastic cola bottle. Hands raised above her shoulders, she approached the bench like a bishop with a sceptre. Tipping her abdomen (the bottle was close to full and heavy), she poured and filled a glass printed with butterflies.

Returning to the lounge, she placed the coke at Aidan's side then walked to the clefts in the fake-tone fireplace on the left of the TV. She withdrew the photo album she had deposited several days before, and walked around the sofa so that Aidan couldn't see her. It would be several hours before Mum rose.

Nonetheless, she slid the album into the dark linted envelope of space below the sofa and went upstairs to get Barney. As she passed Aidan's bedroom door, she couldn't look at it.

"Who's that puffing down the track?" said the TV as she returned downstairs. "It's Thomas."

"Turn it down," Amy hissed and Aidan shrugged, reversing his tiny finger on the zapper, where he had been millimetring the volume to the right. She lost sight of him as she sat on the carpet behind the sofa and withdrew the photo album. She could still hear him, if only his shifting.

Cuddling Barney, she opened the album, held the bear's paw and touched the photo.

IN FRONT OF AIMEE SAT a cake that Nan had brought round. It was white with blue letters squeezed out of icing. *Amy is Five!* it read.

She stood in the kitchen of the house. In the garden could be heard the sound of children playing. Not many. Her mum had many friends, so many, in fact, that Amy never met the same ones twice. She didn't, however, encourage her daughter to bring friends back to the house. Most of the children she played with, Aimee remembered from vague memory, were the children of neighbours.

She wouldn't care about them: she would be playing with Aidan or, if Mum made her play with someone her own age, she would be watching him.

Aimee wondered if she should walk into the garden and play with herself. If she were to do so, would That Place and This, The Other and An Other, all collapse? And would the mess be worse than one she was in already? Or would she just explode in a cacophony of fire? It was easier to stand in the kitchen, staring at the cake. She crept towards the table and, as though untying a shoe lace, carefully unpicked the sugar letters, glancing over her bare shoulder and through the light ruff of translucent fabric in case the patio door started to slide. At her side, a large brown bear said, "What are you doing now, little girl?"

To which she replied, "It's my birthday cake. I'll do what I want."

Aᴍʏ sᴛᴀʀᴇᴅ ᴀᴛ ʜᴇʀ handiwork. The cake no longer read *Amy is Five!*, but *Aimee is   !*

Amy smiled. Then she turned the pages and cakes went by: one, two, three. Now she came to pictures of Aidan as a baby, and there were no longer the see-through blisters of plastic where photographs should be.

Aidan crying. Aidan breast-feeding. Aidan in the garden. Aidan sleeping. Aidan lying down. In the background of most shots was Amy. "Like his bloody shadow," her mum said when Nan was round. Later, Mum would make an effort to make sure the girl was on the other side of the camera but, so focused on her younger brother as she was, Amy could remember when each of these were taken and where she'd been standing at the time. It was all about the line of sight, or line of hearing, to the little boy. As the album reached its halfway mark, he was no longer a baby. Amy's finger dallied on Aidan dressed in a new spider costume at Christmas, smiling out from between fangs of black felt. On his forehead, six white eyes goggled, the pupils finding their rims as if trying to escape. Her throat lumped, and she regarded his face. How could she keep him safe? It wasn't a rhetorical question.

Amy rose and walked around the settee to the TV. She replaced the album in its niche, and turned.

"The fat controller wasn't happy about this," the television said as she turned it off.

"Awwwrrghhhhh," said Aidan. Then, on seeing the teddy in her arms, he sunk into the corner of the cushions and shook his head. "No," he said. "No."

She walked towards him and, by her knees, onto the sofa cushions. Her pyjamas tugged her thighs. She was too strong for Aidan and she bear-hugged him, forming monkey hands on the other side of her teddy, which was now pressed into his squirming stomach.

"No," he repeated. Even now, he would not shout.

Amy held the little boy until his head slumped back against her chin and his lungs emptied onto her right shoulder.

"Give me your hand, love," she said and took his fingers. She placed them on the teddy and closed Aidan's grip. Simultaneously, she grasped Barney's other paw and they travelled together, all three of them falling.

"So," SAID BARNABY. His maw made a slight slapping sound as he talked, as if he were speaking around a portion of human thigh. "We thought we would go on an Expedition, seeing as this is only the third time you've visited This Place." Barnaby paused. He was bent to his haunches and trying to face the five-year-old boy, which was hard as Aidan had his face buried in Aimee's lilac dress. "Does that sound exciting?" said Barnaby, slapping his way through the syllables. To Aimee, he sounded nervous, as he often did when speaking to toddlers.

Barnaby's friends, the Christian and the Piglet, stood nearby. Piglet coughed and scratched his yellowed Y-fronts.

"Where are we going—" said Aimee, to interrupt the silence. "—on the Expedition?'

"Ah," said Barnaby, to Aidan rather than Aimee. "We thought we would try to find a Pole. And we thought about the North Pole, but the north is the land of the Witch, as you well know. So we decided we would find the South Pole." He grunted as he rose to full height, his knee-joints clicking.

Aimee stared up at him and blinked. With Mr Mann's class in the Day School, she had studied European Geography and, while she wasn't as good with maps as she was with plants or stars, she distinctly remembered where the Poles were.

"There isn't a Pole in the south," said Aimee. "The Pole is in the east. It has its own land... And it isn't *one* Pole—there are lots of Poles in their land. So we would be looking for *a* Pole."

The bear and the Christian and the Piglet looked at each other. Piglet shrugged, pulled his face down so that his lips made an *n*, lit a cigarette, filled the top of the letter and shrugged again, inhaling.

The Christian said, "Well, she is a very clever girl... I don't really know... for sure."

"We did it in school. Mr Mann said so," added Aimee.

"Well, if a human said so," said the Christian. "And it would be easier to find one, you know, if there were lots of Poles in the east instead of just one. If you see what I mean."

Piglet grunted, perhaps because he agreed or perhaps because he was scratching his Y-fronts again.

("One," repeated the Christian to himself, apparently because he liked the number. He often said this, or three or seven or nine.)

"Okay, that's decided then," said Barnaby.

The bear bent once more, with a smile that showed his teeth. Aidan, who had mustered the courage to peek past the folds in his sister's lilac dress, buried himself in frills. He was wearing a robe the deep blue of the sky near its highest point.

"Well, what do you think of that, little human boy? We are going on a Pole hunt. Won't that be fun?" Barnaby had put on his toddler voice again, forcing out a tone of placation. Unfortunately—alongside it—there issued a stench of human meat. Aidan shuddered. Aimee thought he might be crying.

Turning away, the bear added in an undertone, "He hates me."

THEY TRACKED EAST FOR several hours, winding some way south and some way north, but taking care to skirt the frozen, icy realm of the Witch. They passed the perimeter of the Night School which, of course, was locked up, as it was Daytime. But the Christian showed Aidan, when he peeked out from Aimee's dress, where the spiders laired in the caverns below the Night School's plateau. The caretaker spent some time locating all of the fetishes he had tied to the fence and retying them all. (At one point Aimee thought she heard a gargoyle, high in the clear Day, saying, "Oh God, it's children. I thought the school was closed. Oh no! My bottom can't deal with any more children!")

In the east, beyond the Night School's plateau, the Latter Wood relaxed its botanical rules and allowed birches, oaks, willows and beeches. Piglet's home was cloistered in the roots of one willow, which did appear to be weeping but perhaps that was because of the smell that rose from below it. The small pig spent half an hour clattering about beneath the hollowed bough (which had been carved into a small trotter-sized staircase) before poking his snout out and announcing that it was now presentable—in an ishy kind of way—and please could they come below, but please could they forgive the mess because he hadn't known visitors were coming. They descended and drank a quick cup of tea—quick because he didn't have any milk and because Piglet's home smelt strangely like a bush that was desperately trying to pollinate as wide an area as possible. There were used tissues everywhere.

They didn't find any Poles. Not South or North or East or even North-East (and they didn't dare go far *that* way, because North-East was the end of the Latter Wood and the boundary between the Witch's domain and that of the Queen of Spades, who was, if anything, even more vicious). Barnaby's mood became increasingly short, which was to say towering, until he snapped every few steps and shouted at the Christian when he suggested they should try to see if there were any Poles in the west.

At this point, Aimee said they should go home to the Other Place. She twisted her brother's hand into one of the bear's paws and, as he disappeared, she took the other.

"DID YOU LIKE IT there?" Amy asked, letting go of her brother's body.

Aidan squirmed away and, running for the hallway, shouted, "Didn't go anywhere!" There was a loose lean to the way he moved, so that he bumped into the jamb of the door on his way out.

His footsteps on the stairs were slower than normal and then were lost in the roar of their mother's voice from its apex, filling the stairwell space as a dragon would with flames. "Shut up, both of you. I'm trying to bloody sleep."

"DUE TO THE MAGICAL nature of This Place," said Mrs Her, who took the anatomy lessons, "nothing can die unless the Witch or her minions kill it."

Before her, on a set of yellow tables that had been drawn to the centre of Class 8's room, was a pig's head on a platter. It looked across the children's faces and said, "Please save me."

Tower vomited in the corner. Mrs Her had placed him there not as a sanction, but because she knew he would need the bin. But Tower missed it, having turned the wrong way. Vomit belly-flopped onto the floor.

Mrs Her sighed. "Please be quiet," she said, talking to the pig not the class, as the children were all, save the dribbling of Tower, silent. She exhibited a scalpel. "This is a scalpel. It is not a toy. If you misuse it—Angel, I hope you are listening—I will not replace your eye. Do you understand?"

"Yes, Mrs Her,' said the class as one. Mrs Her had the kind of dour features that encouraged little in the way of calling out. It may have been her beard.

The scalpel hovered over the scalp of the pig's head. "When you cut, always cut away from yourself. Do you understand?"

"Yes miss."

"Cut what?" said the pig.

Mrs Her's hand sawed backwards and forwards, before slicing into the back of the pig's head.

"Ahhh, argggggggghhh, arrrrrrrgggghhhhhh," said the pig. "By the Witch, that stings. Arggggggghhh… Ah, that's better. Did you stop?"

Ignoring him, Mrs Her said, "Once you are beyond the nerve layers of the head and into the skull, your animal will no longer feel any pain."

"That's quite a relief," said the pig. To Aimee, he sounded sarcastic.

Mrs Her put her fingers into the gap she had carved. With a crack that bought Aimee's adrenal glands to attention, the teacher unhinged its skull.

"Somebody do something," said the pig. Nobody moved. "Spineless bastards," it added.

"Now pigs are generally very intelligent creatures. This specimen may well be an exception, by the look of its brains."

"And human women are supposed to be clean-shaven," said the pig.

Beneath her fringe, which was extensive but not as long as her beard, Mrs Her's eyes glinted. The scalpel did the same as she waved it.

"First—"

A droplet of blood landed on Aimee's upper lip. Mrs Her was exceedingly strict, and Aimee didn't dare move to wipe it off. It headed towards her mouth.

"—you will encounter the parietal lobe. This area of the brain—" Mrs Her picked up the pig's head and turned it.

("I feel dizzy," said the pig.)

"—is responsible for perception, making sense of the world and arithmetic, as well as spelling."

Tower looked up, a stricken pause straightening his lips.

"Don't worry, Tower, I didn't say spelling test. This, according to what Mr Him tells me, is the part of brain you may not have." She pointed with the blade.

Tower blinked then, turning, vomited on the wall.

Mrs Her resumed cutting, pulling the platter beneath the head slightly to the side so as to deposit the gristle of its brain. The scalpel tinkled as she smeared it off.

"So, pig," she said. "What is one add one?"

"Window," said the pig, through gritted teeth.

"And how do spell 'pig'?"

"Are you taking the piss?"

"And how do you spell 'vegetable'?" Mrs Her growled.

"G… E… T… F… U… C… P… T—" it said.

Mrs Her's beard shifted. Maybe, thought Aimee, she was smiling.

"Below the parietal lobe," continued the teacher, "if you dig diagonally forwards and downwards, is the temporal lobe. This takes care of your memory, your understanding and your language."

"Where am I?" said the pig abruptly.

"Oh you are a funny pig," said Mrs Her.

"Who are you?" The pig's eyes tried to peer backwards and failed. "I have a head flake," it said. "It hurts like purple poo pyjamas."

The class desperately wanted to laugh, particularly the boys—Aimee could tell—and they swelled as though holding in mass flatulence.

Mrs Her dispersed the children to their tables. Gulping slightly, Aimee raised her scalpel. In front of her, thankfully, was not a pig's head but a trotter. She brought the blade to it in small, hesitating butterfly strokes of movement but, as the metal touched the skin and raised the blond hairs on it, the trotter jumped off the table. Retrieving it, Aimee noticed her palms were sweating.

"Right," said Mrs Her. "Begin your dissection."

MR HIM WAS WEARING his tweed jacket, the one with the black elbow patches, which meant they were doing Chemistry.

H_2O was written in long laconically sloping lines on the blackboard, which reinforced the impression of Science. Mr Him hit the letters with the end of a metre stick then struck the number, saying, "H_2O. Does anyone know what this is?"

Class 7 didn't answer, apart from Angel, who muttered what sounded like, "Yep. It's boring."

Peter snorted, and Mr Him struck the pocked, yellowed, chemical-stained wood in front of him with the stick. It bounced, as did Peter on his seat, which was a high unbacked stool.

"Water!" said Mr Him.

"Has he wet himself?" asked Brains.

"H_2O is the chemical formula for water. And, Brains, I don't suppose you know what this means, do you?"

Brains did his best, by the look of his twitching right eye, to stare in a straight direction at the blackboard, where Mr Him was pointing to the end of the chemical formula.

"Water," said Brains.

"No. This!" said Mr Him, reapplying the ruler to the *O*.

"Water," said Brains without changing his tone.

Mr Him's sight went limp, lifeless. He kept going, regardless, "The *O* is for *Oxygen*. This tells us that oxygen is in water. *Air is in water.* And what do I keep telling you is in the air in This Place?"

Sunshine raised her hand.

Mr Him looked at it, then at the rest of the class. Her arm was alone.

"Sunshine?" he said, in the same manner as another person might say, "Just get it over with and shoot me."

"Magic," said Sunshine, in the same tone of voice.

Mr Him stared at her, his eyes reanimating. "Yes! Yes!" He struck the desk in front of Tower who started to oscillate as though hit by an earthquake.

"Water has air in it and, ergo, magic."

Aimee, along with the rest of the class, didn't question Mr Him on what Ergo Magic did.

"And that magic can be used to teleport. Remember what you were taught about the power of emotions in This Place?" Mr Him managed to maintain, with his facial expression, that this was not a question and thus did not require an answer. "Today, we will be experimenting on Teleportation via Desperation. In short, we will be teleporting extremely desperate Ink Neepers."

Bending, Mr Him retrieved a shoebox from behind his bench. He put it on top of the wood, opened the lid (which was holed), before reaching in to pick up a man. He was, as Aimee had heard Mr Him say, short; in fact, he was incredibly short.

Aimee had only ever seen an Ink Neeper once before and that had been in a scurry of motion that had sent her class screaming and running for the far wall, and the teaching assistant for the caretaker. The Christian had arrived and cornered the tiny figure in a chest of drawers, which he had wheeled into the playground and left open overnight, before retrieving it, Ink-Neeper-less. About the size of a mouse, but considerably slimmer, the Ink Neeper was a fairy-like humanoid who was addicted to sniffing ink and, when clutched by ink withdrawal, chewed pens until they leaked into his miniscule mouth. Pens often went missing in the Night School and the teachers would, quite accurately, blame this on the Ink Neepers.

The small figure emitted a whining scream like that of a toy fire engine and attempted to bite Mr Him's finger. Mr Him held him by the ankle and, using his spare hand, lifted a length of Bunsen burner tubing, which was attached to a water tap. The tap was, as was to be expected, attached to a sink. The tap was on and liquid dribbled out onto the bench and the floor.

"If you gather round, children—"

They did so.

"—you will see me place this Ink Neeper into the end of the tubing."

Mr Him forced the Ink Neeper's head into the tube. Before disappearing, the mouth wailed then the Neeper was underwater and only bubbles emerged.

"Now," said Mr Him, firmly gripping the Neeper's writhing legs in between his thumb and forefinger. "The Ink Neeper really wants to get out. He is drowning. However—" Mr Him grunted as the fairy kicked his thumb, bending it backwards. "—*little bugger*... he cannot go back, because I am bunging the gap." The creature was now fully in the tubing, misshaping it into the form of a small twitching man.

Aimee began to sweat and realised she was holding her breath.

"So at some point he will bend all of his will into going down the tube—but it is too narrow. Eventually, his emotions will spark the magic in the *air* in the water of the tube, and he will *teleport* down its length—"

~131~

A *POP* interrupted Mr Him. The Ink Neeper had fallen from the end of the second (tubeless) tap of the sink and into the basin. It breathed heftily, arms seeming to conduct its lungs.

"Oh... there! He's done it!" said Mr Him. The Ink Neeper clambered out of the sink and ran, leaving tiny puddle footprints. "Get him!"

As the children scattered after the scurrying Neeper, Mr Him shouted, "The magic can be used to transverse any pipe or plumbing." And then, "He's got my fountain pen! Stop him."

Giggling and gurgling ink, the Neeper ran under a bench.

IN BED, THE WALL stained orange in the same way as her fingers were stained yellow by laburnum pods, Amy stared across at Barney but didn't reach out to him. His eyes were opals, glistening with their own light as though with tears or rage. There would be little point reaching out to Barney as, angled as he was, there was nothing to reach out to. Amy had torn off his right arm and it lay, fingerless, in the utter black beneath her bed.

YES, I HATED HER, and more than I had ever hated another child. But I was proud of her, through the tears of pain, for being by far the cleverest little girl I had ever known. Her brother was getting sicker, and I knew then, you see, what she had planned. Even through the pain I could see it.

It's amazing what children's minds are capable of.

AMY CLOSED HER EYES and shut off her mind and, without Barney's arm to reel her in, swam into blank darkness and dreamlessly slept.

Chapter 4

"WAKE UP YOU STUPID little bitch."

And again.

"Come here you stupid bitch."

Before she could do the first, Amy had done the second and stood, as uncertain on the landing carpet as she was on her thoughts.

Aidan was in Mum's arms, his lips an iced yellow. He had the hue of pork bought from Iceland.

Mum said, "Get a fucking move on, get a fucking move on," as though swearing was about to become unfashionable. Momentarily, Amy thought she had poisoned him too much, but the boy choked and hacked on an unconscious breath.

"Give me him, love," said Uncle Chris.

Amy didn't even notice Mum ignoring him. The sound of Uncle Chris talking was a little like the words he always said when they watched Alien: "In space, no one can hear you scream." Amy was sure she was the only person to have heard him say this, as he said it in a whisper. Somehow, now, he seemed to be screaming. In this case, it wasn't that no one could hear, it was that no one was listening.

Amy was listening to her mum though. "What are you doing just standing there? Go and get dressed."

There was a question in there somewhere and a swear word hidden underneath it. But Amy couldn't feel her legs or her brain, only a growing panic, her heart billowing in her chest and inking her arm with pins and needles.

"Are you trying to kill your brother? Are you trying to kill him? Go and get dressed."

Standing between her door and Aidan's, between the paper-cut of her mother's frame and the odour of Chris (who smelt as though he had been swilled speculatively around a can of Stella), Amy was falling but not in a good way. Her skin was flaking away in thin rubberised curls like the snakeskins of truck tyres on the M60.

Her baby had a mouth dripping with thick froth, like the women in the magazines under Chris's side of the bed.

The sight snapped her out of her somnambulistic state and she receded back down the landing like a turned-off TV set—to her white wooden bedroom door. Brusquely, all thumb and no fingers, all bones and no flesh, she touched it, its truculent thick paintwork, its stiff lips of pine, like it could protect her, like it was solid. She didn't trust it. Her mum had taught her that, by how she was in public. The caresses to her head. The faux grins. The warm words. Her door slid open. The shush of its progress over cheap carpet was restrained—churchy—and reminded her of the sound of falling into the Glade in the

Latter Wood. She wanted to go there. She could see, despite the shadows, Barney in the ravines of her bed. He didn't look too good. She grasped his stump at the shoulder.

"I'm sorry Barnaby," she said.

She let him fall and instead took his arm—but not his paw.

THE HOSPITAL SMELT somewhere between disinfectant and vomit, as if it'd swallowed the first and retched the second. Amy sat and shut off her senses and waited.

Aidan is close to God. That's what Uncle Chris said. Maybe Aidan can smell Him.

Her lower legs, where she sat, fell from her knee in two lines of smudged white cotton and wash-bled love hearts. She hadn't changed out of her pyjamas. She'd forgotten to when she took Barney's arm, and her mum wouldn't wait. Amy couldn't reach the mussed trenches of the hospital's weary carpet with her toes, but she didn't swing her legs. They fell urine-line straight. She tried to recall when her mother had last washed the leggings, but couldn't. Her mum was distracting her. Her mum was screaming at the doctors and nurses with an open mouth like a big round full stop that went on forever. Amy wondered if that was what God looked like. An infinite full stop. She closed her eyes until she could see Aidan. His mouth was off-colour. Amy was not entirely surprised. She'd smeared the yellow stain on his dusky lips, like laburnum trees seen at speed at the edge of a twilight glade.

Barney's arm was inside her pyjama top, cuddling the bottom rung of her ribcage.

"STUPID L----E F-----NG bitch. What does she th--k she is d---g?"

The sound of *her* came and went as fast as he did, these days, in bed. He blocked her out when she wasn't talking to him, and not just her either. He often blocked himself out too. Christopher had become something he could not be. At least he could have a couple of drinks and forget that he had ever been anything better. He came, most often with her, before he had even taken his pants off. She mocked him for it, which didn't help.

Amy stood over her brother's hospital bed, leaning forwards. In her grip, and forced into Aidan's unmoving fingers, seemed to be the arm of a teddy bear.

"Leave the poor child alone," Christopher said, looking at his hands. When he wasn't drunk his voice reminded him of his mother's. She always called him 'Christopher', even though no one else did. Now, most of the time, his name was four-lettered and followed by an 'er'.

"What? What did you say to me?" There was curl of a lip that may as well have been a fist into his. "Say that again... one more fucking time."

Christopher frowned, trying to muster all of himself into his face. There was a weight on his corneas, dragging them down. The hospital room was leaning in on him, walls and all. Panicking inside, he thought he might cry.

The young doctor and a grey curly-haired nurse turned to look at each other.

Christopher didn't say anything. His mouth made the round childish *o* its lips knew from the shape of rum bottles.

"She's not mine," she said. "I swear to God that child is not mine. And she sure as hell isn't yours, you faggot. You being so bloody soft on her, that's what made into *this*." She pointed at Amy. "No child of mine would turn out like *this*."

"Um, I'm sorry," said the doctor. The silence after his word was raw. The ward seemed to hold more blood than it was used to, to have admitted more wounds than it could plaster. "Come and sit down with us, please. You have been through more than we can possibly imagine. But so has your daughter."

"Daughter? What bloody daughter?"

The nurse is looking at me, thought Christopher, like I should do something. He often felt the eyes of the world on him and often when they could not possibly be watching—when he was in the lounge or the garage, when he was alone. His fists narrowed as he found himself unable to move. I've got to help that little girl, he thought, but his hands wouldn't reach out to the child and his lips couldn't speak. All of him really wanted a drink.

Staring at her mother, the little girl removed the brown dismembered teddy's arm she'd placed in her brother's linen and walked away to the waiting room.

AN OLD MAN APPROACHED, bent over and vulnerable like a snail that had lost its shell. He sat on the chair next to Amy, which was pink-cushioned and of a far ruddier hue than his skin.

"Hello there," he said, smiling down at her and inclining his neck so that his head was above her shoulder.

Amy looked up without reply.

"Is that your brother?" he said.

Amy continued to look up without reply.

"In there?" he inclined the already inclining head and his neck creaked as though complaining that it really would rather not.

"My baby," said Amy.

The old man frowned. His hair was tentacles on his scalp, long and thin and black. Amy wondered if there was a monstrous squid on the other side of his head, eating his brains. His scalp reminded her of Mr Him.

"Oh, I see—" said the old man, "—baby brother."

Amy's mum had told her not to talk to strangers. Strangers were dangerous. Besides which, she didn't like the smell of this one.

"Are you worried about him?" said the old man.

Amy thought about this—not about answering but about how to stop the old man talking to her. She didn't want to be rude. After consideration, she waved the old man closer, cupped her hand to his waxy cheek, and said the phrase she had heard countless times before, which she accepted as being the best way to end a conversation quickly.

The old man leaned in.

Amy whispered, "Shut the fuck up, you little bitch."

The old man looked at her with two brown eyes that seemed to be abruptly dampening. Shit stuck to a toilet, thought Amy. He got up and walked over to the pink chair he had recently vacated, his skin flushed close to the colour of the cushion on which he then sat.

THE SMELL WAS everywhere. Not just on her nose or in her nostrils, but soaking her brain. Her organs had the feel of aliens in saline tanks. Knowledge saturated her, as did one thought: I'm running out of time.

But Amy had to wait. No matter if there was little of his spirit left, if she could hear the eek of it eeking away. This was the place, the room, to wait. It said so on the sign. Amy felt her face go burnt-soup red. She sighed a breath fecund with everything she couldn't say and rose. She walked through the closed double swing-doors, by the murmuring doctor, past three cubicles, then right and to her baby: a yellow stain in hospital whites. He had the look of a pod, like in Invasion of The Body Snatchers. The machine by Amy's head beeped. She ignored it. There were purple spots at the edge of the room, mainly on the ceiling. Amy watched them with the corners of her eyes: the pupils were all for him. Her baby was gone, almost. There was the lightest of winds as his soul drifted away. Amy pushed the brown limb deep into the hospital linen, and closed his small palm until it eclipsed the thumbnail shape of the teddy bear's felt palm.

"What are you doing sweetheart?"

Amy half-turned and, inside her chest, her heart did a full turn of its own. A nurse stood behind her, staring at Amy then at the bump of the teddy bear's severed arm below her brother's linen then back at Amy.

"Oh sweetheart, is that part of your teddy bear?"

Amy considered this. In her experience, every interaction with an adult was worthy of careful thought. In the end, she nodded.

The nurse was gun-grey-haired with curls that framed a pasty, wan face. She looked like a grandma. Not Amy's Nan, but somebody's. She smiled at the child. "It'll be our secret," she said, winking. Her eyes were darker than all the rest of her skin tone put together, and they reminded Amy of pulled bath-plugs. Her cheeks were pale and drained. "I'll make sure they don't take it away, love."

THE DOCTORS SAID, "Go home." Amy heard them as she passed her mother, walking back to the waiting room. The doctors said, "There's nothing more that you can do. He's critical but stable." They were, thought Amy, wrong. They couldn't see that his soul had almost gone to the Other Place.

Her mother had gone straight to the taxi rank. She hadn't tried to stay. To cuddle Aidan. She had let him go and had grasped the outer edges of her elbows, rocking on the spot gently. Amy hadn't stopped to watch, but had returned to her seat and tried to pretend she'd never left it.

Amy was lucky. She didn't know what a STD was or how it felt on the skin, and so had nothing with which to compare the itching, maddening sensation of the drive home. The image of her baby brother was inked into her, sharp as any tattoo. She knew where he was right now—in the Glade in the midst of a ring of laburnum trees, in the long grass. In the middle of the night there were things in the Latter Wood that would make man-eating bears seem like vegans. Amy had to get to That Place. It was well past her bedtime and she longed for a teddy to cuddle.

Nobody spoke. Mum was wrapped in her own arms and (having snapped at Chris's sympathy) coated in silence. The taxi driver indicated and pulled onto the estate. There was the clenched-teeth sound of the car coming to a stop on broken glass, and Amy got out before the adults. As Uncle Chris paid the driver, Amy unlocked the door. She hurried in and upstairs, undressed, and slipped in between her under-sheet and her duvet. She didn't look at her teddy bear as she reached out to him, or at the damage she had done. She could feel the wound on her fingertips, rough as old scars, with tight curls of stuffing impinging on the air like the guts of the rabbit she'd once seen on a country road. Her fingers crawled around his abdomen and found his other side, and she took his remaining paw.

THE DROP INTO Barnaby's world was an outrushing breath that was met by one of Aimee's own. She hit its ground running, knowing where her baby would be. He'd been left by her intervention, as exposed in this world as any would-be changeling. His skin would be cold and numb and wooden-feeling, like a goblin child pretending to be human. And grey as well. She hoped his skin hadn't turned blue for if it had, there'd be little to be done to save him—even in This Place, where magic was in the air. Aimee felt panic inside her. It was turning her inside-out, blushing her skin, pushing her heart hard against her ribcage.

She parted the grass like the hand that parted the reeds on Moses. There was no crying—not here—though she knew he lay beyond the silhouettes of vegetation.

She leant in and saw that his eyes were closed, his skin drawn about them as it was about his small mouth, which was a darker shadow of red as if it had rent itself by screaming too long, wailing for help in the alien night.

He's dead, she would have thought if there was time for it, but she didn't and she grasped him up against her bursting chest. She ran. The grass was unhelpful hands on her knees, her hips and her elbows where she swaddled him. Her lilac dress was bunched about his body at the front with its ruffs of white drowning him in material spume.

She ran. Laburnum trees loomed, entangled and noxious as memories of trauma half-seen in the dark. Under their eaves could be heard strange things, crawling. There was a smell on the wind and not that of a baby turning blue. No, it was the odour of a world that was falling into anarchy. Aimee had transgressed a rule. There was something rotten in This Place, and Aimee knew it was what she had done.

She ran under the canopy of laburnum trees.

"Come on, come on," she said. Her breath was hot and fast on the little boy's face. He didn't reply.

She tripped on a tree root, stumbled, and fell into a swell of earth and down a fold. There was a muffled shattering, like glass would make inside a napkin, from her right arm. She looked down, but not at it, at him. He hadn't changed in any way, unless it was to go a deeper grey. Now she noticed a smell of blood. It wasn't his, or hers, though she could feel her own making the arm of her lilac dress darker and longer. The odour was too animal. There were predators here. The minions of the Witch were abroad. Aimee rose and, again, ran.

There was a crash in the undergrowth. Twigs snapped and shredded. Whatever was out here was both uncoordinated and big. The Night School was close but couldn't be seen between the dense bunching of shadows.

A crackling of ripped vegetation came from close by, near her right shoulder. She darted left, her small red right shoe making a question mark in the soil. Whatever pursued her passed over it a moment later. It had breath as big as a bonfire, and hot, and smelling of cooked (if not burnt) meat. Then it was on her, grasping her by her long tawny hair. For the first time in This Place, she wished she had Amy's dank bob. Pain became a lever in her skull, and she jerked still and then was borne back into her pursuer's arms.

Into its arm.

One bear limb reached round and picked her up. She could smell the stump of the other one, leaking and torn. The bone in her arm was a many-forked lightning rod of pain.

"Hold still girl," the bear said. "We're not alone."

"I'm sorry Barnaby," she said through teeth gritted so that they would sieve out the screams.

"Shut up," he said, not unkindly.

There was sniffling in the dark. Amy had watched Chitty Chitty Bang Bang one Christmas, when Uncle Chris had passed out on the settee and Mum was at the bingo hall. The sound reminded Aimee of the Child Catcher's nose. It, the Child Catcher had said, never failed to sniff out children.

Now whatever it was was closing in. Whatever length its nose was, it had wet fecund nostrils like the tunnels of worms. There was also the slapping, slapping, slapping of an awkward eater. Russian Dolls, thought Aimee. She knew the thought was right, but didn't say it out loud. Slowly, Barnaby lowered his bulk to the dirt. They hunkered down behind a holly bush.

"Don't sit on me," said a grasshopper. Barnaby squashed him with a quick anxious step.

The sniffing stopped. "Hmmm," said a voice that seemed to come up from below layers of flesh. "Somebody hiding behind that holly bush, eh? Well you know what they say about little girls hiding behind holly bushes, eh? No? Well I don't either. I don't think they say anything much about that. And why would they? Very unlikely to happen, my dears." The slapping resumed. It sounded for all This Place like the creature was eating its own lips.

"Run," said Barnaby.

"Don't think I will," said the creature, tearing the bush out of the dirt in one looping action.

Aimee did.

As she went, Barnaby charged, one-armed, against the monster. Behind her, she could hear the sound of a mutilated bear being borne to the ground and its roars as the thing bit deep. Then Barnaby's screams sounded as human as his breath smelt. The gates of the Night School came into sight.

HER NAME WAS Disdivanshumayl and, needless to say, it was as hard for Mr Him to pronounce as it was to remember. He did so as: Dis ('insult') Divan (the Spiderish for 'don't')

Shumayl (a spider's family name). Disdivanshumayl was woollen-skinned and blind in seven of her eight eyes. The one good eye didn't look at all healthy and most often not in the right direction.

"What did you say?" Disdivanshumayl said.

"Uh," said Mr Him. It was hard to argue with the teaching assistants. Not only were they, in the Night School, supernatural beasts, but they also tended to be older than the teachers. In this case several centuries older.

"Miss!" said Angel. "Miss! It's Aimee! She's late." Angel seemed to take some joy from this.

The classroom door opened too fast, it seemed, for its safety mufflers, which creaked and snapped. Aimee was surrounded by purple shadows—the last of twilight before it became night—her eyes were set back under her forehead, her petticoat muddied, her shoes nothing more than two clogs of earth. In her arms she held a bundle that looked worse than she did, and which was hard. It also looked rigored by death.

Mr Him said, "What are you carrying, Aimee?"

The girl swayed where she stood beside the lava table, perhaps from the weight of carrying the body of what appeared to be a boy, perhaps because of the fumes that rose from the magma. Mr Him didn't wait for Disdivanshumayl and rose, skirting the carpet-seated children. He walked to Aimee, pulled apart her arms and took the child from her. The little boy wasn't dead; Mr Him could see the stir of artery on his neck, but barely. His lips were open and whispering. His skin burnt hot, but in the way of a firework on the wet November grass, dampened and squibbed yet still dangerous. The boy's hands were clawed, rigid, with each finger pointing at a ceiling tile. Look, they seemed to be saying, dead spiders. It was a good thing Disdivanshumayl could not see.

"Sunshine," he said. "Get Mrs Her." He needed a first-aider. The children were off their carpet bottoms and on inquisitive feet, cluttered around the three of them—their teacher, their classmate and the dying child. "And Mrs Disdivanshumayl, could you take the register?"

Carrying the blue-robed toddler, Mr Him ran to the junk modelling bin. The boy's soul was bleeding out. The door opened as Mrs Her rushed in.

"Put him on the table," she said.

Mr Him swept the volcano to the side. It clattered to the floor and sent out scorching black lines of lava. Small meteors of discharged rock steamed towards the pupils where they sat on the carpet. Mrs Disdivanshumayl shouted as they shuffled away, "Bottoms!"

Aimee's brother lay golemed on the table-top.

Mrs Her plunged her hand into the junk modelling bin and came up with a pair of lungs that sucked in the classroom's air. She loped to the boy and pressed the windpipe that hung, umbilical, from the pair of lungs to his lips. "Hold it here," she commanded. Mr Him did so.

She returned to the bin and, despite her height, disappeared to her hips within it, her beard hanging, Mr Him imagined, in the darkness. She re-emerged, spluttering, with a heart in her hand that spat exasperated flicks of blood. Nothing really died in This Place thought Mr Him, not even the organs of the dead, unless the Witch or her minions killed it. The graveyard was good for school resources.

"Why is he dying?" asked Mr Him abruptly. "Did the Witch do this?"

"No," Mrs Her replied. Tottering to the table, slipping on a line of red that had spurted out from the heart, she grasped a pair of scissors. "I think he's dying on the Other Side." She returned and cut the boy's robes up the centre. Underneath he was naked. Mr Him tried not to look but as at an accident he felt compelled. He blushed the colour of the liquid that squeezed across the boy's belly as Mrs Her went further, dissecting his ribcage with the scissors. The bones made the crunch of eating cornflakes before they softened. Into the rift, she pressed the heart.

"This will massage his," she said.

Lungs and heart flailed while those within the boy seemed still. Beat. Suck. Beat. The adults stood. Mrs Disdivanshumayl had finished the register, and the classroom was silent.

The boy turned his head in a jerk. The boy spat. The boy screamed and Mrs Her, unseen beneath her beard, smiled and said, "Get me some string. I need to stitch this up."

Part 2

Chapter 1

ALL EIGHT OF MRS Disdivanshumayl's eyes jerked wide open as Aimee collapsed. There was the sound of an impact as thick as the spider's hide.

"Ah… Mr Him?" she said.

Mrs Her said to Mr Him, "Get me some string. I need to stitch him up."

The 'him' was Aimee's little brother, but the teaching assistant had none of her eight eyes for the boy, only for the collapsed girl.

Panic made the teaching assistant's legs skittish. Mrs Disdivanshumayl pulled herself together and up to her fullest height, which, of course, was the ceiling. Looking down on the—now bottomed—pupils on the carpet, she said, "Angel, pick her up! Take her to the office! Quick!"

The office was where the plasters were and the skin-grafts and the spare arms for when they were fallen on, as Aimee had done.

"Owwwah," said Angel.

"What?" The teaching assistant's hair bristled, and there was a lot of it to do so. "WHAT?"

"Nothing," said the boy, who rose, straddled the little girl's inert frame, and pulled her to him, pressing Aimee to his chest and struggling against her weight. Aimee's thick hair fell downward. One thin pale arm rose of its own accord and hung out awkwardly. If Disdivanshumayl had belonged to the Other Place, it would have reminded her of Stephen King's Carrie at her prom—all blood and not much by way of visible skin. Momentarily, Aimee looked as though she were about to grasp Angel, though her pale eyes were closed. Being of This Place, Disdivanshumayl thought of a prince and princess before she blinked most of her eyes and remembered that these children were too experienced for such childish nonsense.

"Go," she said, watching the blood welting off the pupil, falling in half-congealed lumps from her hand like Turkish delight.

Grunting, Angel—who was stouter than he looked—swung the bloodied arm around his shoulder, and swung the girl towards the exit.

"Tower," the boy growled, and Tower was on his feet and at the door, opening it.

Made to limp by his burden, Angel walked into the corridor and out of sight.

"PROMISEMEPROMISEMEpromiseme," Aimee was murmuring to the shirt on his shoulder, her voice like a four-year-old's writing, all forgotten finger spaces and missing capital letters.

~152~

'Oh put a full stop in it," said Angel, meaning to say 'sock' but his mind was reeling as much as his body. He had, though, made it his habit not to complain (or his father had), and so he just kept walking.

"promisemepromisemepromiseme—"

They were nearly at the office. Behind them was trail of blood in smudged zigzags.

"promisepromisepromise—"

"What?" he said. It was the last of his breath and it came out viciously, as though it was a kicked can.

Her eyes lolled to him, seeming to stick to his in much the same way as her body had collapsed against his side.

"Promise me you'll take care of him—"

"Who?" he asked, though he knew.

"Promise me—"

There was a crackle of displaced bone as she hefted up her arm and flapped at him with its hand.

"Promise me."

"That's broken."

"A promise on a broken hand is a promise that lasts forever," she whispered, as though she'd heard it somewhere before. Her eyes were larger than they had any right to be. Angel thought she might be about to pass out.

"A promise on a broken hand—?" he asked. It sounded intuitively right, and the children of the Night School put more faith in their guts than other children had to.

"Promise—"

He nodded. Spat on his left palm. Held her hand. Felt the blood rise between his fingers and his spittle ooze between hers. He imagined it mixing. She shook him in three violent jerks, each producing that grazing, gravelly crackle of bones chafing. Each time the sound seemed to say: this is too much; this is the something that should not happen. But she did it again, and again.

"Promised," she whispered.

They had reached the red chairs outside the office where sick or injured children sat and waited for their guardians to pick them up or for plasters to be applied.

He nodded. "Promised," he repeated and lowered her almost gently onto the nearest chair. It was then that he realised she was fading.

His eyes widened, but not to be as big as hers or as large as the gap his mouth made when he shouted, "Help!"

The receptionist ran out—a cockroach the size of a baby elephant. All those legs helped when she needed to carry lunch registers or plasters, as she did now.

"Out way," she chattered.

"Is she dying?" said Angel.

"No." Plasters slapped against flesh and blood recoated the chair. "Passing out. She'll be back."

"promised—" whispered Aimee and she was gone, leaving only the sound of the word and the feel of her blood coating Angel's right hand and the smell of it lingering.

BARNABY REACHED UP to try to stem the lines of blood with his padded paw. The bleeding was a hot wash down his flank and made up—in part—for the lack of feeling in his body. He heard the finger-tapping of dribbling blood in the algaed pools of rainwater and realised, dim as the light in the wood, that his senses were flowing away from him. His sight gruelled into a layer of sleep across his eyes. It was most inconveniencing, thought the bear, to lose one's arm. He couldn't put his paw on exactly what was happening to him right now. He felt dizzy. With his left arm, he hugged a tree.

There was a bumping squawk, like a bird hitting a window, and Barnaby raised his muzzle. It was wet through, from sweat not blood. High above was the sky, just as high as it'd always seemed to be. And there was the Honey Pot Star, hanging in the sweet spot in the centre of a swirling galaxy. It was only visible when the Witch's Moon began to orbit. Across what was left of the moon and across the star passed several silhouettes: wide-winged and heavy-framed, a legion of them, flying south. One of them squawked. There was a laugh that sounded not so different from a scream. The Witch's legions flew on the winds. The Witch would waken and rise soon. Barnaby was sure of it—in his gut; his mind had long since stopped working.

He tried to let go of the tree. He tried to think of Aimee and Aidan, to give himself impetus, but he could remember neither of their names and soon couldn't even move his eyes.

MONEY INFESTED HER mind, as blowflies would a corpse left in the savannah sun. Pound by pound, direct debit by standing order, the pall mounted until it blinded her. It laid its larvae in the flesh of her brain: she could feel it wriggling.

There were bigger predators than money to hunt down her mind out there in the long grasses of her life, not to mention what she had suffered as a child, but she ignored them and they ignored her. She sat on her settee and watched Oprah and shed a few tears. She cried at the smallest thing. Uncle Chris called her a 'soppy shite', but other names hid inside his eyes. The tears were down to her Aidan, she reckoned.

Poor kid, she thought.

Poor sweetheart, she thought.

Poor love, she thought, but she found it difficult to actually think of him. The image of his face wavered in front of her own, not so much as though a veil had been drawn between them, but as though he'd been drawn through one. It was hard to think of her children as anything other than lost pounds. Good money after bad. Her life, she knew, was hard.

Still, her son's image unsettled her, and she got up, and she made a coffee, and then a tea, and then a coffee, and she shifted uneasily through the early afternoon. Later, she would put on her make-up and the black blouse that shrunk with her age. She liked to go to work; it took her mind off money. From time to time, she would pace unevenly around the lounge, up the brown-carpeted stairs, eyes darting and thinned. (Sometimes she felt like a zombie from one of those bloody horror movies Chris was always watching.) On her wanders, she would see the footprints, here and there, of wasted money.

Amy's clothes. Amy's books. Amy's sketchpad. Amy had been an accident—and an expensive one.

She stopped. She'd heard the sound of Aidan crying—she was sure of it—inside Amy's room—she was sure of that as well. Her son's face floated before her, disembodied as her emotions. She opened Amy's door and stumbled into the girl's bedroom. She sat awkwardly on the green carpet. Before her lay the red-covered sketchpad and she opened it, feeling the rough off-colour pages and resisting, for once, the urge to tear at them. She sneered and read the entries, stared at the maps, scratched with long unpainted fingernails at the drawings. She read about forest nymphs, and how a 'Mr Him' never took Class 7 to visit them.

"Bloody ridiculous," she said to herself. "Off with the bloody fairies."

She shook her head a little too vigorously, as though protesting a memory, and her eyes, as much by accident as the girl had been, saw the teddy bear under the bed.

"Bloody bitch," she said in an almost reverent whisper. "She took it out of the bin. Clever little bitch."

She crawled forward, her knees chaffing on the carpet, and slithered into the niche under the bed. When, as now, she was alone—when Chris was at the dole office, or cutting grass, or plastering for extra money here and there—she would find herself in the tight places of the house. Sometimes she felt as though she were hiding from something.

She grasped the arm of the teddy bear and wrenched him down from between the wall and the bed, out from the shadows under the latter, and back to where the sketchpad lay open on a page decorated by a map of the Latter Wood.

The teddy bear, as it turned and rolled out, only had one arm. She stared at it, holding the bear loosely in her arms, then at the sketchpad.

"Loony tunes," she said to herself. "She should be in a bloody loony bin, not in my home. She can't be bloody mine."

Her fingernail traced the outline of the wood until it reached... "The Night School?" she said, but then her hand slipped on the teddy's arm and she grasped at the limb instinctively to stop it falling.

And her hand clutched the remaining paw.

And she fell.

THE WORLD WAS A dizzying spin of darkness, but Barnaby still knew, as through and through as the stuffing in Barney, whenever Amy took the teddy bear's paw and entered This Place.

The shades that haunted his sight were not only because of the late hour but also (mostly) because of blood loss. The stump of his right arm welted as he breathed raggedly and through ground-down fangs. He had been biting on something to stem the agony and only realised it was his tongue when it had swelled. From time to time he would curse the fact that she'd taken his right arm and not his left, but the rest of the time he either howled in pain or couldn't make a sound.

From a slumped position in the bower of the rhododendron bush in which he had hidden himself, Barnaby rose as best he could and walked worse. Bees could be heard in the cramped darkness. The night was clenched hot in the fingers of the twigs.

"Buzz," the bees said.

"Buzz," they repeated, as though they had nothing better to talk about.

If Barnaby could've limped, he would've been pleased. Instead he crawled and hobbled, and fell over, and then did it all again. It took him a while to reach the girl who was holding his paw and, when he did, he saw she was far older than he'd expected her to be.

SHE WALKED IN A DAZE. She felt rather like somebody who didn't believe in rabbits but had fallen down a rabbit hole. The trees, all of them like the one at the bottom of next door's garden (she didn't know its botanical name), had pods that whispered in the wind. After she'd been walking a long time, or so it seemed, they ceased this whispering and began to tinkle like jostled chandeliers. More than this, they were no longer yellow but jaundiced white, and her skin became pimpled and the same hue as the rimed pods. She could feel her nipples without touching them. Beneath her feet, the ground crackled as though she were walking on crisps. She didn't look down, just in case she was. She felt sure she was dreaming but thought it looked far too real. She screwed up her eyes into a squint, balled her fists and kept walking, doing her best not to suspend disbelief. She needed a lack of belief, as she did back in her own world, more than anything else.

There was the tiniest of fairy-tale tinkles as a breeze passed through this section of the forest, collecting motes of snow and crystals and flurrying them before her sight. She absolutely refused to refer to them internally as fairy dust. The boughs of the trees appeared to be roughly painted with ice, but she didn't give them a second glance and certainly didn't peer.

Instead she stared straight ahead and walked, and she didn't see the large, brown, kneeling bear. It was bleeding through a space where it should've owned an arm. It was watching her with the same expression of disbelief that she wore.

THE BLOOD FROM HIS wounds was slowing in the cold of the Northern Wood. Barnaby was as close to the domain of the Witch as he would normally dare to go. The pimples on his hide, beneath his pelt, goosed: not with cold but with fear. Whoever this woman was (and for some reason he recognised her), however she had come across Amy's teddy bear, she'd blundered into a place that she didn't understand, a dangerous realm, and had just kept on going north. They had passed the Chocolate Box Village a while back, and she hadn't even noticed.

He had to stop her but couldn't crawl fast enough, and the dirks of ice that had been grass and the daggers of ice that had been bushes hurt him where he'd been torn. The holly, glazed like Christmas cakes, was particularly painful.

Barnaby slowed and raised his eyes to see that she, whoever she was, had reached the resting place of the Witch.

"Stop... have to stop," he said.

THE FACE SWAM IN THE block of ice before her but, at its depth, its expression was unfathomable. It had smooth skin or perhaps that was the ice shearing it, and was small-headed, at this distance, and so had the look of a child that had fallen into a frozen lake. One arm rose, beautiful and cold and tapering, towards the surface of the ice block, seeming to seek her touch.

"I know you," she said and reached towards the hand.

The face was familiar, she decided, in a part of her brain that could still do deciding.

You're beautiful, she managed to think.

She slouched onto the block. It was warm on her palms, like a prostrate body, and on the underneaths of her elbows. It didn't feel cold at all. It felt like it was breathing... or beating... She reached forwards and down.

The ice parted, and her hand and that of the Witch met.

The Witch's fingers twitched.

There was the crunching sound of a heavy body crashing through the lines of iced trees behind her, but she had no head-space for what her ears told her and she slumped fully against the block, cutting her scalp. She collapsed down the side of it, her left temple bleeding.

By the time the woman had settled on the eiderdown of the snow, she had fallen unconscious and was blonde enough to fade into her resting place—at least until it turned red. The droplet of blood that had left her head infused the ice-block, colouring it crimson, and the white lines of the Witch's lips rouged and curved into a smile. The smile parted with one long juddering breath.

As Barnaby didn't know the doll-like lady, he had no way of knowing what she did to Amy in the Other Place and so tried to save her. He staggered to the block, grasped her and dragged her away. The dragging was an exertion he could've done without. He only needed to hold her hand (she was already fading from This Place), but he'd forgotten this. It was then that he heard the sound of the Witch's cackle, as the ice block in which she had slept began to melt. The laughter bubbled up through the crystalline water, as maggots do through the skin of a corpse.

The bear, against the odds of his broken body, ran.

THE SUSPENDED SILENCE of the Northern Wood spread out across the Latter Wood. The laburnum pods, where they whispered together in the breeze, stilled and held the wind, cupped. Small things in their bowers and in the nooks and niches down by the many rivulets stopped their digging momentarily, before resuming and noticing as they did so that the earth felt chillier on their paws than it had before.

The dying light of one star in the constellated night reached the heavens in an unseen burst. It eclipsed that of the stars about it as it puckered up in one rosy-red, bee-stung kiss and then was sucked in, becoming infinitely smaller than an eye could see, if it were looking. No human eyes were, of course, because it was Daytime in This Place as it was in the Other. That supernova was the Wishing Star. Somehow, in their positions about it, the Needing and the Wanting Stars looked forlorn when night finally fell.

In the Day School in the Other Place, a little girl felt a shiver go through her skin—not so much as though someone had walked over her grave, but as though they had stopped, unshouldered a shovel, and started to dig.

THE WOMAN OPENED HER eyes, pulled herself to her knees, picked up the teddy bear by the ear of his round fat head, and rose. She would sell the bloody thing. She didn't decide this, as there was nothing left in her brain to do so, but she would do it—for the money. The money was important. It itched at her as to why, as an insect does at the skin, but she knew it was. Garage sale, she thought automatically—for no particular reason other than that she often thought this when she thought about money—then left the bedroom and went down the forest-floor coloured stairs, carrying the bear by its remaining arm and not by its paw.

THAT AFTERNOON AMY was at playtime and, though she didn't really have anybody she would call a friend, she was speaking.

"Yes Barnaby, we did it," said Amy. She said it again, louder, dancing about in a circle as though nailed to the playground. "We did it Barnaby. He's safe."

"She's crazy. Crazy Amy has an imaginary friend." Lucy giggled, high-pitched enough to cut through Amy's daydream. Lucy, as ever, wasn't alone and her friends laughed with her.

Amy danced away. She didn't care, not today; today everything was better.

After the whistle at line-up time, Mr Mann, his hair thinning as his eyes did these days, told her off. Amy was still dancing. Even he, however, shook his head, worn down by her constant grin.

"Off with the fairies," Mrs Skinner said.

Amy didn't care. Aidan *was* off with them, and that was the only caring Amy had room for.

She smiled at Mr Mann as she walked by—in the line—and, when she was inside and out of his sight, she danced some more.

During Golden Time, she drew flowers and butterflies and worms, all of them wearing wide crayon smiles. It wasn't until after she'd finished scribbling that she realised she had also drawn a little boy with big luminous wings. An angel. The angel had an upside-down *u* for a mouth and a frown for a face.

"MY BABY WOULD LOVE this," said the woman. She was pregnant and brunette-topped and half a head taller than the man who turned to her.

The man's fingers gaped with his lips. "It's only got one arm," he hissed.

"Yeah, but it's a proper old teddy bear. Look... smell it."

The man did so. He was thin and his round glasses had the appearance of being the widest part of him. His eyelids tightened as he sniffed then relaxed, as though seeing something he hadn't seen for a long time. "It smells of childhood," he said. He had a southern accent.

"Aye," said the brunette (who didn't). "It smells of happy children."

Amy glowered at her. Her fists were balled beneath the table Chris had taken out of the garage. On its surface a sign said *Garage Sale*. It was a school evening and she sat in her uniform.

"How much is this, love?" the woman said.

Amy didn't reply.

"Don't mind the child. She loves that old thing. God knows why." Her mum smiled. "That'll be fifty p, love."

The man looked at Amy, shifted to his right foot, and put his hands in his pockets.

"Well if you love it, sweetheart, why don't you keep it instead?" said the woman.

"Kid's gotta grow up, eh?" said Amy's mum. She looked at the teddy in the woman's grip and her sentences shortened. "Fifty p, please."

The sun came out from behind a skyscape of white clouds and disappeared again. The sky looked like it had snowed upwards. The woman's hand went towards the table. Amy thought she was about to replace the bear, but they (the hand and the teddy) went away again. Her other palm fell on her belly and gripped its crest, rubbing it in a slow sun-shaped motion. "Tony!" she said.

The man grimaced and then the bumps of his fingers could be seen, knuckling beneath the denim pockets of his jeans. He retrieved a pound coin and said, "Keep the change, our kid," sounding more southern than he had before.

"Thank you. Say thank you, love," Mum said to Amy.

Amy didn't but mumbled two syllables that rhymed with it. The man stared sharply at her from within the round rims of his glasses, but her mum didn't notice. She wasn't all there this afternoon.

They left, the woman carrying Barney as though she no longer wanted him. Her hand gripped the bear by the underarm, on the side of his body that still had one. Amy and her mother sat in silence. No one else came, and the clouds darkened as though the white sky had turned to slush, and it began to rain.

THEY PACKED AWAY IN silence, except for her mum telling her what to do and where to put things. When they went inside and out of the rain, Amy could no longer keep in the tears and she started to cry. She curled up in the corner of the sofa and her mother shouted at her, her beautiful face contorting in confused rage. She didn't seem to remember why Amy was upset. Her mother collapsed on a chair beside the round wooden table in the kitchen, letting her head fall into her arms.

"Jesus, kid, you *are* screwed up," she said to the inside of her arms.

There was a knock at the door and her mum's head jerked, her eyelids snarling open.

"Oh can't you all just leave me alone?" she shouted.

Amy sank into the settee's skin-coloured upholstery.

The knock came again.

"Get the bloody door then," her mum said, letting her head sink back down to her elbows.

Amy didn't move and her mother's left eye came back up above her elbow joint, like a dragon staring through a hole in a mountainside. Amy rolled off the sofa and went to the door, opening it. The brunette pregnant woman was walking down the street, the spectacled man pulling her towards the lamppost on the corner. She was too far away to hear Amy if she spoke, but near enough to hear shouting. Amy, however, couldn't raise her voice. The hallway and lounge behind the little girl were echoingly silent and would carry its sound to the mother who slumbered within.

To the dragon, Amy couldn't help thinking, before she thought, please come back. She did this with as much effort as a yell. Her brain hurt until it felt hoarse. Please bring back my teddy bear, she thought. Her fingers splayed and closed as jerkingly as her lips would have, if they could.

But the couple didn't turn back and turned instead around the corner, the man dragging the woman and muttering something that was within only her earshot.

Amy shut the door.

"Who the hell was it?" growled her mother.

"Just kids."

"Bloody gits," her mother could be heard to say and then something else, which was muffled by the crook of her elbow and the creak of the table as her head rested upon it.

"WE SHOULDN'T HAVE bought it," said the woman, staring at the bear. She held it with both hands now, by one underarm and by one white stuffing-clouded spot where an underarm would've been if there had been an arm.

"Did you see that fishwife? I wouldn't have crossed her." Though her boyfriend said 'fishwife', his accent when he talked in their house came from Surrey. When he was outside, she didn't know where the dialect came from. It sounded like a mixture of Irish and Australian and someone taking the piss out of Mancs. Sometimes—quite a few times in fact—the sound of it made her cringe. She'd learnt to drive because she couldn't stand the bus rides and the looks.

"Oh well, what's done is done." She lay back on the settee. She was feeling sleepy. She cuddled the teddy.

"Do you want a cuppa?" said the man.

"No, I'm just gonna shut my eyes. Get forty winks."

"Okay, old lady." He smiled as he said this. She could tell because the sound of it lilted slightly and he sounded as southern as he did when she had first met him. As innocent. She grasped the teddy closer—as tightly as she had when she was a baby, a toddler, a child—and, for the first time, held it by its paw.

SHE OPENED HER EYES.

Is this a dream? she thought.

She blinked. She was sitting on long grass, which was as comfortable as a bed. A moment before she had been lying on a settee.

"Is this a dream?" she repeated.

"Nope," said a nearby dragonfly. "I think," it added. Then, zooming around her face, it muttered, "Oh God, now I'm worried about that... thanks a bundle!" to itself, and droned into a sky that was deepening from the purple of a bruise to the greyish black of a corpse.

She shook her head. The teddy she'd been cuddling was gone.

"Dream," she said to herself. "Dream... dream... dream." She sounded a little too convincing, a little too real.

She stared at where the teddy bear should've been. She was even more heavily pregnant than she should be, and she was wearing the kind of dress a pregnant woman would dream of but could never find. It was beautiful. Yellow prints on a satin of blue that could only be found in a lover's eyes, or in a sky stared at from lying on your back on a grassy verge in midsummer. Blue that didn't know worry, had never felt fear.

Unlike her. There was a crashing in the long grass before her. An insistent closing sound crashed through the shimmering, flickering boundary between what she could see and what she couldn't. In the dusk, it went from a hump of darkness to a shadow to a paw that grasped her by the neck of the dress with one remaining arm and hefted her to her feet. More importantly, it hefted her to its maw as it screamed, "GIVE HER BACK THE TEDDY BEAR!"

It had eyes that were remarkably human, in that they looked quite mad. Its teeth smelt a little like a grill that had recently cooked human meat.

"I DON'T KNOW WHO THE FUCK YOU ARE, WOMAN, BUT GIVE AIMEE BACK THE FUCKING TEDDY BEAR OR I WILL FUCKING EAT YOU."

With this, he dropped her on the ground.

This hurt.

"DO YOU UNDERSTAND?"

It swayed uncertainly on its feet, and she thought it would swoon and fall on her and flatten her. It was a darker brown than a bear might normally be, being, it seemed, slicked by sweat. Not only blood but flesh seeped from the wound that was supposed to be its shoulder.

"DO YOU UNDERSTAND OR DO I NEED TO RIP OFF ONE OF *YOUR* ARMS?"

"I understand," she whispered.

With a growl that sounded like Bearish for swearing, it reached down and, with an almost mannered delicacy, shook her by the hand.

SHE WOKE WITH A scream.

"What?" said the man. As ever, when stressed, he sounded posh. "*What?*"

She cast the teddy from her. She pointed at it. She gibbered.

"What?"

"Give it back," she said.

"I don't under—"

"WE HAVE TO GIVE IT BACK!" The bear's voice (*bear's voice??* her mind managed to whine) was still in her head. It came out of her mouth in a scream. "DO YOU UNDERSTAND?"

She'd never seen him gulp before, but he did so now.

"Yes," he said.

"WELL," SAID NAN TO Mum, her shoulder pads shifting delicately as she sighed, "we're a proper family, love, and nothing brings a proper family together more than trouble for one of its own."

These days, Nan didn't often speak this way. Gone was all the talk of M and S or of baking or bowling. Amy swung her legs and tried to touch the lino with her toes. The kitchen floor was made to look like slate tiles, but even fake contact was better than none at all.

Nan grasped Mum's hand at its back and gave it a quick rub.

"Right love?" Nan said.

There was a knock at the door. Momentarily, Amy hoped it was Barney, but then she realised he couldn't reach the knocker.

"That'll be Cat," said Nan.

Mum didn't ask Amy to get it, and instead rose herself. Amy stared at her nan, who smiled in response to her gaze.

"Don't worry, sweetheart. He'll be okay."

It took a skipped heartbeat to realise Nan wasn't talking about her teddy bear but about Aidan. Her nan was wearing large drooping earrings, like the tears of a pearl that glowed yellow below the kitchen's bulb. There was no lampshade in this room. They sat around the small table, which had once been square but now had worn, irregular sides.

There was the sound of speech in the porch. "Aww, darling," it said. It was Auntie Cat. There was the clinch of silence as the two women hugged and held onto each other, and then murmuring. When Mum came into the kitchen with Cat, her smooth white cheeks were wet as pebbles in a stream. Then Amy understood how the evening would go and felt better. She'd seen this dance before: the falling apart, the coming back together. It was the same as with Uncle Chris, except without the fists, the swearing and the throwing of things. She could put it into a list, like they practised when they made sandwiches at school:

First, Mum has one of her off days, and they fall out, and Mum says bad words to Nan.

Second, something goes wrong, and Mum phones Nan and cries.

Then, Nan comes round and doesn't comment on the wallpaper or that there's no lampshade or the smell of damp, and Uncle Chris has to go to the local.

Next, Mum cries some more and they have a good time, and they're not off with each other anymore.

Finally, Mum has one of her off days, and they fall out, and Mum says bad words to Nan.

This time Uncle John and Uncle Tommy had come round to fix Uncle Chris's car, and all three of the men had gone out to the local together. On special days (like Christmas and New Year), the local would let Amy come in and collect glasses, empty crisp packets and ashtrays. The crisp crumbs made Amy think of Uncle Chris and the way his eyes would go to sharp pieces when Mum talked to and laughed with all the men at the bar. Uncle Tommy had once said that going drinking with Uncle Chris was like drinking with a potato. Mum had laughed too much at this and looked quickly at Tommy's lips, eyes and body, and then looked quickly away again. Mum looked the same way with the men at the bar in at the local.

"Go on," said Nan now. "Make the brews sweetheart."

Amy did so, and the three adults sat around the table while Mum described the night at the hospital. After serving the teas, Amy went and sat on the settee and coloured the edges of the Latter Wood in green, as if the trees there weren't laburnum. She tried to visualise Barnaby's face but couldn't, not because of the passage of time since seeing him, but because a jet black icon of a Witch on a broomstick had appeared on the sketch of the Latter Wood and was moving around. Like an icon on a computer screen. Like it was looking for something. It blipped about the white Northern Wood, then settled in the Chocolate Box Village. For a Witch, it was fat: a blimp on a stick. Shit, Amy thought in her mother's voice. Her mother, meanwhile, was describing being made to wait by the nurses but not describing her swearing at the doctors or the purple spots in the corner of Aidan's room; Amy guessed she'd been unaware of these. Mum often didn't remember what had happened when she'd lost her temper.

Amy stared up at her, then back down again. The Witch hadn't moved.

When her mother had finished, they all sat silently and Cat rubbed her belly—not in the sun-shaped way of the lady at the garage sale, but only on the right like she was charting a crescent moon.

"Can you feel it kicking?" asked Mum softly. She never normally mentioned the unborn baby.

"Nah, it's been quiet like all day. If I have a curry, it goes crazy."

Nan laughed, and Mum smiled. "You don't know if it's a boy or girl Cat?" Mum asked.

Amy's scribbling paused on the page.

"Nah," said Cat. "It'll be a nice surprise." Her words were slow and soft, as feet would be if they trod on eggshells.

"You'll be a good mum," said Mum.

Her eyes looked raw and as young as in the photo album as she glanced up at Auntie Cat, who blushed, her face going long and red as she replied, "Thanks sis... I'm so sorry about little Aidan. And I'm sorry if I've been uppity with you. I didn't mean to be. I'm just happy, I suppose, and I forgot what you've been through."

Mum looked at Amy then glanced at her sister, her bee-stung lips thinning like when she wanted to speak but she didn't get the chance, as Nan smiled and said, "It does me good to see youse like this. I know there's been lot of water under the bridge. I mean, well, you know what I mean. You've had to put with a lot of crap and I'm no different, but it does an old lady good to see her girls getting on. Come on. Let's have a game of cards like in the old days."

"Like with poor Dad," said Auntie Cat.

Mum's eyes snapped away. "Oh don't mention that old bastard."

This was too much for Nan's face, which darkened. "Hang on, young lady. Don't talk about your dad that way. I lived with him for thirty years, you know."

"Yeah I know," Mum said. Amy went back to scribbling. She heard the turning in Mum's voice and knew her head needed to be down. "You don't need to tell me, you know what I mean? He wasn't no angel, was he?" Her eyes sharpened to the side where Cat sat. "And you can drop the whole 'poor Dad' business. You know what he was like with me." The eyes bladed back to Nan. "And *you* know too."

"I'll have none of that tonight," said Nan. "Not with your little mite in the hospital. You need to learn how to curb your tongue, young lady."

"Oh stop young ladying me," said Mum. But she glanced off to the side, her eyes softened by the mention of Aidan.

"Go get the cards, Amy love," said Nan into the pause.

Amy did so and brought them to the table. Before Nan had married Uncle John, they'd played cards every Tuesday. Girls Night In, they'd called it.

Nan pulled up a chair. "Have a seat sweetheart. I'll teach you Chase the Lady."

"That's not what he called it," said Mum, but she spoke sideways—to the wall—so everybody could ignore her, and they did.

Nan taught Amy as the adults drank the wine Mum had brought from Kwik Save. Amy tried a sip and gagged. With each passing hand Mum drank a glass, and with each her gaze seemed to skew as she stared at her hands of cards, as though she saw entirely different pictures. Whatever it was, it pleased her as little as the way Nan kept asking questions about Cat's unborn baby, as little as when Cat had shown everybody her twenty-week scans.

"Three of Spades. Slither under that if you can you jammy bastards," her nan said as she laid a card on the table.

"Ohhh... drawing out the lady, are you?" said Cat, giggling.

"Shit, you mean the cunt, right?" said Mum, who smiled around the rim of her wine glass but to herself, as if she could see her reflection distorted in it. Her smile looked too wide.

Amy glanced up from her cards. The woman in question, she knew now, was the Queen of Spades.

"Oh, who cares what she's called. Just put the bloody cards down," said Nan.

"Here's the *lady*," said Cat, laying down the Queen. Her face was long and red, again, but more watchful and reminded Amy of a lizard in one of her nature books.

"No... you're the fucking *lady*," said Mum, placing the King of Spades. Her lips looked like they were smiling but her eyes didn't.

Nan stared flints at her. "I'm gonna walk away from the table if you don't stop your potty mouth. There's a child here."

~176~

"Oh, fuck the child," said Mum. "The game's called Hunt the Cunt, and she was always called the cunt when we were little. Not the bloody *lady*. Just because you two got old and all dried-up and prissy and all high and mightier than me don't mean a cunt ain't a cunt."

"I've got to go," said Auntie Cat, clasping her handbag with one hand and her belly with the other as she rose. "Early meeting tomorrow."

"Look," said Mum. She picked up the Queen of Spades and thrust it before Amy's eyes, which went slightly crossed as she did so. Despite her constant reading, Amy's lexicon was often restricted as if she were an everyday eight-year-old with everyday experiences. In the field of anatomy—as in the area of cursing—she was, however, an expert. She knew that 'cunt' meant 'fanny', and that 'fanny' meant a woman's private parts, but she couldn't work out what the Queen had do to with either. She wasn't naked for a start.

Her mother continued, "If anybody asks you sweetheart, she's the cunt. These two can call her something different if they like, but I know who I am and I know who she is, and it's best to know yourself if you ask me."

Auntie Cat leaned in. "Never a truer bloody word said," she hissed and turned and walked into the lounge.

"Enjoy your meeting, you bloody *banker*," Mum giggled. The front door banged and she drank. It was possible for Amy to see, because it was dark outside, her mother's tears reflected in the kitchen window.

"Why can't you just leave it all in the past? Like your sister did. Why can't you just move on?" asked Nan thickly.

Amy thought Mum would yell. She didn't. Instead, when she spoke, her lips hardly moved and her voice was bitter like she was chewing on a speaking beetle from the Other Place, and it was speaking instead of her. "Because he left her alone. Because I was Dad's favourite, his perfect little china doll."

Tears were padding down Nan's cheeks and onto the tablecloth. They looked thicker than they should be and glassy, as though they had been forming in her head for years under the pressure of decades, like diamonds did. "I'm sorry," she whispered, "but I can't go back."

"I keep trying to get better Mam," said Amy's mother. She sometimes called Nan 'Mam' instead of 'Mum'. Amy didn't know why. "But I feel like I'm buried underground, buried alive. And every time I try to dig my way out, it's like I get turned around and it all just keeps getting darker, you know? Sometimes I don't feel like I can breathe."

They held hands over the table for a moment, and then let go.

Nan drew the cards in and shuffled. She shuffled some more.

Mum was quiet as she did so. She touched the edges of her eyes.

"Are you going to be alright love?" asked Nan in a murmur.

Mum smiled shortly, and it quickly disappeared. "I think I need help Mam." She looked at Amy but couldn't seem to hold the stare, and her eyes shifted away. "No, I'll be alright... Just can't stop thinking about little Aidan, that's all."

Nan's face crumpled delicately like a bin liner pressed around a dead pet. She sighed. "I know sweetheart, but there's nothing you can do. The doctors know best."

Amy lowered her head and stared at her hands. Now that there were no cards to look at, she saw Barnaby.

There was a knock. Amy looked up. The world swam but badly, as if it were drowning.

The knocking came again.

"Knock—" it said, "—knock."

Like a joke, thought Amy.

"Maybe it's Cat come back," said Nan.

"Will you get it for me love?" said Mum to Amy.

Amy walked to the porch, closing the door between the lounge and the hallway, and opened the front door. It wasn't Auntie Cat.

IN THE PREGNANT woman's hand was a garden spade. On its blade, balanced lopsidedly, was Barney. Next to her, the bespectacled man looked embarrassed, looked up and down the street, but didn't look at Amy.

"Here," the brunette said. "Take it."

Amy stared.

"It's yours," the woman said and shoved the spade at the little girl's somnambulant grip. The teddy bear listed. The woman seemed to be sweating. The teddy bear appeared to be smiling. When Amy took him off the spade, he felt happy.

"Come on," said the man.

The woman stared back at Amy. Her mouth opened and then closed.

"Come on," said the man.

The woman's mouth opened again. "I don't understand," she whispered.

"We've got to go," the man said, dragging at the brunette's arm.

Please don't, Amy thought to say, but they were already at the gate. Look after your baby, she thought to add, but they were walking down the pavement. The man's glasses were fixed ahead.

The little girl walked into the house and closed the door. After the soft click of its closing, there was silence until Nan shouted, "Who was it sweetheart?"

Amy looked down at Barney. She smiled. "Just kids," she said.

"Bloody again," her mum exploded. "I bloody hate those little gits. Wait till I give them a piece of my mind." There was the scrape of chair legs on fake tiles.

Amy stiffened. Her fingers turned to claws on Barney's pelt. It felt good, despite the fear.

"Oh sit down," said Nan. "You're in no state to yell at anybody. Go get me another drink, you funny bugger."

Mum could be heard rising and, beneath its sound, Amy ran up the stairs. Each step she took lifted her smile a little higher. Amy entered her bedroom and replaced Barney, careful to wedge him under the bed so that he wouldn't be visible.

Chapter 2

ANGEL LOOKED UPWARDS. The bell tower that nestled on top of the computer suite of the Night School was tolling. It was the end of the second break before midnight. The children were coming in—Angel could hear them: the sound of talking, the noise of teachers shouting at them to stop, the sound of talking, the noise of teachers being ignored. There was one teacher, however, who wasn't saying a word.

As ever, Angel was where he shouldn't be, having claimed to Mrs Disdivanshumayl that he needed to pee. He stood outside the disabled toilet near the hall. It didn't matter that it was occupied and he couldn't enter, he had no intention of going in as his bladder had no intention of relieving itself in the near future. Instead he was watching Mr Him, not because he'd promised Aimee that he would watch him but because he'd promised he would protect her baby brother. And Angel did not renege on his promises. (Unless they were to a teacher, but promising a teacher was like Brains in Numeracy... it didn't count.)

Mr Him walked by, looked at the toilet, shook his head, and continued on his way. He wasn't alone. Why Mr Him would want to go to the toilet when he wasn't alone, Angel didn't know.

Angel pretended to be opening another child's lunchbox. He'd found throughout his time in schools (both Day and Night) that teachers never ignored you more than when they were in a hurry and they thought you were doing something wrong.

Mr Him was in a hurry.

The little boy with Mr Him was just as quiet as the adult was. Though Angel was only somewhere between seven and ten, he wouldn't have considered himself a little kid and he wasn't, at least not in comparison with this one. The boy appeared to be from Year 1, and Angel was quite sure he'd seen him sprinting up and down the corridor to the dining room just after midnight snack. Normally this boy was giggling and, when he wasn't doing that, he was gurgling and, when he wasn't gurgling, he was screaming. Angel had never seen him quiet.

They walked, the three of them—two of them side-by-side and Angel hidden behind—down to the stairs that led to Key Stage 1, then right, and from there the Key Stage 1 playground. As he descended and his school shoes stepped onto the scrape of the playground's tarmac, Angel felt his breath rise into his chest. His fingers jangled as though his nails were being forced across slate. His cheeks and nape reddened as if he had screamed but hadn't meant to.

Angel glanced behind him. Neither Mr Him nor the smaller child did the same and, when he looked ahead again, all Angel could see of their heads was their hair and, where this wasn't the case, Mr Him's baldness. The follicles seemed to move more than the slight wind demanded. Mr Him had a hand on the child's grey-jumpered back, propelling him forward. The fingers on the fabric were splayed, crooked and still, like the legs of glued insects.

Half of the Key Stage 1 playground was a willow garden, its pathways made of tunnels of bent and woven wood, hung throughout with fairy lights. The globes of the street lamps that lit the playground were, here, scratched out by the lengths of willow; the twinkling of the fairy lights was now all that lit Angel's way as he followed them in.

He lost Mr Him in the dark.

They'll be looking for me, he thought, meaning Mrs Disdivanshumayl's eight eyes. It was long after break. The thought occurred to him that Mr Him must've known he was following, must've stopped, and would now be standing in wait between two ribs of willow. A man who made Angel think of tweed and failure abruptly took on sharp edges, like being hit by a quiet father for the first time.

Angel glanced behind again. And to the sides. He didn't really like the dark—it reminded him of the bedroom he'd escaped from to come here. The Witch's Moon was up but was shrouded by the leaves that adorned the willow-weaving nearer the centre of the garden. His feet wanted to turn around; his toes, if asked, would've gone further, wanting desperately to flee. He could feel them itching, but he'd made a promise—and to a child, moreover. Gripping his fingers into fists, and with his courage like stolen Lego between them, he walked forwards. He could see the breath in front of his face but little else, until the vaguest of breezes touched his cheeks and a dull rotten oval of light could be glimpsed ahead, through the foliage. The middle of the willow garden, thought Angel.

He edged closer to the falling light of the moon. The end of the willow tunnel was a putrid full stop just ahead. His heart thudded, seeming to pause on each beat, waiting for something. He expected at every second to see the tunnel's end smudged out by the ink of Mr Him's silhouette. He didn't. Angel reached the Glade and crouched. (The nearer to the ground his bottom got, the more he wanted the toilet. This feeling reminded Angel of his father and especially the times he asked, "You gonna piss yourself, you little shit?" The circles of willow seemed to noose around his head, and Angel found he couldn't even gulp, let alone pass water.)

The midst of the willow garden held a pagoda and a pond and nothing else.

Where are you? thought Angel.

He stepped out into the light of the Witch's Moon, which was less bright now that he was within it. The pond's surface was threaded with grass and bubbled by frogspawn, which shivered slightly like jelly on a plate. The pagoda was slats of silhouette-black with no sign of occupation.

"Gone," whispered Angel. It felt reassuring to hear a part of himself that wasn't his heart.

(WHAT HE HADN'T SEEN—because it was behind not one willow shoot but many—was the sight of Mr Him holding the hand of a five-year-old child and leading him into a pond. He'd missed the sight of water quickly swamping the boy's tiny black leather school shoes, which were just a clot or two of mud, the frogspawn flooding his white school shirt until it may as well have never been clean, and the grass obscuring his face entirely as though he had never been at all.)

BARNEY SAT IN THE middle of the ruffled duvet looking for all this particular world like a bear going down in a cotton storm. His one remaining arm was raised slightly at the angle at which he sat, as though clutching the air.

Amy gulped snot. She wiped gunge onto her jammies.

She raised her own arm, the opposite one to Barney. She let it fall. She tried again to reach out to him—and let it fall. The waves of duvet were insurmountable, as was her guilt. She swallowed, tried to whisper, "I'm sorry," but though made to say it at least three times a day, she couldn't. Not now she actually meant it. She raised her arm and reached for Barney, didn't let it drop, and soon enough she was falling.

LOOKING UP AT THE night sky, Aimee realised that, here, the moon didn't wane but only waxed. It should now be the time—calendarwise—of the sickle. Its coverage indicated instead that this was a one-and-a-half moon. Again, with the slap of cold air to her cheeks, Aimee was reminded that by bringing her brother here she had broken the rules of This Place, marred nature, rearranged the order of things in the same way as Angel would say, "I'll rearrange your face," if you refused to give him your lunch money.

She brushed aside thoughts of Angel, as thoughts of Angel meant thoughts of the one he was protecting: her baby brother. It wasn't that she didn't want to think of him, it was that she already did and those thoughts were as big and luminous and sky-filling as the Witch's Moon. She couldn't afford for them to wax or they would split her face open and she'd cry again.

There was movement under the treeline of the laburnums but it was slow and heavy, and Aimee knew it couldn't be her bear. She hunkered down between the long fingers of the overgrown grass in the Glade. It was wet beneath her red-shoed feet, mud lapped against her white sock-line, and she guessed it had been raining. The wet was already turning to frost in places and the breath from her mouth was cloudy. Heart thrumming, she pressed her face to her ruffed shoulder, trying to douse the smoke signals. She didn't want whatever was out there to be alerted to her position. If it wasn't Barnaby, it was big (it sounded big) and must be a minion of the Witch. She glanced again at the sky for some sign of the Honey Pot, or the Wishing, Needing or Wanting Stars, or just for some sign.

She spotted nothing but the blanched, crated features of the moon itself. She'd never looked at them before and hadn't noticed that the pocks could be read as a sharp-toothed grin. She decided not to look much now either but couldn't ignore the noise of breaking vegetation and hacked breathing, and she knew that the thing in the night was closing in.

"Where are you Barnaby?"

She bent lower against the mud, careful not to touch any of the tendrils of green and yellow grass. The vapours that rose from her mouth were thinning now but only because her throat was tightening. She wondered momentarily if breathing came from the heart, before recalling the anatomy lessons of Mrs Her. Still, she caged her lips with her pale fingers, little good that did. The noise of the Glade's transgressor was coming ever closer. It breathed as no creature had any right to, in long wet exhalations and fast snakeish hisses of inhalation. Whatever it was, it didn't sound as though it were supposed to be alive. This made Aimee think about rising and running. But to do so would be to invite it upon her. The bear knew this spot. He would come. If she ran, she'd have nothing to fight for her. But if she stayed, it would close in (as it did now) and not only close in but touch her with whatever it had for arms.

Aimee tried to put this out of her mind but could do little to dispel the images of fangs and tentacles and claws.

When it came, she discovered she was half right.

It had fangs and one paw of claws but the other was missing and, in its stead, was the smell of blood and broken fur.

"Barnaby," she breathed in relief.

The bear made a sound in its throat which may have been 'Aimee' or may have been vomiting; the girl couldn't tell because the bear then collapsed at her shoes.

"Barnaby!" she repeated.

She crouched to the earth. Her hands and palms and fingers found his fur, cradling it where she could. It was wet underneath, at the skin.

How could she have been so cruel? How could she make him crawl out there? Why couldn't she leave the poor bear alone? Amy didn't put any of these questions into words, not even inside her own mind; she was too young to do so, perhaps.

But she could articulate their answer: Aidan, she thought, as she often did.

She cradled Barnaby in her small arms and raised his snout and head (which was now unconscious) onto her lap. She stroked him and cried onto the tuft of his forehead. It was matted and not at all looked-after, as was the rest of his pelt. His pride, it seemed, had gone the way of the blood he had lost.

Aimee considered dragging him back to the treeline, where he would be covered by shadow and have more of a chance to rest, to heal. But she knew she didn't have the strength, and wouldn't have even if she were a full grown woman. So she gently lowered his head into the soft mulch between the foliage and collected arms-full of grass and built him, sheaf by sheaf, a hut as low-lying as his frame. It was all she could do.

"Won't help if the wolf comes to blow it down," she said, her head giddy from exertion and from the lateness of the hour by the time she was finished. Dawn was visible beyond the wall of the Latter Wood.

"Sleep well bear," she kissed his snout. "I won't bother you again—" She didn't apologise, figuring he would've heard enough of this even when unconscious. "—until you're healed... find somewhere safe."

With this she reached below the skein of interwoven grasses, found his paw, and took it.

THE DARK BRANCHES were darker with rain and, in the lantern lights of the five-child party, appeared as would snakes newly shed from their skin: eager, slicked, ravenous. Tower's heart fluttered somewhere between frightened and excited, its thump-thump unable to settle on either. He didn't know what it was to be indifferent as much as he didn't know what it was to be cool. His hair, the way his clothes hung to the swollen front porch of his gut, his gait and its endless swaying between left and right—he couldn't do easy. His fingers misbehaved when he drank tea and he spilt it. His eyes couldn't look you in the eye.

Tonight in the Latter Wood, the dribbles of water seemed to have tortured everything else into silence.

"Ah, ah," said the Christian, crossing himself as he often did (before they'd left the school he'd faced east, bent, knelt and prayed to Allah for at least five minutes on a small rug). "Watch out for the—"

Tower ignored what he was supposed to be looking out for. He had enough to worry about: the way he walked, for one.

He'd tripped and fallen five times, and his face was covered in muck. His mouth had the taste of dirt.

"Stop here," said the Christian. Not, it seemed, because the ground was favourable for the planting of the potato seeds they carried but because the two nearest laburnum trees were arranged (due to the collapsing of one) into the figure seven. "Who's got the trowels?" asked the Christian. It was difficult to tell in the dark, until Tower turned his lantern on the group. (He was one of two children who'd been tasked with the job of light-carriage. A very important job in the coal-edifice of the Latter Wood at night, when the Witch's Moon was eclipsed by the drape of laburnum seeds. Also a very easy job, and one where the Christian could easily see if Tower had dropped the lantern or otherwise left it behind.) It turned out, via the medium of light, that the Christian had forgotten to give any of the children the trowels.

"Oh bugger," said the Christian. "Oh the bad number," the Christian added as he double-checked his lack of equipment. "Help," he said finally.

Except he said it in a child's voice.

Tower stared at him. The lantern to the side of Tower's right temple cast the Christian in fish-lips of light and gave the man, momentarily, a halo of his own.

"Help me!" said the Christian, in his child-voice. Except through the use of peering, Tower could tell it wasn't the Christian who had spoken. His lips hadn't shifted. There was a slight wind in the forest and it touched Tower's cheek, which shook like the syllables of a stammerer.

"S-sir?" he asked, sticking up his hand.

The Christian ignored it. He had more pressing worries, it appeared—these being trowels. Tower twisted his hand.

"Sir?" he repeated.

"Please... anybody—" the child's voice was raised again. It had a ghostlike quality, borne on the wind as it was, its tone plucked of any solidity. Tower staggered slightly to the side, as though drawn to it. He felt quite unable to stop himself.

"He's taking me away. He keeps touching me. Please make him stop," said the whisper.

"Um?" said the Christian. "Um?" he asked again. "Where are *you* going, Tower?"

But Tower wasn't listening or at least, if he was listening, he wasn't listening to the Christian.

Tower's feet, almost of their own accord, stumbled into a jog and then a run.

"Where is he taking me?" the wind seemed to ask. But if it was the wind, it was a young wind and a scared one.

Tower darted from treeline to treeline, past bushes. The darkness around the ring of his lantern light took on a new meaning, like swearwords to a child who was beginning to understand them. The world shifted without actually moving at all. But Tower didn't stop. His run became more of sprint.

The wind was moving away from him, carrying the words on it in snippets.

"Help... Please... It's... Him... Stop... Him... Help—" it said.

The terrain was hardening beneath his feet. The soles went this way and that, as they always did, but no matter where they trod they stepped on frost. The laburnum pods occasionally, when Tower was more concerned with following the voice than his own eye-line, cut across his cheeks. The air felt as hard as a coin-hoard and just as chill. His skin and blood were hotter than before, at least at his cheeks, as the blood rose to combat the lowering temperature. Tower didn't notice this, because all he noticed was a voice—not many years dissimilar from his own—saying, "Help!... Me!"

And then Tower suddenly stopped. And then Tower suddenly saw where he was and everything that was in that place with him. It was one of those moments of clarity only available in a frozen forest where nothing moved bar the thing that you hoped never to see. A thing so heart-rending it reminded Tower—and most forcibly—of bedtime.

Tower tried to scream, but all that came out of his mouth was the vapour of his breathing, and he turned and ran in the opposite direction in as straight a line as he had ever managed.

THEY STOOD IN THE KEY Stage 2 playground—Tower and Angel and Sunshine—below a lamppost that must have been of Victorian descent. It looked like it needed a blue police box and a red postbox to complete the set.

"A village? Are you sure?" asked Angel. His face carried its usual expression of contempt, in the same way as a medieval peasant might have carried the pox.

"He's said so three times already," said Sunshine in her most pleasant voice, which was reminiscent of tuberculosis. Autumn seemed to suit Sunshine, perhaps because it was the cloudiest season in the Latter Wood.

"Y-yes," said Tower.

"Full of children? Children that have gone missing from this school?"

Tower nodded. He didn't trust himself to talk—stammer and all—but his nod went several directions at pretty much the same time and could well have been a shake.

"Mr Him," repeated Angel. He'd said this since the beginning of the conversation. "Mr Him—"

"You said that—" said Sunshine. "—before."

Angel ignored her. (He'd been taught by his quiet father to ignore women, especially the ones who felt at liberty to give their opinions. He'd been taught more than that, in all honesty, but didn't attempt to pass his teachings onto Sunshine for fear she would hit him back.) "We have to stop Mr Him getting to him," he said.

The other two children nodded solemnly. They both knew the 'him' he meant: Aimee's baby brother Aidan.

AMY SANG SMOOTH Criminal:

"Aimee, are you okay, are you okay, Aimee?"

As children do, the first time she had heard Smooth Criminal she had misheard the lyrics but had then stuck with the mistranslation.

"—the bloodstains on the carpet, then you ran into the bedroom—" she sang accurately. She loved Michael Jackson. Ever since hearing that he lived in a place called Neverland,

Amy had felt a connection with him and his songs. Sometimes it felt as though he were singing directly to her. Jackson, perhaps because of his position above her bed, seemed to be keeping an eye on her while she slept.

Amy stared out of her window at the wine-gum sunset and, below it, Manchester's lights arranged into the outline of tower blocks. Her eyes dropped as she murmured along with Jackson on the secondhand CD player, "You've been hit by, you've been struck by, a smooth criminal—" Her eyesight fell through the park, past the swings and the bouncy cookie-dough asphalt the council had baked the ground in, and, finally, she looked to her left, to the picture on her wall. Before this song, she had been singing Man in the Mirror and, though she had to sing it nearly silently, her throat was rubbed raw and her eyes looked redder. Quite often she saw the Little Man in the bathroom mirror: Aidan. He looked safe for now, and like he was hidden in the Nursery of the Night School. She never saw herself, but this was down to a want of looking more than anything else.

The picture she now stared at on her wall was one of a set of three, but her mum had sold the other two at various car boot sales. It was of a hill with a lamppost upon it, lights hanging from its bulb, making it appear Christmassy. (With *Fairy Lights No.3* written below the painting itself in a ghostly shade of grey.) Amy was unsure what the picture had been painted with, but the colouring had a blue, ethereal quality, almost as though it were not there at all and that explained, to Amy's mind, why her mum had missed it on her many car boot clear-outs.

Amy mumbled, "Aimee are you okay, will you tell us that you're okay?"

If Amy was anything to go by, she probably wasn't.

There was movement in the picture.

Amy blinked. Billie Jean was now playing, but Amy was straining to hear Other speech. In the foreground of the picture, there were three children under the lamppost. They were talking. One of them looked as solid as a tall building, another wore angel wings, and the third shone out of the canvas like a star. (Amy was unsure which one—maybe the Needing.)

"People always told me, be careful of what you do, and don't go around breaking young girls' hearts," whispered Amy, knowing Michael Jackson off by heart. "And mother always told me, be careful of who you love, and be careful what you do, 'cause the lie becomes the truth—"

"PLEASE IGNORE THE monster at the back of the classroom," said Mr Him. This was proving troublesome for most of the class but not for Angel, who was paying attention for a change. "What did I say, Brains—eyes to me! Both of them please."

Though he focused on the teacher, Angel could hear the crate at the back of the room shifting and bellowing or, more specifically, he could hear the thing within it.

"Any guesses, children, as to what is in the box?" Mr Him rubbed his hands together. Angel could've sworn they'd left slime behind—the palms glistened.

Angel put up his own hand.

"Mmmmn?" said Mr Him.

"A Gorilla of the Witch," said Angel.

The face of the teacher fell around his glasses which, rigid, seemed to be the only thing keeping the façade up, like scaffolding. "Well yes," Mr Him agreed. His gaze nailed itself to Angel for a moment then moved on. In his crossed legs, Angel's fingers knitted into each other.

"Today's lesson," continued Mr Him, "is death. How you can die in This Place—" He walked behind the carpeted area of the classroom and the pupils' heads followed him owlishly on top of their shoulders. 'Death' had caught their attention. The back of the classroom was a space cleared of its normal orange-topped tables. In the centre of the puce floor stood a dark coloured crate, which shifted and trembled to the breaths of the Gorilla within it.

"Science! I know—so boring most of the time. Thermometers and weighing scales and yawns, yawns, yawns… But this Science lesson, you get a chance to feel what dying feels like. Real, hands-on learning… The Gorilla's hands, that is… Any volunteers?"

No hands went up. Not even those of the girls who sat along the carpet's front row.

Now Mr Him was holding a length of string. "Oh come on! It's only a little winged monkey." The crate careened about the floor, as whatever was inside took exception to this description and bellowed. "Come on, it's not dangerous. Perfectly safe! I'll just let the Gorilla hit you until you nearly die. But I won't let it actually kill you. I wouldn't do that, or you'd never come back. Look, I'll keep this—" He twitched the string like a marionette cord. "—tied to you and pull you out when you've lost enough blood. All that will happen is that you'll pass out of This World and wake in your bed in The Other. Easy as pie, dying is." He grinned nastily. "So... volunteers then?"

Mr Him had wandered to the front of the room again.

"Just a little monkey... Little winged monkey. I'll have to pick someone, I guess—"

Every one of the children's hands could well have been rooted in the carpet. There was the distinctive sound of mouths holding their breaths. Mr Him crouched in front of Sunshine, whom he often smiled at. He put his hand on her shoulder and Angel felt his stomach do something strange—something adults did with pancakes on Shrove Tuesday.

"Come on, Sunshine," he said. He smiled at her.

Angel put his hand up.

"You trust me, don't you?" Mr Him touched her shoulder. "You know I would never let anything bad happen to you."

"Angel put his huh-hand up," blurted Tower.

Mr Him's upper lip twitched as he let go of Sunshine and rose to stand. "Brave boy," he hissed. "Showing the class how much of a big boy you are, eh, Angel?"

Angel stared back. He didn't speak.

Mr Him smiled as he tied the length of string to himself and then said, "Stand up boy."

Angel did so, and Mr Him tied the other end around the boy's belly.

"Now," said the teacher. "This will be painful, I'm afraid. So, a little bit of advice, if I may. It will be tempting to move as quickly as you can inside the crate, because the Gorillas are strong but slow. I would say: don't. Take the beating and I'll pull you out all the quicker."

Take the beating, Angel could hear his father telling him in his head. Angel licked his lips, which felt surprisingly dry against the bottom of his tongue, and Mr Him led him to the back of the classroom.

Now the teacher was whispering, "There's a small door on the other side of the crate. Big enough for a human but not for the Gorilla. I'll push you in and you'll be gone." The last seemed to be for Angel's ears only. There was a look in Mr Him's eyes that suggested he was thinking about all the times Angel had misbehaved.

Angel smiled his most beatific smile and said loudly, "It'll be okay, Mr Him. Don't you worry about me."

"I'm not," hissed Mr Him, swung open a small mahogany coloured door and hefted Angel in. Inside the crate smelt of faeces and was as black as the underarm of an ape, until Angel realised that was actually what he was staring at. The Gorilla's wings made its underarms cavernous. Then the Gorilla turned and bared, not only its fangs but a monstrous set of biceps. Its wings shook the confined space. It bellowed and Angel felt his hairline waft and his nostrils wither.

Angel rolled around the Gorilla as it sprang. The crate skittered to the side, scraping across the polished floor. The classroom outside screamed and Mr Him shouted, "Don't fight it. Make it quick."

Angel tried to flinch away but recoiled into the skin of the Witch's minion. It stank. He was tangled about its upper right leg. With a huff and a snarl, the thing turned to bite at him but missed. It couldn't smell him, Angel realised, because of its own stench. He slipped a finger inside the knot of his string and untied it from his belly. Then the Gorilla seized him about the waist and began to pull. Wind knocked from his body; stars made a light inside the crate but a fake one. Angel had to stare between the coronas to retie the string, which had now completely encircled the Gorilla's right bicep. With a wriggle, Angel freed his arm and pulled insistently at the rope.

Mr Him, at the other end and unseen by Angel, tugged back.

"Hummmnn?" the Gorilla asked. Its grip eased on Angel enough for the boy to play dead. It took all of his willpower not to wheeze. Mr Him tugged again.

Angel could see the rough length of string and the ape pinching it with two fingers, curiously wrapping its entire hand around it. The hand, thought Angel, was about the size of a tyre. He reckoned its punch would be like being hit by a truck. Angel liked trucks even more than he liked Ferraris.

He could hear Mr Him saying loudly, "We'll leave him in there a little longer, shall we class? All the better for this experiment." Then the teacher whispered into the hole, "Goodbye Angel. This will stop you following me around school."

Mr Him gave the string a tiny mocking tug.

The Gorilla wrenched back, and there was the sound of Mr Him hitting the side of the crate.

"Agrhmm," Mr Him said.

The Gorilla pulled again and wrenched Mr Him into the crate, or at least wrenched his head, which the Gorilla punched. Blood splattered on the crate's straw.

"Arggggghhhhhh," screamed Mr Him, his voice muffled by his shock.

As the Gorilla pulled the rest of Mr Him's body into the darkness and continued to pound it, Angel crawled out of the crate and lay—smiling—on the polished, slightly scratched floor of Class 7.

"ASK HIM!" SAID ANGEL.

He stood, his expression balled up as a clenched fist. The Headmistress would've thought he was about to cry if his eyes weren't so defiant.

"Ask him!" the boy repeated. "Tower saw it all. Where he's taking the children. That's why I let the Gorilla have him. He's kidnapping little kids! I wish the Gorilla'd killed him."

The Headmistress—an owl who wore horn-rimmed glasses and, quite often in the winter, cardigans—leant back. Her eyes blinked in shock which, given the size of them, made her entire face blink in shock. "You don't mean... That's an awfully... serious accusation Angel."

"It's true!"

"Well I mean... I'll have to talk to your guardian. It's the snake, isn't it?"

Angel didn't answer this but said, spittle falling seemingly accidentally out of his lips, "How could you let him teach here?"

"That's enough now Angel." Her feathers stood on end, as they did when she flustered. "Go back to class."

The child did so, and the Headmistress leant back into her leather chair (made from the hides of mice). Eventually she flapped, rose and flew to the reception. "Could you get Mr Him for me please?" she asked.

MR HIM STOOD BEFORE the Headmistress. She stared at him and tried not to notice how sweaty he was. (The bruises, however, were impossible to ignore.)

"It's a serious accusation," she said after the teacher didn't reply.

"You know that's in my past. You know I changed... healed. It was a devil inside me—the Witch's devil—" He was looking at her, but somehow not. Again the Headmistress tried to ignore this. If she'd been wrong about Mr Him... She couldn't entertain the thought. The thought certainly didn't entertain her.

"And the boy saw you at the village?"

She made it—pointedly—into a question, but he didn't answer, at least not for a while. Then he said, "If I am to spy on her, as I agreed, that's where I need to be. The village well leads... well, you know where the village well leads—"

There were too many pauses in the conversation for the Headmistress. Her stomach crawled as though she'd just eaten her favourite meal. She decided to visit the village and soon.

She hadn't—not since the last time the Witch had woken. She didn't like to reacquaint herself with that time and so kept away. "And what have you found out?" she asked abruptly, as hard and sharp as her beak.

His eyes flicked over her feathers. "No more than you already know. The rumours are the Witch is abroad again. Something to do with Aimee and her younger brother... What was his name again?" The Headmistress didn't reply so he continued, "Something she did with him? Something wrong... unnatural? The small creatures of the forest whisper that the Witch is searching for the boy. It would help if you told me where he's hidden. I could help keep him safe."

"The board of governors have decided that should remain... confidential... for the time being," said the Headmistress.

"I understand," said Mr Him. Apart from his skin and the bruises the Gorilla had left, he looked calm. "Is that all? I have a lot of planning to do."

"HI." THE SNAKE NODDED and lent against the radiator. He stood as he imagined a human would stand, slouched somewhere about where he imagined a human's shoulders would be, as if he had them. When picking up a human child he felt it appropriate to act like a human. If he'd been asked, he would've been unable to explain why.

The dragon didn't ask him. "Hi," she said in reply.

The snake nodded, nonchalantly he thought. He wouldn't normally stand near enough to one of the other guardians to actually be able to converse, but he'd been held up at the

Headmistress's office being told once again just how wayward Angel was. He was late, and the normal standing spaces were gone.

"You're Angel's guardian?" asked the dragon.

"Yesss," said the snake, surprised enough to drop accidentally into Snakish. "Yes," he hurriedly corrected.

"Energetic boy," the dragon said after a moment, huffing out a line of ash across the polished floor as she did so.

'Energetic' was Schoolish for 'trouble-making'.

"Yes," said the snake, with an increasingly more clipped (and human sounding) syllable.

"Mine's Tower," said the dragon by way of introduction. She smiled at him.

"Good boy, bit shy," said the snake and that meant 'boring stammerer'.

The dragon smiled again, a grin now as long as the snake's body. "I'm Betsy," she said, extending a claw, which was not a simple feat as she was large and wedged into the corridor to the hall.

The snake put his tail into the claw and they shook. To do so he had to abandon his human pose, and this didn't please him at all. He didn't like the reminder that he was a reptile.

"Hisssss," he said.

"Sorry?"

"Hisssss—that's my name."

"Oh." A pause. "Can I ask a silly question?"

Hisssss stared at her. "I don't know any snakes," he said.

"No, that wasn't what I was going to ask. I was going to ask how snakes tell each other apart if they all have names like Hisssss?"

The snake continued staring at Betsy the dragon. He eventually repeated, "I don't know any snakes."

"Oh I see." Her grin became apologetic, which must have been difficult for a dragon's mouth. "I'm sorry."

The snake made a noise in its throat that sounded a lot like his name and turned to look stoically at the classroom door. Luckily it opened, and he slithered forward with a quick, "Nice to see you, I'm sure." He always found it embarrassing talking to other guardians.

IN THE BORING FILMS Mum watched, Amy had seen adults putting love letters in small, metal, paint-chipped boxes and secreting them away somewhere hidden, somewhere safe. The grown-up would then say something like, "It was the putting away of my heart," or, "That's where my love stayed, hidden in the dark, and every emotion I had, afterwards, was nothing to the feelings that I locked in that small old metal box." Amy, and not because of her age, knew nothing of love but she knew the feeling of taking the one thing you cared for (and the one thing that cared for you) and putting it away.

She carried Barney to the bed, crouched, and winkled her body through the fusty black under the mattress, as one would winkle out a divot of chocolate ice-cream. She pulled aside her discarded books and toys and hid him at the back of them all, in the corner of the space below her bed. She was about to return her books and toys to their original position and come back out from the shadows, when she caught a look in Barney's eyes. It wasn't of sadness, or of love, or of any other emotion for that matter; he was *looking at* something and she saw it. What he was staring at was the ground—the grassy Glade—from the same kind of height as Amy and in the same kind of winkle-esque movement that suggested he was crawling along it. She saw stars in the black hemispheres of his glass eyes and she knew it was Nighttime in the Other Place, but early. The moon had not yet eaten up the sky. His sight shivered as though he shivered, and he glanced around in that furtive, fearful way the injured have when they know they can't take any more shocks without dying (and when they know that something is hunting them). Amy's fingers tremored as she reached to his scalp, touched its roughness, and repeated herself, "I'm sorry… sorry—"

She put back the toys and the books, and shuffled out from the space, and left her teddy there in the night.

Chapter 3

PIGLET SAT LISTENING to the rain slapping on the mud above him. More puddles than mud, he guessed. It had been raining for some time in the Latter Wood. It was unseasonably cold, though just the right amount of wet. The stool below him was round and short so his legs formed a triangle, rear trotters pressed to the wooden floorboards. As he listened to the droplets chattering excitedly on a roof made of roots, Piglet wondered what he should do with the day.

"What should I *do* with the day?" he said to himself, emphasising the doing.

First, he thought he might try and find Barnaby Bear and see if the bear was interested in hearing all about how he had found the bear. He guessed maybe not. Then he thought he might think very hard and try to move today to Friday, in the hope that Friday was sunny and, after a moment's contemplation, reckoned that if he wished for long enough that wish would certainly come true. However, he worried that falling asleep might ruin the wishing and decided that he couldn't stay awake for so long a time.

Finally, his thinking ran dry and the rain refused to do so, and so he settled on masturbating vigorously and then getting stoned. Or getting stoned and masturbating with less vigour. He didn't really mind.

It isn't easy, as you can imagine, for a piglet to masturbate. Trotters tend to be ungentle instruments to use on the small curl of a baby pig's manhood. So Piglet would sit on his stool, lean forward, and scissor his knees quickly as though jogging in the air, until the job was done.

Piglet did this while thinking of the nipples on a sow. He was done by number five.

Post-masturbatory, Piglet lit a cigarette. It didn't help the drippity-drip of boredom through his mind but it helped to pass the time.

Piglet wore a Hawaiian shirt. He loved that shirt. He liked its overstated tones. He reckoned they distracted from the fact that he wore no trousers. Also, he had a bushel of exceptionally curly hair (like a head of pigs' tails), and the shirt seemed to suit this.

Instead of trousers, Piglet wore Y-fronts, more yellow than white, and it was debatable as to whether he could've removed them if he'd tried.

"I'm going to find Bear," Piglet finally said. "Maybe he'll know where to find some honeys," he added, by which he meant female piglets. He looked down at his yellowed crotch. "You haven't been in a honey pot for too long." He sucked on his cigarette and stared at the beaded curtain of the rain all done in grey. "Ain't that right," he said as he got up.

Outside, away from his home, the water spiralled from the pod-lines of the laburnum trees; the flow was dyed yellow, as if the trees were urinating on the dirt. The sky was drawn and quartered by the sharp branches. The clouds bled down and through. Its pall fell on his head as he slouched through the mud.

Today, the Latter Wood hung above the ground: its smell, its chill, its discontent. He sucked a cigarette and let his lips think of teats.

After a while, he thought of a tune to lift his mood: "Ho hum, ho hum, ho hum… They sing when you're up their bum… Ho hum."

He sucked, and there was a swishing sound as he left the Latter Wood and passed into the Glade. Amongst the long grass there were signs of the passage of the bear in tufts of torn pelt and smeared sweat. There were also dried welts of mammal-blood. Piglet sucked on his cigarette and, as with smoking and cancer, tried to believe the blood and the bear were unconnected.

The Glade soon stretched into the plains and the swishing became a swashing. Piglet waded Y-fronts deep through a brook at the southern end of the grassland, and then to the border of a dark wood. This wasn't the Latter Wood and wasn't formed of laburnum trees—at least as far as Piglet could tell, and it was very difficult to tell when you couldn't see. This wood was shrouded, its canopy too thick to allow the droop of the draped clouds, let alone the sun above them. It was named

The Copse because, Piglet supposed, it was dark as a Corpse was when buried six feet under. (He didn't know why the name had dropped its *r*—some things were just lost in translation, he guessed.)

"Bugger," he said. "I hate this dark wood. Can't see a thing." He considered his cigarette. "Maybe this light can show the way."

Lighting up a new smoke, he walked in.

His trotters scraped on the dirt and sounded desperate, like claws on a blackboard. Piglet stumbled and then tripped, falling headlong onto his cigarette.

"Ouch," he squeaked.

The wood didn't reply.

"Ouch," Piglet repeated, in case the wood hadn't heard him the first time.

Eventually, he found his way into verdant foothills, which became barren foothills, and then the feet of mountains. The altitude welcomed him with all the warmth of autumn turning into winter. A slashing wind made his cheeks a deeper pink and snow fell in scurrying swarms.

"Bloody nice day this is turning out to be," he said.

In between the clumps of cold, he sought the bear's cave. He smelled the opening before he saw it—an odour, high as the altitude, of broken fur and blood that had taken its time to congeal.

Inside the cave's entrance it was dark and dank with the smell of a large beast that had come here to die, and of lumps of faeces that had fallen off or adhered to its pelt, uncared for.

"Bear?" said Piglet into the shadows.

There was the sound of shallow breathing and then, "Piglet?"

"What happened to you Bear?"

"Aimee pulled off arm."

"*She* did this to you?"

A pause. The brown bear wasn't considering, he was breathing, and it seemed to take everything he had. Then he said, "Yes."

"I'll kill her," said Piglet, becoming so agitated he jumped up and down. In Another World he would've been inaccurately described as *Tiggerish*. "I'll poke her eyes out and put them down her panties so she can see just how shitty she is."

"No, don't do that. She was only—" Bear paused.

The silence was as fetid as the cave, hung with shadows and threats and a smell close to puking.

"Bear," said Piglet, "you have to get out of here. The Witch has woken and is abroad, and so are her followers. I saw a Russian Doll in the Latter Wood just last night."

"I know." Bear shifted, as though an uncomfortable fact was poking into his back where he lay.

"They'll come for you now they know you can't fight them."

The black shadow sighed. "I know," he said.

"Come on then. I'll help you up." Piglet scurried forward. He reached into the shadows for the bear's paw so as to lever him up. It was like putting a trotter into a pocket of worms. His nails scraped over soft, pussing, broken skin.

The bear growled. "Wrong arm," he said.

"Sorry Bear."

Piglet stretched across and found the long fang-like claws of the bear's remaining paw. He pulled Bear up.

"I hate this wood," Piglet said.

"I know," said Bear, leaning at an acute angle above Piglet's head. A ribbon of bear saliva added a curl to the piglet's hair.

With tiny squealing grunts and breaths meaty with old blood on gums, Piglet and Bear, one leaning on the other, entered The Copse.

Inside the canopy, a stumble could be heard (but not seen) and a trip.

"Bear, you're on my neck," said a whisper.

"Sorry."

Groans as something hefty was lifted.

Stumble.

Then trip.

The bear wailed in pain.

"Oh, I give up," Piglet whispered.

"WE'RE GOING ON A bear hunt, we're going to catch a big one," Amy said the next day. "What a beautiful day. We're not scared."

From the side, Lucy watched her lips move out of the corner of an eye. Hanging somewhat in the way an immaculate crystal of blonde pigtail. Amy looked a little like a shadow cast by it.

"Uh oh. A forest," mumbled Amy. "A big dark forest. We can't go over it. We can't go under it. Oh no. We've got to go through it."

She repeated the lines after Mr Mann who sat before them, left arm at a right angle, holding open the pages of the book so the class could see. His face was expressionless as Lucy's was, though inside she felt burgeoning joy. She had kissed Adam at lunchtime; she had kissed him on the lips. That wasn't what made her happy though. It was what Adam had agreed to do so that he could be the first boy, the very first boy in the year, to be kissed on the lips. (And for Lucy, golden popular Lucy, to be his girlfriend.) He had agreed, and it was coming, as sure as the bear in the storybook.

Lucy watched Amy as Mr Mann ran his fingers over the lines in which the hunt party ran back out of the cave, through the snowstorm, through the forest, through the mud, across the river, through the long grass, into their house, and up the stairs to their bedroom. Amy tensed, as she did every time. She would curl up sometimes as well. It fascinated Lucy: 'it' being Amy.

"It's a bear!" said the class.

What did you expect? Lucy would normally have thought. Not this time. This time she thought: *Now!*

And Adam did too because he leant forward and roared in Amy's ear, "RRRRRAAAAAAAAWWWWWWWWR!"

"Adam!" Mr Mann looked like he was about to say but he didn't, because Amy turned around and punched Adam in the face.

Screaming inchoately, the little girl crawled over the little boy, wrenching at his limbs.

Lucy sat very still and very prettily, managing not to laugh as Mr Mann pulled Amy off Adam. The little girl wouldn't let go of his right arm though. She seemed to regard it as an abomination, wide-eyed and spitting at it, as she twisted the limb this way and that as though trying to pull it off.

Lucy had never enjoyed We're Going on a Bear Hunt quite so much.

MR MANN WAS HAVING A bad day. Both Adam and Amy had been stood outside the headmistress's office at lunchtime, and now his class had worked their way through to the Bs. Belinda stood outside the door, as she had done since the beginning of the Maths lesson. Mr Mann cast an apprehensive glance at Catherine.

Both Amy and Adam had been returned to his Maths lesson and now sat at opposite ends of the carpet.

Mr Mann had, rather cleverly he thought, based the lesson around a game of cards. He may be a southerner, but he knew how much the natives loved their games of cards. He guessed many of the children in his class would've played and would be used to adding card scores together. The way their faces lit up and their hands went up, he had been right. A feeling of confidence glittered back through his skin. Moments like this made teaching worthwhile. It was the panhandling of gold—thirty rapt, illuminated faces turned to his lips or to the board. The silence of expectation. Mrs Skinner was laminating, which only added to his mojo.

Twenty-nine faces, Mr Mann thought, noticing Amy.

"Oh let's see," he said, as he held up a large laminated card—the Jack of Hearts. "I need one of you to do me a big favour, if that's okay." He dwelt on each word, as though he were an actor owning the boards of a stage.

"Me," said Adam, seemingly unable to stop himself. "Me."

"Now I wonder who's sitting quietly and really well."

The class placed their fingers to their lips, as though to staple them.

Mr Mann put the blade of his palm horizontally to his forehead, scanning left and right with his eyes. "Weeeeellll—" he said. Inspiration came to him. It came easier, it seemed, when he wasn't sweating. "Adam! You *are* sitting so well!"

Adam smiled.

"Will you go to the door please, open the door, and ask Belinda to come in and sit down."

Sprightly, face-muscles jangling, eyes shining, Adam stood.

"And Adam—?" Mr Mann rearranged his features into a stern expression. "I picked you because you can show Belinda just how to walk to the carpet and sit quietly on it. I picked you because you are *so* good at that."

If Adam had shone more, his skin might well have dissolved. Instead, he walked to the door and did what Mr Mann had suggested he was very good at doing. Belinda followed.

"Nooow," said Mr Mann, watching the door and hoping he had given Mrs Skinner enough work. "Who can tell me how much this card is worth when we are adding?" With a flourish, he used a metre stick to point at the Jack's hat.

A class of hands shot up.

"Lucy?"

"Ten!"

"Yes. Well done. And what is it called?"

"The Jack of Hearts," said Lucy, before he could pick anyone else. She smiled at him.

Mr Mann couldn't help but smile back. She was his favourite and one of the few he could count on not to cause trouble. "That's right sweetheart," he said, unconsciously copying Mrs Skinner.

"And this one? How much is this worth when we are adding?"

The Queen of Spades appeared in his hand, looking diffident.

"Hmmm... Catherine?"

"Ten!"

This was going well. For one of the first times in his teaching experience, Mr Mann felt like doing a little dance. He didn't, and would later regret that he hadn't.

"And what is she called?"

The class sprouted arms and hands like leaves.

"Hmmm—" he said. Inspiration struck again as he saw a little grubby girl on the edge of his carpet. She had stretched up an olive limb. She strained as though she could touch the sun.

Mr Mann was reeling them all in today.

"Yes Amy?"

"She's the cunt," Amy said.

The arms went down as the class, as one, turned to stare at her.

THE ROADS WENT BY like a bomb countdown, but in letters. When the countdown reached A, Amy would be home, Mum would reach zero, and Mum would explode. Mr Mann's words hung between them like the little girl's hand did, yanked by her mother.

"I know Amy is going through a lot at the moment, but this kind of behaviour just isn't acceptable. She's been to the headmistress's office twice today—"

As ever, Amy's footsteps slowed as she approached her porch. The sun flattered the afternoon, momentarily making the grass all the more green as the porch door closed, cutting the garden off. Amy's wrist clicked and her back thumped as her mother twisted her, throwing the girl into the alcove below the coats.

"Get your shoes off." She wasn't looking down. From below, her mum's eyes looked as flinty as an overhanging avalanche. Amy quit looking and unlaced her school shoes, palms clumping on the black leather. Her socks were grey from a lack of washing. Amy laid the shoes symmetrically, side by side in the corner of the alcove. The door to the stairs had opened quietly, and the volume of her mother's voice followed suit, low and sibilant, "Get inside."

Amy did so and turned to face her mother, careful not to stare at her eyes but at her waist. It was slim as ever, though Mum would change her wardrobe at least twice a month due to 'getting fat', and would put off nights out until that bloody belly went away, and Uncle Chris only made things worse.

"What did you do?"

"I punched a boy and said 'cunt' in class," said Amy. Her voice was loud enough to be heard, but flat and unobtrusive.

Mum punched Amy in the stomach. The fist caught the base of her ribs, which creaked and felt as though they had splintered. Breath was forced into her gut. Her entrails were like balloon animals about to pop. Amy slumped onto the bottom step of the stairs. There was a loose feeling of sharded bone just below her ribcage.

"Don't be fucking clever, you little shite. What did you do to your brother?"

Her mother grasped her lank shoulder-length hair and twisted it up above her head. Amy whined, unable to keep her mouth closed, and her mum's thin, wrinkled, black-nailed fingers pressed the girl's chin into her jawbone. A line of snot popped out of Amy's right nostril.

"I spent three fucking hours with a social worker today, answering fucking questions about poison. Seems my baby boy was poisoned. Well, I told *them* he's always running around the garden, so you won't get me that way. *Nobody will take my little boy away from me, do you understand?*"

Amy tried to nod, but couldn't.

"Think you're so clever, don't you love? Eh? Think it would be better if you lived with somebody else, you and your brother, yeah?"

Amy tried to shake her head, but couldn't.

"Well he's back where he belongs now. Safe in his home with his mum. You little back-stabbing bitch. You don't know you're born."

Her mum pulled her head to the side and clipped her round the ear, hard enough to bounce Amy's scalp off the stairs. Amy yelped in pain. She couldn't help it.

"No bruises now, eh sweetheart? Nothing to tell the socials now, eh? And what is this, mmm? What is it?"

Amy stared out of tears and confusion at an object her mother held. It was brown and long and dappled with a darker brown at the end. Her sight congealed around it. It was the limb of a teddy bear.

"More poison?" Her mum was throwing Barney's arm up and down. "Sometimes I think about killing myself, I've told you before and little you care. You'll drive me to it, won't you? You try to drive me to it, don't you?"

The carpet at her forehead scuffed Amy as she shook her head.

"Sometimes I wish, I wish so hard, that I could just go away, go away forever—" Her mum pointed at the sketchpad on the floor, where Amy had left it that morning. "Like you, off with fairies, off in bloody Never Never Land—"

Amy watched the arm as it went head-over-heels through the air and into Mum's hand. Her mother's eyes, as contact was made between the palm of a human and the palm of a teddy bear, became distant. She collapsed against the banister, which creaked, and down onto the square of carpet at the bottom of the stairs.

"Mum?" Amy tried to rise and small clouds of darkness floated into her sight. She blinked until all but one dispersed. The remaining smirch seemed to be sinking from her mum's deep blue eyes into the sketchbook. Amy squatted on the step and rubbed her eyelids and saw what was happening. Her mum was going to the Other Place. She was sinking in like an ink stain. Quick as her addled arms would allow, Amy slipped forward and gripped the brown pelt of the severed limb. Her coccyx jarred as she fell from the final step, sending her teeth together with a clack. She wrenched the arm from Mum's hand; her mother's fingers twisted open, and her eyes widened and turned back on. She mustn't have gone completely, Amy realised. She breathed with relief but didn't dare sigh.

"Give that to me." Her mum reached for the limb.

Amy took it and ran up the stairs. Her palm worked its way up the limb, fingers making for the patch of palm. Her mum followed.

There was the knock of knuckles on the door.

Her mother made the sound of an unbasketed cobra and turned back to the porch. Amy could hear the shouted word from outside, "Avon!" As she entered her bedroom, she closed its door, fell on her bed, and hid the arm behind the mattress.

She lay listening. The door below closed and footsteps began on the stairs, dull and distant and creaking. They ceased, and the sound of her mum went down and away. Amy lay still, afraid that if she moved she would change her fate and her mother would come again. But she didn't.

As far as Amy could tell, her mum lay on the couch until Uncle Chris came back from work, curtains drawn and complaining of a migraine. She didn't go to work that night and was asleep by the time Amy dared go downstairs to cook tea.

"Don't know what's wrong with your mum tonight," Uncle Chris said in a low tone, as they ate fish fingers and chips in the kitchen. Both of them glanced at the lounge, but fleetingly, as though the weight of their gaze could wake her. "She's been off with the fairies all evening," he said.

Amy stared at him.

"What?" he said, a finger of fish wedged in his cheek.

Chapter 4

HER MOTHER WOKE AND bathed Amy, despite it being Friday and bath day being Wednesday. And though her mum stripped her and sponged her, she didn't touch her. Instead of focusing on Amy's naked body, on her back, her front, her thighs, she stared at the sudless water. There was nothing strange, though, about the lack of foam.

"We're too poor for luxuries, right? Closest you'll get to bath salts is spit. Ask your Uncle Chris to get a proper job if you want the high life."

Now Mum said nothing and her daughter could see why. She could see what her mum saw. At first she thought it was her mother's reflection in the water, pallid and jaundiced like the off-cream enamel, spread about as it was by the tiny ripples of Amy's ablutions. Soon she realised the reflected face turned when her mum's did not, its eyes roving across the bathroom. Like Mum's, the lips weren't thin but they were mean. There were jowls though, where Amy's mother would not have allowed them. And at the edge of the reflection, there was the suggestion of obese breasts. The figure's hair was not a bob, but shoulder-length, tussled and blonde like Amy had once seen on a black-and-white poster of Marilyn Monroe. But the face, somehow, was paler and just as dangerously beautiful.

It was searching, searching, searching for something and was reflected from a world entirely apart from the bathroom. The thin lips were moving, twisting out sausages of speech that, though unheard, could only be commands.

Absentmindedly, her mum mumbled to herself.

The face banked to its left, Amy's right, and passed below her leg, where it right-angled out of the water. In the shadows below the girl's bare skin, which puckered despite the steam that rose from the bathwater, there was the impression of an obese woman on a broomstick thin enough to be a thong. Around her, in the shaded water, Amy could see the shapes of Gorillas on the move—Gorillas with wings so grey they were almost silhouettes. Then they were silhouettes, as the fat witch and the winged apes crawled up onto the bathroom wall and, like a shadow play, flapped and flew past storm clouds and over mountains and hills and trees, searching, searching for somebody.

My baby, Amy thought, and her skin broke into a rash of panic.

"Where are you?" whispered her mother, looking for something neither she nor Amy could see.

"STRANGE THINGS ARE happening," said the Christian. He scratched at the scalp under his hood, fingers searching for a forelock to tug. He settled for saluting, though there were no magpies nearby (or swallows or sparrows or any other bird he could believe in).

"What's happening?" said Disdivanshumayl, leaning closer as they walked away from the locked Night School gates.

From somewhere in the mists above the school a gargoyle could be heard yelling, "And don't come back!"

"More children are disappearing than usual," said the Christian. "And I keep finding sand."

Disdivanshumayl shambled down the alley of laburnum trees beside the perimeter of the fence. She spidered to the side to listen, finding it more difficult than most of the spiders in her family to lip-read as her eyesight was fading. The fence continued along the edge of the forest for some while; the Christian paused, as he did every dawn, to tie protective idols and offerings on the green metal. The alley dipped as the fence took a turn right, the Night School having been built on a plateau.

"Finding and... what?"

"No," said the Christian. "Finding *sand.*"

"Oh," said the giant spider, "it'll be from the malleable areas. It helps the children to learn writing. You know... writing in the sand. It helps their motor skills."

"Yeah," said the Christian. He was distracted. He thought he'd heard a flushing sound and it reminded him that the toilets needed cleaning, and whenever he thought of cleaning he thought: Unclean.

"And children go missing all the time. You know the home lives these children have. Poor little mites."

"Yeah," said the Christian.

"Okay, this is me," said the giant spider. "Off to clean up after more bloody kids."

"No rest for the wicked," said the Christian.

He thought: Damnation.

They stood beside the jagged grin of a thin-entranced cave. She waved two legs at him casually and tottered in, gulped down, it seemed, by the shadows. The Christian stared after her and wished he had a family. It wasn't a momentary wish. But he couldn't, not again, not after finding out what kind of man he was. He gulped, genuflected, and moved on.

SHE SHOULDN'T HAVE been able to see what Barnaby saw. Not in the ill-lit bedroom, beneath the shroud of her linen. Not in the dead black eyes of a teddy bear. But there it was: the passing of the Latter Wood across Barney's glass eyeballs. The trees were slanted. The long grass waved obliquely. Sweat drifted across the glass, and the brown, ponderous, fabric forehead seemed to wince.

She had been unable to resist, unable to stop herself retrieving the teddy bear from the shadows under the mattress.

Amy didn't cuddle him, but held the teddy at arm's length.

She shouldn't have been able to hear him, but she did. His breath, fecund with damage, with pain, with pauses. The crunch of his heavy paws on fallen leaves and scattered twigs. Piglet saying, "Dear Witch, you're heavy."

She shouldn't have been able to smell the faeces plastered to his pelt, where he'd been unable to reach and brush it off. Having one arm wouldn't have helped, she realised.

There was a wind in the Latter Wood, focused and insistent as though blown from a single screaming mouth. In the enclosed tent of her duvet, Amy's own breath lengthened, her lungs stretched in her chest, clawing for her throat, and her skin crawled with droplets of sweat.

Abruptly, the bedroom was an explosion of light and Amy wrenched her head out from under the sheets. A coffin of yellow light fell on the wall to the girl's right. A shape twisted in the doorway, backlit by the landing. "Are you alright" it whispered.

It was Uncle Chris.

Amy nodded, eyelids weighed by sweat.

The head disappeared behind the shadow of the door, but quickly reappeared. "Your mum'll be up soon," it said. There was fear in the shape of his silhouette. "Go to sleep."

Amy nodded and the door closed. In the new dark, Amy ran her fingers over the teddy but withdrew. She couldn't hold him close, not after what she'd done to him. She didn't know how she could look at Barney.

"I'm sorry, Barnaby. I'm sorry for what I did. I really am sorry."

~225~

She hugged herself and cried and wondered if she could ever go back to That Place.

PIGLET HAD BROUGHT Barnaby here to the Christian's hut in the ribcage of the Latter Wood, where the canopy curved in and even Piglet's thoughts seemed to echo between the trees. Luckily, Piglet didn't have much in the way of thoughts, and those he did have tended to involve sows.

Here, there was a silence that could only be described as preverbal.

The Christian opened the door to his hut and jumped. He tugged at his cowl and appeared to decide that the brown bear and the piglet weren't some unnatural hybrid, but one animal leaning on another.

"Piglet," he said. Then, "Bear." The Christian's voice was as fast as a stutterer's, but managed to fit whole words into the space in which a stutterer would have crammed a consonant. "What?" His fingers perpetually twitched and fluttered, a sign language only his toes could fully see from beyond the hems of his sleeves.

"Arm... Ripped... Off... Bare... Bum... Er... Eh?" Piglet said, in between breathing.

"What?"

"Arm!... Off!... Bare!... Bum!... Er!... Eh?" With a strain that made his snout wheeze and run slightly, Piglet raised the brown bear, exhibiting the scrape where his arm had been.

"Fell on something sharp?" asked the Christian as he let them in. Piglet could hear him chewing his lips as he pottered through his hut. They sounded disconcertingly like crackling.

The Christian moved to help him, holding the remaining pelted arm, and the air in Piglet's lungs came out with a rush of words.

"No, something stupid. Little girl called Aimee—his ward— ripped his arm off just to get her brother into the Night School. Ripped his whole arm off. Bummer, eh?"

There was one room and an en-suite toilet, segregated by a curtain. The whole structure smelt of incense, with sticks of the brown spice porcupining idols of Gods that Piglet did not recognise. A smorgasbord of shrines and their edible offerings lined the walls as well as a large table in the room's centre. Piglet glanced at the figurines, but couldn't believe the Christian had that many ancestors. Some of them were black, others Chinese.

"Just in case," the Christian had once said. Now he said, "Put him on the table." He carefully rearranged what seemed to be a family of midgets.

"In case of what?" Piglet had said in reply. Now he didn't speak but huffed, rolling the bear onto the boards. A small father went clattering to the floor.

"In case my parents lied to me, and I was adopted," the Christian had replied.

The father figurine looked at Piglet forlornly, and still did several hours later. Throughout that time, as he worked on the bear, the Christian whispered to himself from between still lips, his eyes squinting at the broken, rent armpit.

Eventually Piglet said, "Could that be your ancestor?"

The Christian had been working the stump of the bear's arm up into a dough of powdered flesh and stitches. Herbs stuck out from between the needlework as though from the skin of a roasting chicken.

"It's unlikely," said the Christian. "But you can't be too careful."

Piglet stared at him. It wasn't often that Piglet realised something, and less often that he realised it was important, and hardly ever that he got to share this realisation.

"What?" said the Christian, looking up. The bear twitched on the table.

"You weren't whispering then."

"What? When?"

"When you were talking. I thought you were whispering before, but you can't whisper when you talk."

"What?"

Piglet didn't answer and let the night do his talking for him. Outside, beyond the hut's door, they could both hear a susurrating sound in the silence at the heart of the Latter Wood.

"Get windy down here?" asked Piglet.

"Never." Touching one after another of the heads of his idols and, in between each, his own, the Christian made for the door.

Together they stepped outside.

"The trees are talking to each other," advised Piglet. "Do you know what they're saying?"

The Christian had gone pale. Even from inside the hole of his hood, Piglet could see his pallor. He shone with fear.

"It isn't the trees. It's wings. The succubus is coming. Oh Witch, the succubus is back."

Piglet opened his mouth to ask a question but, high in the sky and far to the north, a cackling could be heard, so he lit a cigarette and put it in his mouth instead.

THERE WAS SCREAMING in the photo album. A stain of black swirled in and out of the Polaroids, taking the colour and people they contained with it. The stain had the vague shape of a woman, bloated by power and by flesh and with the eyes—so very blue—of her mother.

Amy shut the photo album, but she couldn't let go of its edges. Her grip was all that kept her pinioned to reality—or, at least, to this version of it.

Glancing to the door that led to the square of carpet at the base of the stairs, she wondered if the adults had heard. Mum had gone to bed early. Christopher, after trying to watch Aliens (which he did at least once every month), had too. The DVD had been ruined, its scenes catching, then flickering black before a snapshot of a metal corridor returned. And when the girl Newt froze on the screen, a hissing sound like someone screaming above the ceiling tiles had filled the room. Amy had stayed up past her bedtime with Christopher, who'd ejected the DVD and polished it five times. Each time, his head bent to the ring of silver, he'd missed the two blue irises that had appeared, staring out from between the buzzing static like the eyes of a spectre in the snow. On each attempt, the DVD would judder to halt as though it had realised someone was watching.

Amy saw her.

The Witch was in the air vents.

The Witch was behind the steel shutter doors.

The Witch was impregnating the aliens.

And now the Witch was in the photos, stealing away her relatives. Circling, taking them one-by-one, until she came, last, to Amy's baby brother.

Amy turned off the light, opened the door to the stairs, passed between the jambs, and closed it behind her. The planes of it on the carpet whispered at her back. There had been whispering in the film and in the photo album, but not once the Witch had closed in. Amy rose up the first step, placing her left foot alongside her right. Her feet crawled, the skin itching to stay utterly still. She didn't dare to put one foot in front of the other.

Never split up, Amy thought. Christopher's movies had taught her this.

She took the next step.

This was taking a long time.

Shadows moved on the wall next to her. They had the look of women on broomsticks and gorillas (or Gorillas) with wings. The wallpaper had the appearance of bubbling sulphur, yellowed and curled by the cigarette smoke of her mother and previous householders. The Gorillas flapped behind and across the discolorations, as though through a cloudy and evil night.

Amy ran to her bedroom, closed its door, sat on the bed, reached beneath the mattress, and drew out her sketchbook. She flopped it open and stared. The bedroom's harsh unshaded light stared down with her. The world she had crayoned and biroed and pencilled was desolated, hit by a hurricane of black swirling shadows. The stain of black—an ink blot on the move—was swallowing tree after tree in the Latter Wood, drawing the yellow from their pods, crackling against the Christian's hut, sucking from the letters of the description Amy had pencilled next to it, draining the Christian, pulling at his thumb-nailed cowl, disrobing him. Amy reached down and shut the sketchbook. She lay on the bed and turned out the light. Barney was a lump behind her, stopping her lying still or comfortably.

She knew she should reach out to him. She could see what the Witch was doing in the world she had made. She knew her baby wasn't safe, but couldn't move her hand.

Next door, she could hear her mum snoring.

"I can't," she whispered to Barney. She couldn't even turn around. "Don't make me do it."

Nobody did, and she fell asleep.

THE TODDLER FELL over a brick of wood and seemed to forget she had hands, using her mouth instead to cushion the fall. She stared at Angel long enough for him to see the scream coming.

"Okay," Angel said, gathering up the little girl. "Don't worry, it's okay, it's okay. Let me have a look."

The girl slowly allowed the boy to prise apart her hands. Her lips weren't bleeding. Angel checked her teeth.

"It's okay," he gathered her again, patting her back. "You're not bleeding," Angel said.

"Is she okay?" said Ms Lydia, the Nursery teacher.

Angel looked up and nodded. "Not bleeding," he said.

Ms Lydia smiled at him and walked back to the other Nursery room through a low, wide arch in the open-plan play area. She disappeared behind a colourful display of wind and magic dust and flying houses, which had all been laminated. Even so, some of the houses had cracks in their paper masonry, formed by little, pulling fingers.

Angel could hear Ms Lydia on the other side of the blue, yellow and red bricks. "He's a real sweetie, that Angel. He's great with the little 'uns."

"Ye-ye-ye-ss-ss," replied the teaching assistant—a large grasshopper.

Angel glanced across to the window.

"Hey, Sunshine, keep the bricks over there. They're tripping over them."

Sunshine returned his gaze then looked at the sallow green carpet. She was supervising the construction area, but her site had been demolished by the Nursery children, its wooden bricks strewn by their energy all the way to the Small World area.

"Yes, fine." Sunshine walked over, picking up and carrying a little boy called Gypsy. She stopped above Angel. "You know who's in the Quiet Room?" she said to Angel.

Angel shook his head.

The child in Sunshine's arms had quietened and was trying to explore her pockets. Sunshine guided the fingers away and put the child on the carpet.

"Aimee's brother."

Angel looked up. "I thought he was older."

"Yes. He is."

"Go and play. No. Go and play," said Angel. Sunshine's toddler waddled off. "Why's he here?"

"Think they're hiding him."

"Who from?"

"The Witch's people."

Angel frowned. "Mr Him?"

"Yes." Sunshine leaned in, glancing around, not for children but for adults. "Three kids disappeared last night. It's more every time."

Sunshine watched as Tower approached from the other Nursery room.

Angel's face hardened. The skin around his mouth lengthened as his lips constricted. "They won't take him."

"It's time to go to class," said Tower, jabbing his finger at the clock that read Five Minutes to Hard Work. Tower looked worried. It was difficult to tell if he felt worried. Angel had never seen his face look any other way.

"How do you know?" said Sunshine to Angel.

"I won't let them." When he looked back to Sunshine, Angel glared.

Sunshine shrugged with her mouth and cheeks and shoulders. "Okay," she said. "Keep your knickers on."

"We'll protect him," said Angel, in the voice he used to ask for children's dinner money.

"Fine," said Sunshine.

"Swear it," said Angel. He spat on his hand, in the V between the first finger and the thumb.

"Okay." Sunshine smiled (she loved spitting) and spat in turn, and they shook hands.

Angel turned to Tower, proffering his hand. "Swear," he repeated.

Tower nodded uncertainly. "Crap," Tower said, after a moment's thought.

Angel stared at him.

"Poo?" Tower said, a little more shakily.

"Retard freak boy," Angel said.

"Oh, okay," said Tower. "We have to go. We're gonna get in trouble."

THOUGH THE NIGHT SKY was flooded with cloud, the great yellow Witch's Moon still shone through it, like a skull from the bottom of a pirate's cove. None of its light illuminated the forest below, and the colours picked out by the swinging lanterns of the school party were unrealistic—too pale or over-gaudy. The Latter Wood looked for all the world as if it had been coloured in by a child.

The Christian gestured for the small group of children to descend into the trough of a dale that had once been a river, but had become a muddy natural road, and then had overgrown into barely a path between low, humping, scraggly plants and holly bushes that did their best to lean in and pick at the caretaker's robes and prick his skin. This, for the caretaker, was not an unusual sensation. His skin, even at the best of times, had a tendency to crawl. At the worst of times, it was his brain that crawled. This was one of the latter occasions, and had started when he'd heard the Witch and the wings of her minions in the wood. If he hadn't been so scared of spotting a single magpie, he would've spent the night staring at the sky.

Cursing the Gods (which, for the Christian, took some time), he waved his right arm, and the group lowered into the mud at the bottom of the dale. He was breathing, in the hushed wood, as though it were going out of fashion and touched wood continually, pressing his fingers to a twig of birch sellotaped to his index finger. He also touched his forehead.

The Christian tried to avoid stressful situations but, on Tuesday nights between 1.00am and 1.30am, he had to teach Ornithology. There were only five children in his group, but the Christian itched with tension. He was aware, in a way that

~235~

others were not, of the luck in the universe, both good and bad. He was mindful, as often as he could be, of the increasingly unlikely run of good luck that meant his parents had met, his particular sperm had impregnated her egg, he had survived infanthood, and he hadn't, as yet, unexpectedly died. He expected to die by many ill turns (a rotten egg, a hole in the forest floor, a dragon burping, et cetera, et cetera…), but it was the unexpected that really scared him, especially at one o'clock in the morning.

"Children." The caretaker breathed to calm himself but found this difficult. He panicked as dizziness set in. Where was Mr Him? he wondered. He wasn't supposed to be left alone with the children. ("Not supposed to be left alone with children," echoed in his mind.) "Children!" he repeated and waved at the edges of the group. The bank of clouds was thickening, an incoming tide over the sky. "Please stay quiet. You'll scare the birds." The magpie aviary was nearby.

In the dark, lanterns bobbed. Gold light limned the leaves.

"What birds?" a boy's voice said.

"Shhhhh," said the Christian, as he often did.

Feathers erupted out of a holly bush, and a girl screamed. It was a magpie.

"Shhhhh," said the caretaker again and reached for his forehead. "Morning, Jack," he whispered.

The first bird was followed by a second, and the Christian breathed silent relief. A third magpie flew overhead, crying out, its shape an unmistakable taper. A fourth, then a fifth, followed.

"Gold," whispered the Christian, as the lanterns rose. "Stay down." An unpleasant feeling was rising close to his heart, unsettling it.

A sixth.

A seventh.

There was a movement in the Latter Wood. Two-footed. A man, or a child—the Christian couldn't see through either the foliage or the lack of light. The group of schoolchildren quietened. He could hear the squelches of them pressing their small bodies into the mud. The Christian rolled prayers around his mouth like gobstoppers. There were paws moving on dirt, audible through the forest floor: squirrels and moles on the move. They were fleeing. The shape out there was muttering. It sounded as though it were saying, "She needs me, she needs me, she needs me."

Then, between a thumb of leaf and a finger of twig, the Christian saw it. A child so pale it gave off its own pallor. The child's eyes appeared to be as much gouges as its mouth (blood-edged and slitted vertically) did, and they widened as it continued to moan, "She needs me, she needs me."

Its fingers twisted back over themselves, touching the back of their own hands. They caught the opposing wrist regularly and strangled it.

"She needs me," the child repeated. A line of tears, as much snot as water, fell from its left eye and hung from its protruding lower lip. The Christian shivered like the child did, before falling.

One of the children in his group (Sunshine, he thought, though he didn't really know their names) gasped.

The figure stopped and stooped and turned towards the bush that hid it. It was a boy of sorts, or used to be. "The Witch is visiting," it said. "We are so very lucky. I can't tell you what she does to me."

The prayers in the Christian's mouth began to go off. To falter. He forgot the names of half the Gods he believed in.

A bell tolled, somewhere far to the north, and the child-figure raised its head and moaned, "She needs me."

It turned awkwardly—with arms as contrary as the ends of a pinned worm—and ran.

"Thank Fuck," said the Christian, subconsciously adding a new God to his list.

The Christian stumbled home through the greying forest, touching the wood taped to his finger. He touched it nine times, then seven, then five, then three, then one, and then did it all again. The morning had the feel of a time that would require all the luck he had.

Arriving home, he pailed water from a trough that trickled from his overhanging roof tiles. He didn't have a well, as he didn't trust them. He had read his tales, and strange things hid in wells. Also, you could never be entirely sure where wells led, even if you'd dug them yourself. Wells were slippery things.

"Piglet, is that you?" he said, as he approached the shade of the porch. It had yet to see the light of the dawn sun and, given the canopy, wouldn't do so until the afternoon. A dot of light nodded.

"Yep," said Piglet, removing the cigarette.

"How's the bear?"

"Still asleep… He keeps fading."

"Yeah," said the Christian. Through the open door, he could see the large brown bear, larger than he should've been and swollen with infection and rot. But then—in a blink—he couldn't. Barnaby shimmered, seeming almost see-through when he shallowly breathed in, like a sleeping God no one believed in anymore. "She needs to come back here," he added. "She needs to return for him, or he'll go out—"

It had been a hard night, and the Christian walked past the little pig where he lay staring up at the eaves of the hut. The door scraped fully open as the Christian entered. He turned, began to light one after another of the incense sticks and bent to the shrines. Beyond the huffing of his sackcloth as he bowed and the crackling of incense sticks as they lit, he didn't hear the wings of Gorillas until Piglet ran in.

"It's the Witch," said the little pig. "It's the Witch."

The Christian stared at his assembled Gods and at the Bear, swallowed and said, "Help me hide him. Then hide yourself."

PIGLET HID BEHIND the curtain, beside the hole in the floor that was the Christian's toilet. It didn't smell of incense in here. In the main room, Barnaby sat by the door, still comatose, incense sticks stuck in his ears and in the stitches of his arm. Some of them were smouldering.

"What is that?" the Witch said.

"An offering to the Bear God. You can't be too careful, not with the mountains nearby."

The Witch's voice was as thick as chocolate melting in a cauldron, "Smells fresh."

"Make a new offering every week," said the Christian.

"You're always so careful, aren't you, my little man?"

The sound of the Christian's gulping would've been enough to flush the toilet near Piglet's feet, if there'd been a flush. "You're not invited in—" he said, "—succubus."

The Witch laughed. It was a giggle more than a cackle, despite her girth. She was beautiful, with hair blonde and dress dark, the satin of which was split up her left leg. But Piglet had no idea how her broomstick flew. She was *big*. Piglet watched her from between the gaps in the lining of the curtain as she walked forwards. She looked directly into the Christian's cowl. He cowered backwards against the table.

"You are a silly boy," she said, touching his cheek. "Pathetic boy. I'm not a succubus, and I'm not a vampire. I'm a Witch, idiot, and I don't need to be invited in. I'll come anyway. Just like you do, when you see me."

She pulled down the Christian's hood as he blushed. His ugliness was the opposite of her skin: clumps of scarred cheeks and a forehead and chin that looked as though he were half-made, while she was finished. Hers was the kind of face that made men think 'yes', while his would make women say 'no'. She rose over him, and shadows of her huffed out half the incense sticks in the room with a sound somewhere between sibilance and sighing. Smoke curled around her head and arm, as her perfect hand found the nook between his robes, below his waist.

"You're in love with me, aren't you? You see me in your sleep. And to think, even the thought of your face is enough to make me gag."

The Christian looked past the Witch, at the bare floor. His will seemed to be spreading as thin as the straw scattered there.

"So bashful. Your eyes may be looking down, but your snake-eye is looking up. Is this what it wants to see?" She drew satin back from her left breast. The cloth sounded like it rather enjoyed it.

The Christian's pock-riddled cheeks bunched and withered and bunched as he swallowed and gulped. His eyes found her nipple. Her hands were moving against him. Her body pressed him to the table, his buttocks below the rough ends of its top, his knees bent before hers.

"Tell me, my pathetic little man, what I want to know."

"No." But his breaths were louder than his mouth, and his head was nodding in small, frantic jerks.

"All men are mine," the Witch whispered. "I have Gorillas outside, hairy and strong. They'll beat it out of you, or I could get it out of you. You like the way I do it, don't you?"

He was shaking, fingers out of control of the table-top. They were clawing. The Witch's hand stopped moving.

"Please," said the Christian.

She smiled. The twist of her lips said 'pathetic' better than her tongue.

"The world is out of joint," said the Witch, leaning in to speak against his earlobe. "A little girl broke the natural laws and brought in a little boy who was not allowed here. That little boy belongs to me."

Her hand began again. Her eyes danced on his face, sharp as stilettos.

"Give him to me," she said.

"The Night School," he gagged on his words as his body jolted.

"Yes, of course."

His robes dampened below her hand.

"The Nursery," he said. "The boy with blue eyes."

The Witch withdrew, wiping her hand across his face.

"You are an easy little bitch," she said. She laughed. "And you get easier every time." She stopped laughing. "And now I'm bored of you."

She reached across the table, clutched an incense stick from the head of a black ancestor, and stabbed the Christian in the throat. There was a mild hiss and the escaping of a bubble of blood. The Christian collapsed fully to the floor, gagging, pulling clumsily at his throat.

Piglet's trotters sprang to the fabric of the curtain, but he had the heart of a very small porcine creature, which is to say the heart of a coward, and he couldn't part the cloth. The Witch picked up a burning incense stick, reversed it, and put it into the Christian's eye and into his brain. She repeated the action with a second stick and the other eye.

"Well," she said, glancing at the halves of incense sticks that could still be seen quivering as the Christian did. "You should always touch wood. It's lucky—hadn't you heard? Now you'll never be unlucky again."

With a laugh short as a slap, she walked out of the hut.

Piglet rushed into the room. The Christian had stopped moving. Outside, heavy wings began to flap, and the twigs at the end of a broomstick could be heard mildly thrumming as the Witch took to the air.

"No," said Piglet, trotter to his mouth. He rushed back into the toilet and vomited into the hole, not helping its smell at all. When he'd finished voiding his stomach, he straightened, wiped his mouth, plastered back his pigletty curls, and walked out of the hut to the nearest tree.

He knocked on it.

A horseshoe of bark opened up, and a squirrel's face peered out. "What? I've already paid you for this week's milk," said the squirrel.

"Shut up," said Piglet. He didn't think he had long before his guts found something else to chuck at his mouth.

The squirrel wrinkled its small, black, wet nose. "By the Witch, are you alright?" it asked.

"Listen." Piglet lent in, which the squirrel's nose didn't seem to think much of, and whispered, "Tell everyone: the Witch is coming. The Night School will be attacked. Tell all the guardians."

"Oh bugger," said the squirrel, before closing its front door. Piglet could hear the scamper of small feet inside and the chatter of a small mouth talking at speed. Piglet slumped against the tree's root system and went back to simply breathing.

THEY WERE IN OCTOBER and, as such, the clouds were out, the sun was not, the rain was down, and the children were in the classroom at lunchtime. It was wet play, but Mr Mann couldn't afford to let the children do so, especially in the water area. Playing would mean far too much mayhem, noise, and, most of all, violence. (He had, on several occasions, thought of providing their dressing-up area with a stick and a pig's head to see how they would combine them.) Instead, he'd turned the lights off and put on a film—it was the only way to keep them sedated. The glow from the television lapped over the flowered faces of the children, which were turned up to face it, eyes wide as opened petals.

Mr Mann hated the new school year.

He turned his mind to the end of the previous year, and the degree of cheating the previous teacher must have perpetrated to fabricate the levels the children had arrived with. He wouldn't have said this—in his thoughts, let alone out loud—but he knew already he would never find a way to deal with several of them, and with Adam and Amy in particular. Mr Mann was a reflective teacher and had a good awareness of how little behavioural control he could exert, and of how near to a complete breakdown he teetered. This was just another thing that he wouldn't say out loud, and he shared this reticence with at least one of the children, who was thinking as she watched The Wizard of Oz: I've got to save my baby. The film is lying. The Witch is alive.

None of this reached her lips nor, in any discernible way, the rest of her face, which was unmoved as it stared at the screen. She saw the Witch in the background of every scene, be it Dorothy dancing on the Yellow Brick Road, the flying monkeys, or the green wizard operating his machine. Even in the shadow cast by the balloon.

There were shapes moving in the cornfields.

The shadows of the trees were Gorillas on the wing.

In the aisles of the Emerald City, a long, female, taloned arm reached for a baby. Outlines moved on the keys of the wizard's machine, and they weren't his fingers. An organ played an unknown tune. Amy didn't like The Wizard of Oz. Its inaccuracies seemed to mock her, as did its jolly singing. Adults forget how uncomfortable it is to sit cross-legged on the floor for long periods of time. They have no idea of how uncomfortable it is to sit cross-legged while your younger brother is being kidnapped and you can see it happening.

Amy bunched her fingers around her skirt.

I've got to save my baby.

She had to get back home, back to Barney.

Amy put her hand in the air, the elbow seeming double-jointed the way it bent back against the air, as though trying to throw itself off.

"Miss," she said. Like most of the children, she forgot, often enough, the second syllable of Mr Mann's title.

Mr Mann looked up and answered, "*Yeees?*"

"I need the toilet." She crinkled around her crotch, as though dissolving.

"Go on then," Mr Mann sighed.

Amy rose, her mind a tornado of superheated thoughts. She crossed in front of Lucy, who shifted slightly, as she always did, to surreptitiously trip her. Sidestepping, Amy considered kicking the blonde girl in-between the pigtails. She didn't, but continued to the door, leant her frame backwards to open it, walked to another, opened that, turned left into a corridor that was carpeted but smelt of old urine. She stopped. Out of the side of her eyes, she'd seen the line of coats on her class's pegs. Looking to one end of the corridor and then the other, Amy listened. Close by, a child was being taught phonics.

"A digraph is—" said an adult.

"Two words make one sound," said a child.

"Two—" The teacher paused. "—make one sound."

"—words?"

"No! Two—"

"—sentences?"

They wouldn't be moving for a while, thought Amy, crossing to the pegs. Her eyes scanned above the top of the curves of red metal until she saw *Lucy*, decorated by a scenery of butterflies and stars and hearts. She took Lucy's coat, which was thin and light pink, off the peg and hurried into the toilet. It was Nike and Lucy always wore it at break-time, even in the sun.

Amy didn't have long.

Closing the cubicle door, Amy pulled down her tights and underwear and peed for a while, letting out what she needed to, staring at the coat on the floor. She kept some back though. Over the years, Amy had become an expert at controlling her body. Reaching forwards she grasped the coat, opened one of the pockets on its side, and crouched again.

LUCY WAS STILL CRYING when Amy's mum came. The little blonde girl sat in the corner of the carpet, desperately scraping at her coat pockets with damp paper towels. She'd refused Mrs Skinner's offer to take it to the kitchen and clean it, and the fabric had threatened to rip when the teaching assistant tried to take it out of Lucy's small hands. The sun had peeped out and shone down on her in the reading area, making bright crystals of her tears. Her sobs were loud enough on their own and needed no highlighting. Amy's mum, for the first time, blushed when she collected her daughter, which was not a good sign.

"The break-time monitors had to pull them apart," said Mr Mann. "I'm afraid your daughter was saying some very nasty things about how Lucy smelt. And, of course, she admitted to urinating on her coat—"

At this, the sound of Lucy's scrubbing increased in ferocity and Amy was dragged from the classroom.

AMY STOOD IN THE centre of her bedroom and tried to smile. This hurt where she'd been pressed to the window, her mother having applied the double-glazing to her face. As her mum had crushed her against it, she'd said, "Do you think anybody cares about you, love? Do you, eh? Them out there don't care, get it through your thick skull." And she'd pressed the back of Amy's scalp until the girl thought that the glass would make its way through. Luckily, the window had been double-glazed by the council two summers before, and so didn't break. Her mum, though, had been right about one thing. An old man had glanced up to see Amy being rammed against the upstairs window, and had looked away, shaking his head as if to dislodge a daydream. And another thing, thought Amy, now I know why they're called window pains. Slowly, Amy found she could smile and did so fully, her lips picking their way around aching teeth. There were no bruises on her face. Her jaw throbbed from the clenching the window had given it. Her kidneys and bladder ached from the fists that had fallen there, but still she stood tall as a lightning conductor in a gathering storm. She could feel it coming. She'd reached home in time. She was going to save her baby.

Hurrying to her bed, she drew its frame back and withdrew Barney's abdomen and severed arm. Having stolen a sewing kit from the downstairs cupboard (under the stairs, behind the iron, on the shelf by the red linen basket—Amy knew the cupboard well), she crouched, then sat, and went about reattaching Barney's arm to his body.

She stopped only once, despite all the shouting from downstairs, when her mother put her face to the bedroom door and screamed, "I'm going out tonight and you'll not stop me, you ungrateful brat. You can just stay in there—no tea—and no bothering the babysitter. *And stay away out of your brother's room, you sick little shit.*" Amy's heart had expanded with blood it couldn't handle and her nape had drained, becoming pale. But her mum hadn't come in, but instead had dragged at the door, jangling it though it was closed tight against its jamb already, saying, "I don't want to see your ugly, ungrateful face. If you want a piss, do it in your clothes instead of some other poor kid's. Don't you dare come out."

Then, the sound of steps on the stairs.

Then, the lounge door slamming.

Then, vaguely, the television.

"I'm sorry Barney," Amy said, on each needle stroke skewering his brown skin.

Sweat rose up her hairline and finally stood on the skin of her forehead. She squinted and sewed. Outside, dusk crept in with long fingers of dark cloud, each shaped into the form of a Witch or a Gorilla to the girl's quick glances. She spared nothing more of her eyes. She wasn't good at sewing and had more work to do besides. Her sketchbook was ruined, and she knew she wouldn't get back into her world if she didn't rewrite the pages that her mum had stained.

Amy finished Barney's arm, patted him on the pelted forehead and put him on her bed. Downstairs, she heard Uncle Chris rush in and the patter of her mum's nagging. It sounded like rain falling from the moss-hung gutters. Not long after, there followed a knock. The babysitter.

Amy coloured, working yellow backwards and forwards over the Latter Wood.

"Oh, she was tired from school. She went to bed early." Her mum said this loudly, loud enough for Amy to hear. "She won't come out, not tonight."

There was the noncommittal, gum-spooling grunt of a female teenager. "Yah, hah," it said.

"We won't be late, alright love?"

"Alright." The voice was brighter, happier sounding at the adults going. "Have a good time."

Uncle Chris said, "Aye, thanks love." His sentence was awkward on the last word, like Uncle Chris's eyes were when Amy wore her skin-coloured pyjamas.

She coloured The Copse, the Glade she landed in, the Under Hill on the northern horizon, and the Dark Tower Block of the Witch that lay below it. She sketched the Night School and its gates and the Christian's hut, but her pencil nib chipped when she tried to draw his convoluted face, and then snapped entirely as she tried to pen his biography. Amy knew better than to try again, and—after sharpening her pencil—moved on, switching colours as she went, until the world map was drawn and the characters written next to it with thumbnail sketches and quotes from her flora and fauna and mythology reference books, all of which readily came from memory.

Breathing heftily, unlimbering her fingers (which felt like icicles of lactic acid), she leaned back. She was ready, and so was Barney.

There was a car on the drive, distant as hailstones. Amy's hips sent flares of pain into her legs until they met the pins and needles of her lower extremities, which were numb. She tottered to the bed and nearly fell onto its duvet.

I'm coming, she thought, her brain anything but numb.

The front door opened as she took Barney by the upper arm and pulled him down to the green carpet next to the sketchpad that lay open on it.

There was the sound of kissing on the stairs and that of fumbling at outerwear. The babysitter giggled, the sound of laughter rising and falling like hands around the man Amy could hear on the stairs. His breathing was heavy, and the stairs creaked slightly below his weight.

Amy looked up, concentration broken.

"Upstairs," said the babysitter. "They've gone."

The landing creaked, as though nodding in agreement, and the man said, after a breathless pause, "Aye." Then he added, "You make me so horny."

The giggle. Amy imagined eyes like her mum's at the local, when she was flirting with a man who wasn't Uncle Chris. They would be downcast, almost far enough to meet her own lips, which would be smiling in a funny way, as if they weren't really laughing but thinking about something else. Amy, despite her experience, never knew what.

Amy sat as their feet went past her door.

"In their bed?" said the man. "They'll smell it."

"Jesus, you're a pussy," said the babysitter.

"*Your* pussy, you mean," said the man, and he laughed.

Amy couldn't tell what was funny.

The babysitter laughed but it didn't sound real, then said, "What about that one?"

"Nah, too small. *And* the little kid is in there. He'll bawl if we wake him."

Amy looked down at the sketchpad's open pages, placing her hand on it. If her arm was a root, it shook as if in a quickening wind.

"What about that room?"

"The girl's in there. She's sleeping."

"Kick her out. She'll not know what we're doing. Give her a DVD and she'll be away with the fairies. Put the sound up loud."

"What like?"

"I don't know. Disney or summat."

Amy closed her eyes and gritted her teeth and subdued an urge to scream. Her bedroom door shifted, like the first impacts of aliens on a metal blast shield, and then, inevitably, opened. The babysitter stood in it, with a fake smile as big as the space between the jambs.

"Hiya love," she said. "Oh you're awake, that's great. Come on, do you want a film on? Have you got any good ones?" She held out her hand. The nails were pink and black and shiny.

Amy nodded, her head numb as her feet had been.

The babysitter reached forwards and took her by her fingers and, before the girl could refuse her, pulled her to her feet.

"Come on. Up and at 'em."

Amy grasped her sketchbook, touting it by a page which, thankfully, didn't rip. Amy's heart did though, when she grabbed Barney and his arm fell off. Or rather, his body fell off, hit the floor, bounced apathetically and rolled to the side, half under the bed.

"Never mind," said the babysitter, all smiles and breezy syllables. "I'll fix him up right as rain." Her voice was several octaves higher than when she had been talking to Amy's mum. The babysitter extracted Barney's upper arm from Amy's sweaty grip, held it by a wisp of stuffing, put it on the floor, and pulled Amy through the door.

Listening to the sound of the man's heavy body easing onto her mattress and the moaning of the springs under it, the steps passed under Amy's feet in a blur of brown. Above her scalp, Aidan's bedroom door passed out of sight. It was closed. She wasn't allowed in, not since Mum had found out about her poisoning him. Not a sound drifted down from the chipped white door, and hadn't since Aidan had returned from the hospital. He seemed to sleep all the time. Amy had heard her mum say, on the phone to Nan, "The doctor said that's to be expected, after what *she* did to him." Her voice had dribbled venom into the receiver. Nan hadn't asked to speak to Amy on any of the last three times she'd rung. Amy missed her nan.

In a moment, she was downstairs in the lounge, staring at a selection of DVDs through eyes that were doing their best not to cry.

"Oh look," the babysitter said. "This one's good. How about Labyrinth?"

Amy nodded, distracted by the thought that the evening couldn't get any worse.

As SHE SWOOPED through the trees, the Headmistress thought it was colder than she remembered, here in the north of the Latter Wood. The Witch's realm was on the spread. Global cooling, she thought, and had no idea why. It didn't take her long to reach the folds of white land, which had the look of light wrinkles in a tablecloth (from the air at least), and shorter again to reach the village outskirts. She landed on a branch, silent except for the slight crunch of frost. Her white plumage left her feeling safe—camouflaged. Night was falling; the dusk was dusting itself off. There was something luminously yellowed about the frozen north, as though it kept the light long after it should do, hoarding it. If the Headmistress had lived in the Other Place, and had been a reader, she would've been put in mind of Miss Havisham in Great Expectations, and of wedding cakes and wedding gowns.

All was quiet on the northern front, and the Headmistress's lungs opened as, finally, she felt she could breathe. Her lungs had been cramped since her talk that day with Mr Him and the boy called Angel, little tumorous growths of worry worming their way into them and constricting her oxygen intake. She almost didn't hear the sound of screaming over the sound of her relaxed breaths, but then she did.

Gulping as though swallowing down a whole mouse, she flapped to the snow and hopped and skipped to the side of the first house. She bent her head to the chocolate bricks of its exterior. She could hear a mole fart from a forest away and so had no trouble hearing the screaming again, and her mind took even less time to remember what it meant. Children were in the house, and the Witch's minions were doing things to them. And if children were in the house, someone at the school must have put them there, and that thread of thoughts led only to…

With a leap, the Headmistress took to the air. Her eyes were large enough to cry great bells of teardrops, which quickly froze to her feathers. She'd allowed this to happen on her watch. The guilt burned even more than the wind, though it was coruscatingly cold. So consumed was she that she didn't look up and see that the unveiling stars had been blotted out by a swarm of wings, like locusts but bigger—Gorilla wings, in fact—until they took her in mid-flight, and snapped her spine, and one of them ate her in a single gulp. The last thought to go through the Head's mind, apart from Ouch, was that she'd got Mr Him completely wrong.

MRS HER BRUSHED HER beard (which had a habit of growing all the way around her head) away from her eyes. She didn't watch the charity drive, which had been merged with a talent show under the heading of Children Need Talent, but stared at her class. They sat with the precision of broken minds, a moulding process Mrs Her had perfected over three decades of teaching at the Night School.

Mrs Her's attention was taken, and with some glee, by the class that sat in front of hers. Angel and Tower were talking, which they did whenever Mr Him avoided assembly, and were comparing Top Trumps cards.

"Angel!" Mrs Her said, a little louder than she needed to. "Be quiet! Do I need to remove you from this assembly? And Tower... I expect better from you!"

At the front, a Year 6 was making a balloon dragon. The boy's intent stare seemed to squeak as much as the rubber did in the attempt. The dragon's tail abruptly popped and the balloon sped away around the hall, piffling gently in a way that would have embarrassed Fáfnir. It had the same effect on the boy, who went red as a burn.

Angel looked directly at Mrs Her and resumed his conversation. Mrs Her rose. "Fine," she said under her breath and her beard. Glaring at him, she walked to the boy, grasped him by the ear, and dragged Angel from the assembly. She only had to glare at Tower to make him follow, his face exhibiting more agony than Angel's.

"RIGHT," SHE SAID, levering them against the wall outside the hall. "I'm going to talk to Mr Him about you two, and—"

"Where is Mr Him then?" said Angel.

Mrs Her drew herself up straight, her beard bristling. "What business is it of yours where a teacher is?"

"Mr Him's taken Sunshine."

"What?" Below her beard, Mrs Her began to colour, and the colour wasn't pale.

"That's why he's always missing assembly," said Angel. "Didn't you see him leave with one of the Year 2 children last night? And tonight—" Angel's eyes curdled, "—he took Sunshine."

"Now, look here you two—"

"Huh-he's right." Tower didn't stumble on the 'right'.

Now they mentioned it, gears were beginning to click within Mrs Her's brain, cogs were starting to align. She'd seen Mr Him escorting the child out, when the girl hadn't made a sound all assembly. She remembered the times she'd gone looking for the teacher but he hadn't been in school. She recalled the way he looked at some of the pupils.

She gulped.

"Well… look… you two will stay here and I'll find Mr Him, and I don't want to hear any of you making this kind of accusation again."

Mrs Her hastened down the right-hand side of the stairs that led down from the hall, her feet stumbling.

With that, Angel left his position on the wall. "Let's split up," said the boy. After he'd moved away from the wall but Tower hadn't, he turned. "Well, come on Tower!"

With a sigh, Tower pushed himself from the wall, looking more like he was unsticking himself from honey than moving through thin air.

MRS HER STRODE DOWN the corridor to the dining hall and from there, down the corridor to the staff room, and from there, down the corridor to the reception. In each room there was a clock and each clicked closer to one in the morning, the time the assembly would end. For some reason, the clocks' hands tickled up the feeling that it didn't matter if Mrs Her was there to collect her children. She just needed to find Mr Him; though, for some reason, she couldn't ask the receptionist or any of the other teachers.

Cat's got my tongue, thought Mrs Her. In actual fact, it was the knowledge that the children were right that had got her tongue.

Then she saw him at the end of the corridor going back to the dining room. He was with a small boy.

"Mr Him!" she shouted. He didn't turn but walked through the door, letting it close behind him.

She paced then strode then jogged after him. Soon she was running. A guardian came the other way, and Mrs Her had to pause to keep the door open. In the Night School, etiquette was a paper/scissors/stone situation. Children held the door for teachers, teachers for guardians, guardians for their children. Mr Him was in too much of a rush to play these games, letting a door slam in a guardian's face. The teacher was nearly at the hall but—she saw—didn't continue to it, turning instead to go inside the disabled toilet… with the child. He didn't even bother to look around, thought Mrs Her. For some reason, this struck her as important though it wasn't until a few minutes later, when the Witch attacked, that she realised why.

She ran to the door and, feet jiggering on the blue carpet before it, waited. The disabled toilet made a flushing noise. Mrs Her waited. The cistern began to refill. Mrs Her waited, until she noticed the toilet door was marginally ajar.

She tugged at her facial hair, growled, and then entered the toilet. It was empty.

Mrs Her turned then closed and locked the door from the inside.

"SHIT," she said as loudly as she could to the toilet bowl. The toilet bowl stared at her but didn't answer. "SHIT," she repeated, unlocked the door, and stepped into the corridor.

An older child stood there, staring at Mrs Her.

Mrs Her opened her mouth, closed it, opened it, and said, "It helps me to go."

She walked away.

THE SPIKES WITHDREW and the gargoyles rose from their points on the apex of the fence.

"Thank the Witch for that," said one, clutching his buttocks. He quietened when he saw what was coming.

Around the perimeter of the Night School, a phalanx of gargoyles took to the air and turned north.

In front of each of the external windows, corrugated metal shutters rattled down. Doors were locked from the inside and the staff near the reception began to gather in the staffroom. There were assembly points for this kind of thing, as there were for Fire Alarms and Bomb Alerts. The Witch and her minions hadn't attacked for hundreds of years, but the last time they had, they'd come through the front door. This time, the staff would be ready.

The teachers escorted the children back to their classrooms and locked the doors.

AMY STARED AT THE television and at the sight of the shadow of Tower's dragon. It was curled around the Goblin City in the film. As the silhouettes of Gorillas filled the air, the dragon launched, sanguine in all but the darker line of determination that was its jaw. Its wings beat above the Labyrinth and the stocky butterflied figures surrounded it.

Black blood spread in the Labyrinth's streets.

Even Rainbow Brite was made entirely of black cloth cut from another reality that montaged with this celluloid one. She bounced from Gorilla to Gorilla, but the outline of the Witch's minions dragged her down.

David Bowie sang, "You remind me of the babe," and Amy stared as the cut-out of Mrs Her ran through the corridors of a school that could only be seen in impressions of charcoal.

Mrs Her's mouth was opening and closing.

"GET IN YOUR classrooms," Mrs Her ran down the corridor towards the hall shouting. "Stay in your classrooms children!"

News of the attack had spread quickly.

She didn't see Angel and Tower running from Class 7. Angel carried a dining knife as though it were a sword.

Above her, the roof reverberated to a blast that could only be a dragon killing a Gorilla. Through the window to the inner courtyard she saw a gargoyle hit the floor. It had shattered long before it reached the flagstones, and fragments of it pelted the window pane.

Mrs Her—her heels especially—screeched to a stop, as she stared towards the hall. Mr Him, more in shadow than not, more made of silhouette than lit, was struggling with an invader. Mr Him was wet through.

Mrs Her ran towards him.

"What do you think I come to this school for?" she heard Mr Him say. "I'm your teacher. You'll do as I say."

On the blue carpet, a lion lay dead, gutted from its entrails to its third rib.

Mrs Her rounded on Mr Him's assailant.

It was Sunshine.

Mrs Her blinked, her eyes narrowing between fringe and beard.

~260~

He had a knife against Sunshine's pale throat. The girl's neck was stretched and turned toward Mr Him and pallid even where pressed by the blade. Sunshine was sweating and crying, and a dark patch made a pool at the front of her black skirt and down her grey tights. Mr Him was wet through, and not just his moustache and his palms.

The figure in the sign of the disabled toilet was sitting bolt upright as though it had heard something. Mrs Her imagined the sound of flushing.

"You—" Mrs Her couldn't put a word to the shape of her lips.

"Yes. Me," said Mr Him. "They love me. They're mine. They certainly don't belong to their parents."

Mrs Her could hear it now: a rattle of pipes.

Mr Him backed away from the toilet. "She's coming," he said. Toilet water dripped from his moustache and into his open mouth.

Mrs Her drew herself up. She thought he meant Sunshine. "She most certainly is not. Not with you," said Mrs Her.

But he hadn't meant Sunshine.

The disabled door exploded open. Mrs Her watched but not for long, as the disabled figure came towards her on half of the door. The blue stick-figure had disposed of its wheelchair and, for that moment, appeared healed.

What was left of the door hit Mrs Her, and she collapsed below it.

When she came round, it had all already happened.

TOWER RAN ACROSS THE inner courtyard, his stride a line of tics and shakes and convulsions. A gargoyle plummeted to where he stood, and Tower dodged right with his gait's natural confusion. It saved him, as the gargoyle impacted where he had, a moment before, ran. Tower was breathing hard enough to dry his tongue. His cheeks were constellated with dots of red, his eyes with stars. He didn't think he could keep going, but he could see his guardian curled around the gazebo in the courtyard centre, fending off a ribbon of Gorillas. They clustered at him and struck and hissed, and their mouths gaped as wide open as their fangs were long. By contrast, their wings seemed scarcely able to hoist them, thin as the slips in photo albums before you put the pictures in. Tower bent mid-stumble, scooped, and pitched a stone at the closest Gorilla, hitting its right wing and tearing it. The ape roared, tore at its chest and turned to face Tower. Tower shook. He was no longer running, but his lungs pounded like they hadn't been informed.

His guardian Betsy, with a gecko-esque snap of her head, turned and bellowed fire across the Gorilla's right flank, blackening it, and the ape fell to the earth, no longer roaring. With a leap, the dragon jumped to earth, landing beside Tower. The boy grasped her spine and, with an aptitude lacking when attached to the ground, scampered up to sit behind her head.

"Fly," he shouted, in the kind of tone a child would use with his teddy bears—or dolls—and not with a fifty-foot purple dragon.

"Easy. You're right by my ears. Scream like that and you'll give me a stroke," said Betsy.

Betsy flew and, before long, Betsy fought and Tower had her back.

AMY HAD TURNED OFF the television, leaving the DVD running, and sat in the corner, mapping out the stars above the world she'd created in her sketchbook. By the sounds from upstairs, the babysitter wasn't coming down anytime soon and it didn't sound like she was sewing.

Her next best hope, she knew, was that her mum came home. Amy picked up the pad and walked softly to the other side of the room. She turned off the light by the door and listened to the babysitter saying, "Not yet, not yet, not yet, I'm nearly there, nearly there."

The little girl shrugged and sat down in the curve of the alcove at the end of the curtains, where she liked to sit, where the light from the orange streetlights outside slid down into the well between windowsill and cream curtain lining. Peeking above the sill, she watched the street. It was quiet in the Place, and humid.

The wallpaper was a cool hand at her back, reassuring in the heat. The pale vertical bunches of the curtain wrapped around her, like giant fingers. She thought this was how Sophie felt in The BFG. She thought about children's stories, as she was wont to do. Amy liked children's stories. She didn't believe any of them, but it was nice to imagine that, somewhere out there, there were children who did.

She didn't mean to but, closing her eyes, Amy fell asleep.

HE SAW RAINBOW BRITE flickering in and out of existence and jumping from the cupboard to the table to the chair, searching for Sunshine instead of rainbows.

Tower couldn't help, which for him was nothing new. He was an inaccuracy of a child, good for nothing but an occasional kicking. More tellingly, his dragon Betsy was rent down the ribs by scores of scratch marks. She'd been losing blood, dribbling red down through the air like spilt wine and had now faded from her purple hue to a tinged black. It was the colour of twilight giving up the ghost.

"Come on, Betsy. Come on." Tower was no longer shouting and had rocked forward to cuddle the dragon around her throat.

"Umf erg flee," said the dragon.

Tower sat up straight. "What?"

"You're strangling me," said Betsy. Even unrestricted, her voice was weak.

"What?"

"I have to land," she whispered. The boy didn't need to hear her; the dragon came to a rumbling bad landing on the Key Stage 2 playground.

There were no apes to be seen. The school building to their right reverberated with the shock of magic being unleashed within. Tower's ears ached with the vibrations of wind and screams.

He swung one leg around the dragon's neck and was about to dismount when he saw her eye beside his left fist. It was closed, and the lid jostled as violently as Betsy's body did when she breathed.

"Betsy." He hugged her again.

She seemed to smile, though it was difficult to tell with a dragon.

"How can I help you Tower?" she said in a whisper.

"Are you—?" Tower's voice shook as his body habitually did. "Are you—?"

"Yes."

Tower's voice hardened. "Thank you for bringing me here Betsy. I've really enjoyed it."

"Tower." Blood wheezed out with the words. "You're stronger than you think. You'll make it through. You'll be big one day."

"I know," said Tower. "I love you."

Betsy breathed, and Tower held her until she stopped. The boy faded out of This Place and back into The Other.

A CAR PULLED INTO their drive, its tyres gritting both Amy's teeth and the gravel. She sat abruptly where she'd been slumped in the lounge, in the dark with the lights off. She needed to go to her room. For a minute, she couldn't recall how she'd gotten here at all. She needed to be in the Other Place. These were her thoughts, and they went no further. Her limbs, her arms and up-drawn legs, were a tight cage around the canary of her heart. It was still beating. It fluttered, and then started as the car stopped. The headlights whitened the cream curtains. The lights clicked out as a car door opened with the sound of another being slammed shut. A second slam followed and, hot after that, speech.

"You stupid bitch. It's one rule for you like and another—"

"Oh yeah? One rule? You need your rules, don't you sweetheart? Like the rule of your fists."

"You can talk," the male voice muttered.

They were at the door in a new silence drowned in drink. Amy looked over to the opened-up hallway and, left of it, the stairs. The babysitter was up there in Amy's bed with the boy who had a green car the same colour as Nan's curtains. The car that made the same noise as Nan's throat after her cigarettes.

"You can talk," Uncle Chris was saying, tone pitching up masculine then feminine, on waves of inebriation. He seemed to be trying to find his voice. "You can talk. Yeah right. The times you've hit me—"

"Ooooh… you poor lad. Hit by a women eh? How do you get by? Big strong man like you." Her mum's words turned, instinctive as a snake under the edge of a knife. "Little wimp. Little wife-beating fucking wimp."

Uncle Chris was finding his keys. They crankled rather than tinkled under his fingertips.

Amy's bedroom door opened, whispering light and words down the well of the staircase: "Quick, quick, get 'em on man. They're back."

"Alright, keep your fanny hair on."

"Shut it, right. I get twenty quid for this. I'm not blowing it 'cause you can't find your dick and put it in your pants."

The front door opened.

"Oh hello, love." Mum, smiling as wide as the fattest lie, came through the door. "How are you? Have a good night?"

"Aye." A pause, nakedly self-conscious. "Was just checking on the kid."

"But—" Mum turned her head. "—she's right here."

"Oh... yeah."

Silence. Then to break it, "Jesus, you are an empty headed child." Mum shook her head at Amy and laughed for the baby-sitter. "I could clean the house with the cloth in her head. She's a funny 'un alright. You never know where she's snuck off to. What you doing behind the curtain love?"

Amy couldn't answer.

The babysitter laughed. "Aye."

"I'll stick the light on. Would you like a brew love?"

"Or something stronger," said Uncle Chris, squeezing by.

"GIVE YOUR MUM A cuddle."

Amy's brain numbed: going to Mexico and ordering a tequila, as Uncle Chris would say. He was in the next room. At her mum's words, Amy's skin puckered into a rash of kisses that made her think of May Day and of ribbons.

Her mum was watching a repeat of Bullseye. She flicked her right hand with each shot while exclaiming, "It's a one… the useless bastard… one again… triple bloody one—" and leaning forward more intently with every 'one'. Uncle Chris's cheeks flinched on the wrist-flicks. Amy liked Bullseye because of the presenter. His name was Jim. She'd close her eyes and listen to his voice, which made her think of the kind of bear a small, old, grey teddy would turn into in Another Place.

Mum drank Southern Comfort and sat nearer the edge of the settee as she tilted the glass too far, honey-hued liquid slipping down her chin. Her lips twisted as though they couldn't catch enough and wouldn't be satiated. Amy stared at them.

"Jesus, that's easy," said the lips. "W… E… I… R… D—" she shouted at the TV. "Can you spell 'weirdo' instead? Look at your fucking eighties hairstyle!" She giggled and drank and peered sidelong at Chris. "Mind you, he's got big muscles, eh love?"

Uncle Chris muttered something Amy couldn't hear, but which didn't appear to be the answer to, "In 1960, who became the world's first female prime minister following the assassination of her husband?"

Amy tried to listen to what Jim was saying.

"Come on sweetheart." Her mum's voice was as brusque as her fingers on Amy's skin. Amy sat down on the settee and allowed her mother to pull her in close, under her armpit. She could feel her mum's skin where it was peppered with hair yet to fully grow, yet to be razored.

"What do you think the answer is love?"

Amy shook her head. Her mouth didn't move. She tried to appear tired, stretching and yawning. She'd pretend to drift off as soon as the going got good. Uncle Chris sat down on the armchair, eyes pinioned to the TV and its faux-rock surround like a climber who was scared of losing his grip. A woman with the same hair and height as her mother appeared on the screen, throwing darts at a board. She had a different face though. Mum was good at darts and played at the local with Uncle Tommy. They always beat Uncle Chris. It was all the practice with kitchen knives, Amy thought.

A man was throwing darts now. He had grey hair and grey skin and threw into the 5.

"Look at those eyes," said Mum. "He's a loser. He knows he's going to miss. Oh I recognise that particular look, I do." She peered at Chris.

He remained staring straight at the TV, but his eyes shied, as though he couldn't hold its gaze for long.

"Ignore Uncle Chris. He's in a little boy's sulk," her mum sneered.

"Bitch," Chris said, almost to himself.

"Aren't you?" she said. Amy's mother was watching the screen. Amy tried not to. In the dark segments of the board she could see a white outline—like crime scene chalk, but around a face instead of a body. It was the outline of a witch.

"Yeah, that's right," said Chris, drinking and spilling. The sentences dribbled out. "Sit with the kid. That way you're safe."

Amy's mother lent towards him. "Does that help, sweetheart? Give you a bit of a chance. Think you could hit me now?"

The short blonde woman was throwing again. Her dart landed in the red bar of the *20*.

Amy closed her eyes. She'd seen Aidan in the borders of the screen.

"180!" said the man who wasn't Jim, somewhere in the space between her mother's chin and Chris's fists.

"You'd like that wouldn't you?" said Uncle Chris. His feet could be heard striding across the carpet and out of the room.

"No, I'd like you to act like a man for a change."

"Always got to have the last word, don't you?"

"No, you do."

"No, you bloody do." His footsteps were on the stairs. His voice was with them.

"Prat!" yelled her mum, cocking her head backwards. Her neck clicked like the loading of a gun. The footsteps ceased. Then resumed. "Wimp!"

The footsteps returned in a rush.

Amy's mother tensed, stood, and hurried to the door. She was shouting as she reached it. Amy closed her mind and didn't listen. Her mum's lips curled all the way around her teeth. Her back was arched, but so were her arms and at the end of them her hands formed downward-facing claws. She looked like she was dowsing. Uncle Chris came through the door chest first. His shoulders rolled as he threw his arms, wrists first, at Mum's abdomen. His face was a snarl of red and a rictus of shadows. Whatever was going on behind it had frozen his cheek muscles.

The sound came back in for Amy.

"You fucking want this, don't you? You fucking want this, you sick bitch?" he said. His eyes seemed to have bubbled up to the surface. Amy thought they might pop.

"Want what?" She shoved back, taking care to claw his arm and drawing blood where she'd been in red lines under his elbow. "You're too pathetic to beat me. Call yourself a fucking man? Sitting in this room all day long. Or playing with yourself and thinking about me. You pathetic little shite." She twisted down to the settee, grasped the remote control, and threw it at his face. There was a clack as it clipped his teeth.

Uncle Chris screamed and bent. He hissed through his tooth-line and spittle tentacled to the carpet.

"You bitch," he spat again and looked at his hand for blood. His eyes bulged all the more, as though daring the red.

"Oh hurt by a little woman, were you? You prat! I should get myself a real man and not a useless little prick like you."

"Oh—" he breathed, still bent over, "—like that boy that was here just now. You were all over him, you soused bint. You know the looks he was giving his girlfriend?"

Amy backed across the lounge carpet as her mother turned to her. But Mum wasn't looking at her. She grabbed a DVD box off the mantelpiece—Child's Play—and threw it at Uncle Chris. It missed. Child's Play, though, was not without sequels and she clutched the next and then another. Then she was onto Invasion of the Body Snatchers, but Uncle Chris ran at her, bent double, and the DVD soared over his head, sprawling against the uplighter and swinging it before falling to the floor.

Shadows swarmed and scattered below the light like cockroaches. Among them, Amy saw a witch.

Jim said, "What a smashing little lady she is, isn't she?"

Uncle Chris reached her mother, slamming her against the fire. It clanked and listed. His hands reached for her throat and closed. He didn't say anything, the words he wanted to speak swarming around his facial muscles like an alien in a chest. He was now bleeding from his upper lip.

Mum bit his right hand and the fingers shied away.

"Can't even kill me right," she said. "I need a real man. A real man like Tommy."

The hand closed back in. His gaze locked down on her eyes. He lent his slight weight against hers. Her hands skittered across his skin but left no indentations. Amy stared at the last DVD she'd thrown. On its cover, Donald Sutherland pointed like an accusation. It gave Amy an idea. She pointed at the two adults and screamed, "Arrrrggghhhhhhhhhhhhhhhhhhhh—"

Amy was a quiet child, but the scream wasn't. It didn't sound human, and it wouldn't stop.

"—argggggghhhhhhhhhhhhhhhhhhhh."

Uncle Chris lent back on his heels, his eyes reeling, his fingers unravelling.

"Please stop," he said. "Please—"

Amy closed her eyes as she closed her mouth.

Her mum's breath came louder, ratcheting her throat. Amy imagined her pretty, thin lips opening. She could hear the sound of Uncle Chris crying.

"Get off me," her mum said, and there was the sound of a shove, the exclamation of carpet under a foot that didn't know it was about to move.

Her mum's footsteps went past.

Her mum could be heard ascending the stairs. Chris, unbeknownst to Amy, had silently sunk into the settee, his eyes staring at her eight-year-old face.

After a pause, Amy opened her eyes. The cartoon bull was pointing at circular board and the number three. "Iiiiiiiiiinnnnn three... you'll get a great reception if you win this 22 inch colour television—" The television was brown at the back and black at the front, apart from its screen, on which Bully was pointing at another TV. This one, however, showed a toddler in a cot made of rot, of things that used to be fabric but had gone green and decayed. The little boy was crying. The little boy had blue eyes.

Amy fled upstairs, not stopping until she reached her bedroom. Carrying the sketchbook in her armpit, Amy shut the door and walked across the carpet. The light was still on, and her duvet was cratered by the impact of buttocks, elbows, feet, from where the babysitter and her boyfriend had lain. They hadn't bothered taking up the duvet or getting under it. Amy could smell something high and floral, like the hedge on the left of the garden in midsummer, when it flowered and leaked liquid from its petals. It smelt of Piglet's home.

Barney had been strewn across the room. His eyes were glazed and stared at the ceiling.

Arms vacant with exhaustion, Amy gathered her bear back together and sat on her bed, cross-legged as ever, sewing the limb to its shoulder. Her hand felt like a clutch of thick needles. It was all she could do to keep her eyelids pinned open. She sewed, stitch after stitch, until it was done, then opened her sketchpad and turned to the thick creamy beige page that contained the Latter Wood. Rising with zombified precision— all straightnesses of limb—she turned to her school uniform, took three laburnum seeds from her dress pocket, and popped them like sleeping tablets. Equally efficient, she then switched off the light, returned to bed, cuddled her teddy bear, held his hand, and fell sideways through sleep and to Some Place beyond it.

THE LATTER WOOD HAD the odour of broken fur and of spilled blood and, not too far off, of death. In this way, and certainly not in the clumsy, shambling, fern-breaking way in which he walked, Barnaby blended in. The green of the trees and the gold of the pods had been blacked out by the night. All colour seemed, like a Blitz window, to be afraid of the sky. Strange things passed overhead.

Barnaby tried to think about these and occasionally managed, his mind trailing off in fits and spurts, not unlike the paths in the Latter Wood. The undergrowth closed in, or that may have been the framing of unconsciousness. Being unconscious, he didn't realise that these were the times he faded. He was powerfully bloodied, and by his own arteries.

Following the crumbs of his consciousness that stretched out before him along the forest floor, Barnaby closed in on the school.

He could hear her laugh.

There was something about the Witch's laugh—it was as cold as her tit yet as wet as her crotch. Barnaby shivered. The crumbs of consciousness were spacing out. Pretty soon, he couldn't see the next one. He fell. When he came to, he crawled forwards. Twigs crackled beneath him. He blacked out, came to, spat bile and blood, and crawled once more. The laburnum pods above him reached down, seeds bleached by the second moon that had risen in the east and shed light beneath the foliage cover of the canopy. Barnaby hadn't seen this moon before and wondered what it portended. The moon shafts looked like knuckle bones on an intricate hand. Death would have a hand like that, Barnaby thought, and crawled further. His head was swollen and numb and filled with frostbitten thoughts. Barnaby laughed—he was unsure why—and sent a hiccup-cloud of mosquitoes into the warm cosy space beneath the trees. He could just stay here, he thought, let down his snout, press his muzzle and wet nose to the forest floor, and let go, as his shoulder had let go of his right arm. He could, if not for the girl. She'd left him here to guard her baby. Moreover, if he died, she wouldn't be able to find a way back.

He was going on a human hunt, and he was more than a little bit scared.

Barnaby rose to his haunches, then to his feet. He blundered into a tree. Pods fell in a squall.

"Sorry," he said. There was a tingling at his shoulder joint, as if someone had walked across the grave of his lost limb. He stared at it. The limb was no longer lost. He flexed his paw. "You fixed me," he said to himself. He stared at his right arm, a blob of dark brown on black in the dark. "You fixed me," he said and began to run.

THE WITCH STOOD BY the window of the Nursery. Her black clothes were wet, damp enough to look like velvet. Angel hissed and inched closer, gripping his knife. Though the sand table was empty, the Witch had sand on the ends of her stilettos. Angel didn't know where it was from but, despite only coming up to her breast height-wise, he wasn't staring at her feet but at the little boy. She held a broom in her other hand, and Angel ignored this.

The Witch grinned sweetly at him. Despite holding Aimee's little brother from the right angle of her elbow, she turned the key at the side of the wide window. The metal shutters on its other side jarred and rose upwards. Behind Angel were the sounds of Gorillas and teachers fighting and the screams of small children. Ms Lydia lay—beaten by Gorilla fists—at the entrance to the Quiet Room. Inside, the remaining four-year-olds could be heard screaming or, where they had screamed themselves dry, hoarsely sobbing. Ms Lydia's mouth was open as though trying to join in.

"Let him go," said Angel. His teeth were gritted and felt as intransient as the serrations on the knife. Sweat buttered his grip.

"He's mine," said the Witch. She held the azure-robed boy against the curve of her bosom. The child had gone quiet, his eyes wide and glinting as he eyed first the Witch, then Angel.

"You won't take him," said Angel and lunged.

The Witch dropped the child. Angel's blade faltered as he watched the little boy plummet. Angel gasped and stabbed towards her, but his left foot slipped to the side. There was a doughy crack as the toddler slapped against the tiles. He began to wail. Angel's thrust came up short and the Witch said, "You made me do that."

Angel looked up, as open mouthed as Ms Lydia would be from now on. The Witch, as he gaped at her, swung her broomstick through the air. The shaft of it struck his right temple. There was a fizz like ginger ale inside his skull and he fell, as Amy's brother had. When he hit the ground, he didn't scream but passed out. He knew no more, the Witch using his knife to stab him in the throat. The boy, while unconscious, bled to death.

AIMEE PASSED THE staffroom, her feet on their tiptoes from running flat out, her eyes straining down the corridor ahead of her. She saw Barnaby, caught amidst a tangle of Gorillas in the dining hall, but didn't see several of the teaching staff as they fought a Russian Doll.

She slammed through the door out of the canteen, then along one corridor, then through another. Unnoticed behind her, the bear followed, nestled in a melee of apes. The Nursery loomed, both its safety door and its main entrance unlocked and wedged open, which they should never be, she thought. It was against Health and Safety, with small children. Someone could just walk right in and take one. And when she raced into the Nursery, she knew someone had. The door to the playground was ajar, the shutters were up and her brother was gone. There was a screech as a Gorilla impacted against the laminated display behind her and a scattering of construction bricks as it fitted on the floor, its spine severed. The bear roared as he mauled his way towards Aimee, but she heard neither this nor the screech, as she sank to sit, legs at a right-angle, on the puce storytelling carpet.

HIGH IN THE GLASSY night were stars. The Witch flew amongst them, casting a shadow as much upwards as down.

Tell it, her mind said, as it so often did but, as ever, it refused to go any further.

"Tell it," she said. Up there, nothing heard her but the alien cold, and that wasn't telling.

Her Dark Tower Block approached and inside, in her room, a cot waited. In her arms lay a toddler, seemingly asleep but strangely listless. The Witch giggled. Her inner child wanted to play with it. Her adult wanted to join in.

Part 3

Chapter 1

THE BEAR HAD FOUGHT like a wild animal. He had shanked to the right, the stench of his pelt following him, and thrashed his claws through the edge of the Gorilla's wings. Thin, ethereal, they'd ripped. The ape had bellowed, not bothering to strike at its chest as it drove at Barnaby, knocking the air from his gut, careening the brown bear back against the wall of the school reception. There had been the intimate sound of glass smashing on his skull and the clean, clinical crinkle of the exposed shards. The ape had grasped Barnaby's head, and the bear had chewed long gashes of grey and black—then red—flesh from its forearm. The Witch's minion hadn't let go, but had pushed the bear's right eye down towards the toothy grin of broken glass. From the corner of his sight, Barnaby had seen a folder with a label reading *Visitors Sign In Here*. His eyes hadn't caught a glimpse of the broken glass, but he'd known it was there, too close, too fuzzy, to be properly seen. It had been as clear in the Gorilla's eyes as pure expectation. Reaching out, Barnaby had taken a fistful of the Gorilla's fairy-wing and, with a final spin, had brought its bulk down via his flank and onto what remained of the window. The ape's head had juddered, but not too much, as it was speared on the glass. The remaining wing had flapped all the more, making a sound more like a death splutter than a death rattle, and then, waspish, had closed around the ape's body as it stilled and became a corpse.

Barnaby hadn't stopped to feed, but had loped down the hallway that separated the reception from the dining room.

At that point, Aimee had run right past him.

AIMEE SANK HOLLOW-mouthed to the floor. There was nothing to say, not now, and no use in her having a tongue to say it. Even her sharp raggedy breathing was nonsense to her, foreign as swearing in Finnish.

"I'm not going to see the wizard. I'm not going to see the wizard," someone was saying. "The wonderful Wizard of Oz."

She realised it was her, that she was singing but brokenly, like the gargoyles' mouths in the playground. The Nursery lights caught her in their luminescence. She existed, the lights maintained. The shadows had sharp edges; they were solid; they were sure. Aimee felt less so. The tables had snapped legs and bowed, dispirited. The sandpaper alphabet had been strewn around. The *i* had gone missing, along with a child. All Aimee could care about was Aidan, but then she'd failed to care for him. The water table was overflowing with blood. The body of a snake had been dumped there. Too weak to rise as it drowned. Its thrashing had sent splash marks to the ceiling. Aimee would've thought it was Angel's guardian, but her head

~282~

was no place for thinking. A line of lava hung from the edge of the magma area, gunging up and down as it spewed onto the tiles. Aimee closed her eyes on her crying, and her eyelids rapidly filled.

PIGLET RAN A TROTTER through his curly hair. The bear lay slumped beside his ward. By the looks of the smashed cabinets and sharded shelving, he'd used the Nursery to fend off the attacks of the three Gorillas that lay against the walls. One was still breathing, though it didn't look like it wanted to be. Barnaby had, Piglet assumed, inserted the Barbie doll into its ribcage.

The small porcine creature wasn't related to the sidekick of Winnie the Pooh. Firstly, he was rather different in appearance, wearing, as he did, a Hawaiian Shirt the colour of a Hawaiian pizza that had been eaten and then vomited. He also wore Y-fronts, disconcertingly stained yellow. Then there were, of course, his habits. Piglet ran his trotter through his hair, lit a cigarette, and wondered what to do next. He was immensely strong, a trait he may or may not have shared with A.A. Milne's creation, as the earlier incarnation never had a fistfight on which to be judged. Piglet, however, had been involved in several, particularly when drunk. Fewer when high.

He dowsed the cigarette in a pool of blood, bent, grasped the bear's right hind leg between his left trotter and his Hawaiian shirt and the girl's red-shoed limb between his right trotter and the same shirt, and began to drag both of them out of the school.

Though he was sweating, it was not lost on Piglet that his strength was quite supernatural. Considering this (and whether or not he should rename himself Superpiglet), he pulled the comatose human and the comatose bear down the steps from the Nursery (the bear's head hitting those steps with a thunk) and decided this was down to his seven-a-day habit. All that masturbation must strengthen the muscles. It stood to reason.

Piglet dragged the bear and girl through the Latter Wood until he reached the Christian's hut. He didn't know where else to take them to recover. He'd considered his own undertree home, but it was an embarrassing mess and not entirely suitable for a young girl and, besides, the Christian had herbs and such like and these would help them heal.

"Bloody… hell." Grunting and snorting, Piglet backed through the door of the hut, jamming it open on its hinges with his hips. With some effort, he hefted the two unconscious creatures onto the table in the centre of the room. The Christian still lay on the floor with incense sticks in his eyes and, caked in flies and a growing clothing of larvae, was beginning to smell.

"Got to do something about that," Piglet muttered to himself. He thought of how, bent and pulled the incense sticks from the corpse's eyes, re-inserted them the right way up, and lit them. The flies thinned.

"Good thinking," he said with appreciation.

Piglet surveyed the hut, hands linked in his Y-fronts. He scratched his genitals and farted. This normally helped him to think, and did the trick this time.

"Ah," he said, when he could be heard over the sound of flatulence.

In a spot on the right of the toilet curtain, there was a bluish white powder, which he'd seen the Christian use to cauterise Barnaby's wounds.

Grasping a trotterful, he approached the bear. "This should bring you round," he said and massaged it into where the bear's pelt was torn.

With a roar that rolled the bear's own eyes, Barnaby sat straight up on the table. His fangs bit into his lower lip as his skin began to steam.

"That worked well," said Piglet. His jaunty tone was on a quite different pitch to the bear's scream.

Barnaby turned to face the piglet. His eyes filled with rage, before they filled with vacancy as he passed out once more and fell back against the table. The hut juddered.

"Maybe not," said Piglet and decided to wait in the toilet. That way, if he thought a lot, he wouldn't make a mess.

THE CABIN DOOR REELED before him with a creak and swung back as Barnaby stumbled onto the porch. It—the door— looked drunk. The bear wiped the back of a paw across his forehead. Under the fur, he felt liquid. Sweat, he realised. On the porch's step sat a piglet who was smoking what looked and smelt to be a joint. The small pig rolled its head back over its shoulders, stared up at the swaying bear and giggled. The piglet seemed to be high.

"Dear Witch, you look like you've been in a beehive," said Piglet.

"Shut up, or I'll step on your neck," said Barnaby. Instead, he sat beside him on the step, which creaked. "Oh my head," he added.

Piglet took a draw and offered it to Barnaby, who shook his head.

"Don't like it," he growled.

"Whitey much?" said Piglet.

Barnaby shrugged, releasing an odour from his armpits that made him wish he'd said, "Whatever," instead.

The small pig smoked in silence before raising the tight nub of light into the night air.

"Have you ever connected all the dots in the sky?" he said, moving the joint erratically across the constellations above them. "See what words they makes? Could be a message. God's shopping list, maybe… Maybe an apology."

Barnaby released a long breath. "Nope," he said at the end of it. "Don't believe in God."

Piglet took a puff. "Doesn't say anything," he said. "Just meaningless scribbles." He giggled, but the sound of it was forlorn.

Barnaby felt like shrugging but didn't, unsure if his head could take it.

The bear sat and the piglet reclined in silence, before Barnaby bent forward and rose. He staggered back through the cabin door and into the gloom that hung about Aimee. She didn't move. She wasn't asleep. He drew himself up to crouch beside her. He touched her forehead, a small, pale slab of meat in the half-light. It was pallid and moist.

"Aimee," he said.

"Time to go home," he said.

His paw stroked down her shoulder to her arm but went no further. He couldn't send her back—not like this.

"I'm sorry Aimee," he said. He held her forearm, careful not to nick her with his claws. She didn't respond and, to fill the silence, he began to softly sing. It was, he knew, one of her favourite songs, and she'd sung it before, many times, just holding Barney.

"Somewhere over the rainbow, way up high," he sang, "there's a land that I heard of, once in a lullaby. Somewhere over the rainbow, skies are blue, and the dreams that you dare to dream, really do come true."

He whistled once, as though a bird, and the hut fell like into silence. Barnaby found he couldn't finish the song and simply sat, holding her arm, instead.

THE RAIN HAD WELLED UP outside until it was a downpour, the forest floor a frothing, rabid place where mud went to drown. Barnaby stood on the dead Christian's porch and watched the rain fall, staring across to the shadows under the laburnum trees at the southern end of the Glade. There, in an unmarked grave, lay the Christian. Barnaby stared some more. The water fell in front of his face, and behind it, through the leaks in a roof that had seen better days. Yesterday, thought Bear. It hadn't been raining yesterday.

He turned (slow because he didn't want to turn) and opened the door to the shack, and he entered the darkness. The dark dribbled, and Bear could see intermittent spots of light in the corners of the room. The leaks were winking and weeping.

Where the rain came in, it quickly left via cracks in the floorboards. The table had been made up into a bed using shredded linen from the Nursery and various articles of unwashed clothing from Piglet's hut. The air didn't smell good and Piglet's Y-fronts probably didn't help, though Barnaby was unwilling to investigate. Aimee didn't seem to care. She shifted uneasily as Barnaby entered the room. She was still awake. The little light that occupied the Christian's hut glowed in her eyes, as it would in a cat's. She was staring at the ceiling. Despite the holes, it was robed in shadow, though that didn't seem to bother Aimee's eyes as she didn't appear to see what was before them. Even here, even in an imaginary world, she was off with the nymphs. She was off with the Witch. Or, more precisely, she was staring, staring, bending her entire sight to see the little boy who had been taken by the Witch, or so the bear guessed. Her baby.

"How are you feeling?" said Barnaby.

As ever, she didn't reply.

He was only glad she still went to the toilet.

"Come on girl," he'd said, in the intervening time. "Up and at them... You won't find your brother this way... You have to go back home to your world... The human mind can't stand this much escapism. You'll go mad."

The words had done little though, bar measuring out the elongating intervals of her disconnection. She'd begun by saying 'no', over and over, before working up to a strange, ashamed, half-choked moan, then to tense shifts of her abdomen, and finally to this—utter catatonia. Barnaby was scared her mind had broken. The darkness and the stench in the hut drew together, thickening like a sauce over heat. The raindrops kept falling, and the cracks in the roof got wider.

After a while, Barnaby could no longer stand in the hut, not even to cuddle her, not even to sing, and left, shutting the door behind him.

"AH, THIS IS THE LIFE," said the Longworm.

"Oh Witch, yes, beautiful weather," said the Notsolongworm, squirming as he did so, happy as a pig in mud. If that pig were a worm, of course.

"Funny, you know, these storms coming."

"Why?" said the Notsolongworm, lying back. If he'd had arms to rest behind his head and elbows to spread to the sides of his ears, he would've used them.

"Well, people say these storms are a bad omen. Like something bad is going to happen."

"You're crazy, Longworm."

The Longworm didn't so much bristle as constrict, and the Notsolongworm remembered the pecking order of things and that worms should respect their elders. After all, he had no way of knowing whether or not he was made from the tail of the Longworm, or his head. That would be embarrassing, he thought.

"I'm sorry," said the Notsolongworm after a pause. "I mean—storms are a good thing. Good things happen when storms happen. Like rain… and… more rain." The Notsolongworm could've been smiling; it was difficult to tell, what with his segments.

"Yes," said the Longworm. "But things aren't the way they used to be. Take birds, for instance. They don't know their place anymore, you know? In the natural scheme of things."

"Peck you to death."

The Longworm nodded absently. "And things are just, you know, *thinning*."

The Notsolongworm sat up with a start. "Yes! Yes! Just the other day I was tunnelling around, only a few feet down, under the Wood, and guess what—"

"You came through the Other Side?"

"Yep," said the Notsolongworm. "The world just came to an end."

"You know why?" said the Longworm, in a tone that indicated he hoped he didn't.

The Notsolongworm shrugged with his lower body.

"Kids," said the Longworm.

"Yes! Pissing on the ground and pretending it's rain. Disgusting."

The Longworm stared at him, his tail curling like a lip. "What? Are you nuts? *No!* Kids don't have belief these days. They don't believe in this world. It's all this liberal teaching, you know. Laissez-faire, and all that. Teaches them to think. I ask you—who wants a thinking kid?"

"I don't even want a talking kid."

The Longworm stared at him, in much the same way as he had before. "They think. They doubt. They don't believe. Next thing that happens, they get all depressed and start figuring out that this world doesn't exist at all. That there isn't that, you know, magic in the air. That worms don't talk."

"That bears don't shit in the Wood."

The Longworm ignored him. "And when they don't believe. Well, let me tell you something about not believing. When you don't believe in something, that something just stops working. You know?"

The Notsolongworm nodded, although really he didn't.

"Enjoy the rain, I say—" said the Longworm. "—while you can. Because it'll be sunny days from now on around here. From now on. You mark my words. Endless bloody sun."

PEOPLE MAKE THE mistake of thinking the countryside is a good place to live. Particularly human people. In reality, it's a rumour-mill and, here, in the Latter Wood, it was doubly so. It ground its inhabitants into their constituent parts, analysed them, and spat them back out. Even the squirrels bitched about each other: who had the most nuts, who had the smallest. And so it was that Piglet knew Bear was still at the Christian's hut.

Not wanting to waste his remaining nicotine (which he was in the middle of smoking), Piglet circled the shack once before turning in to knock on its ashen door. As he approached, he dropped the fag-end into a hole that he quickly realised was a footprint. Piglet stared at it. The footprint didn't move. It sat still, drooling a little at the edges where the rain had gotten in.

"Oh," said Piglet. "You're a footprint."

Perhaps it was the primordial dark at the centre of the Latter Wood, but the print appeared to shrug.

"*What of it?*" Piglet said. "Well… what made it? is the question, and what is what made it made of? is the other question."

Piglet didn't like to ask himself this and so didn't. It sounded complicated.

He traced the footprints. Tracked, he would have said. "Somebody has been walking around the Christian's hut," he said to himself.

He arrived back at the front door. He couldn't help but notice that he was sweating. A line of it ran into his eye, stinging him. The bees on his floral shirt looked frightened. Piglet clutched his penis in order to steady the shaking of his fingers, as he knocked with his other fist.

"Ho hum," he hummed to himself and tried to think about buggery, but nothing came to mind. He knocked again, meaning to do so three times, but doing so seven times in a stutter of a tiny trotter, before the door stopped him by moving.

"Oh Bear," said Piglet. He could've cried out with joy, and took the opportunity to do so. "*Oh Bear!*"

"What is it Piglet?" Barnaby sounded weary.

"Oh Bear. There's a monster in the Wood."

"What kind of monster?" Bear's voice smelt of fish.

"I don't know." He squinted up from behind his sweaty, curly fringe. "But it's got feet," he whispered. "And that type of monster is more dangerous than the ones without feet. Please help me, please," said Piglet, trying to roll a roll-up. He littered the doorstep with tiny abandoned leaves.

"Okay," said Barnaby. He ducked under the door's lintel and stepped out from the light.

"Look, look," said Piglet. He lit his deflated roll-up and proffered the light of it to the ground. The footprint took on a brimstone appearance. "See? See?"

The bear didn't reply.

They circled the hut.

"Oh my God," said Piglet. He stared at Barnaby. The cigarette shivered in his grip, making the light twitch. "There's more of them. Another monster has come."

"Mmmmm," said Barnaby. He was smiling. Piglet could see long fangs. He didn't like them. "So, let me get this straight," said the bear. "You walked around the hut. Then you noticed there were footprints going around the hut. And now, having walked around the hut again, you've spotted another pair of prints."

"Yes," Piglet could barely say it. But he managed and felt proud, so he did it again. "Yes," he said.

"Well Piglet. I think I know exactly what the monster is."

"Oh." Piglet went quiet. His ears tried to draw in. They were open enough, though, to hear the spittle of a mouth trying to chew its own chin—trying ever so hard—and then the parting of leaves.

"It's one of them," Piglet said, pointing a trotter. "It's a Russian Doll."

An aged lady stood where a parting of leaves had been. She went as far sideways as she did tallways, with a dress that was either lilac or mauve. It was hard to tell in the lack of light. Her hands, with fingers that seemed too wide for the knuckles, rested uneasily in front of her girth, as though longing to smoke a cigarette or pick at food. She wheezed at the bear and the small pig and stared through wide, thick glasses with rims the same dishwater colour as her hair. She had the look of a granny dragged backwards through a bush. The thick lenses gave her the impression of tearfulness, but perhaps she was crying, thought Piglet, because her lower lip was hanging by a string of flesh.

"What's wrong with her mouth?" said Piglet.

"Don't speak," said Bear.

"My mouth, dear?" The old lady's mouth sounded perfectly normal for an old lady, despite the lip. She raised a clutch of the thick-girthed fingers up and pushed the lip into the small wet hole above it. "Nothing wrong with my mouth, dear little pig. It tastes quite lovely." She pulled what she had been chewing from between her teeth. The canines were small but overly sharp. The lip had burst, like a salted slug. "Would you like a nibble?" she said.

"No," said Piglet, before he could think: Don't say no.

"Stand behind me," said Barnaby. While Piglet was still thinking 'say', the large brown bear thrust his small pink body to stand shivering behind the crook of a shaggy right knee. Piglet peered around the leg.

"We haven't come for the girl, you know, Bear. We've come for you."

Piglet could see her gum now, as she spoke. She was still sucking on her lip, and it was unravelling into her mouth like the loose end of a sweater. The threads started to eat out her cheek, revealing a juncture of jaw beyond.

The bear lowered for a fight, hunkering his abdomen down, his bottom pressing on Piglet's head. The pig shifted, but not far.

"You can't fight us, Bear. There are so many of us in here. Look."

The granny tore open her dress, then her bra, revealing large breasts that had thinned to insulation above her belly. Using fingers that were already moist from her mouth, she wormed the entire hand into the place where her sternum should have been. The violation made a suckling sound, entirely unlike bone being cracked, even as she jacked her ribcage apart. Inside her chest, Piglet saw faces. They were all grinning and licking their lips. He didn't know how many faces and didn't bother to count, as one of them ripped out its eyes, ate them, and revealed other eyes with different coloured irises directly below. Now Piglet could see why they were called Russian Dolls.

Laughing, the granny said, "I really like this bit. It tastes *scrumptious*," while she ripped flaccid lines from her breast and uncovered, as if by archaeology, a nose. It sniffed and wrinkled around the nostrils, possibly in distaste. The little aged lady gave herself a mastectomy, ate it, and licked the area around where her lips had been. Her teeth looked sharper and longer now.

Barnaby said, "I will fight."

"Okay dear, if that's what you want." She reached into the cave of her chest, which was much larger than a body cavity had any right to be, and tore off a strip of male face inside. "That's my daddy," she said. As she ate his flesh, she ground her teeth. "He always was a bitter little man. Oh don't fret, little pig. You should see what he did to my flesh when I was little."

The bear didn't reply. Piglet was backing away through the puddles, leaving footprints of mud. They looked guilty and as teary as the granny's eyes. His heart was swelling with revulsion.

Chewing nonchalantly, the little old woman, who was now a little less chubby, launched at the bear. Barnaby leant to the side, his right paw branching back, brown and wet and striking at her as she closed in on him. There was the rip of dress and skin as his claws bit in. This didn't seem to help, as a set of arms birthed from the rent wounds. There was no blood, but the old woman was sprouting limbs, and they grappled around the bear's pelt. Roaring in pain, the bear started to do what the woman did not—to bleed. He went to the wet forest floor, sending out rainwater and blood in fronds. Piglet's feet were noiseless in the trotterprints they made. He could hear his own breathing. He could hear the bear's screaming. He could hear the sound of the granny chattering, like she was discussing the weather or bingo, and more mouths clamped down on the bear, taking parts of him.

Barnaby was losing, both his hide and the fight. His left arm flailed and tore away an arm that had emerged from the overhang of the Doll's right flank. It was replaced by another—this one suited in black. A gentleman's liver-spotted hand pinched at the bear.

"Don't worry, Daddy," said the granny, referring to the disconnected arm or so Piglet supposed. "I'll eat you later."

"No," said Piglet, forgetting his promise not to talk. He was trying to get to, "This can't happen," but only reached, "No," before he ran. He wheeled away, and the water of the puddles cartwheeled behind his trotters. He ran and, in running, his heart swelled and yammered until the organ felt not only bigger than his chest, but bigger than he deserved. He was a coward. On a rise, folded up from the forest floor, in between drifts of fallen laburnum pods, Piglet fell. He crawled into the roots of an old tree.

Piglet didn't know what to do, in which way to express his shock. He tried to masturbate with his right arm, to smoke with his left, but the cigarette wouldn't light and what little hard-on he could muster quickly went out.

He opened his eyes, looking back to where the Christian's hut sat silent in the quiet of the Latter Wood. The animals and insects were too busy staring at him—judgementally—to chirrup or cicada or even talk.

Piglet closed his eyes. It seemed his only option. Shivering and weeping and changing the mud and rainwater and rotting vegetation not at all, the small pig fell into sleep, unconsciousness taking him up in mawkish, felt, black wings, not unlike the colour of depression.

Not long into the sensation of falling, Piglet dreamt a dream. It was of a little girl. Not very pretty, she looked as though she might have a slow mind. She had skin the colour of the pale mud he was lying in and lips smeared with yellow, as though she'd been chewing on the tree above Piglet. She was asleep.

IT WAS ONE OF THOSE times when the Other Place was not a dream, but was dreaming. The Latter Wood lulled. The wind couldn't get up the huff to wave so much as a leaf. The wolf packs in the cold north couldn't get up the huff to go hunting. Even the trees sagged.

Below the shade of one such laburnum, a worm decided that he would do less wriggling and have an afternoon nap. It seemed like a good time for this, it being the afternoon. Lying in a frown of furrowed earth, the Notsolongworm dreamt of flying. He'd done this for as long as he could remember, though the Longworm always seemed disappointed he didn't dream of sailing. Worms were supposed to have aspirations towards the wet and not towards the high but, for the Notsolongworm, flying had always been his secret thing.

He dreamt he had wings.

It was always the same dream.

He soared amidst the clouds. He dipped and watched the Latter Wood drift below him like a jaundiced sea. He jacked to the left, swooped, and, exhilarated, entered the cave-like bosom of the wood, flitting between branches. This was normally where the dream ended. Not this afternoon. The Notsolongworm would have smiled in his sleep, if he'd had lips. He swooped, and would have whooped, if he'd had the mouth for it.

There was something pink and wet on the earth. In his slumber, the pink wet thing fascinated the Notsolongworm, so he landed and pecked at it.

Why, isn't that fascinating? he thought, at the same time as thinking, Pecked? And at the same time as thinking, Ow!

The Notsolongworm woke as he was hoisted from the groove of soil. He dangled from the mouth of the bird he'd always dreamt of being. It certainly had the wings. It also had a beak.

At that moment, the bird was hit from the side by what appeared to be a cat. Whatever it was had fur and fangs, and moved at speed. The bird sent up a plumage of unattached feathers that took some time to settle back onto the forest floor, and the Notsolongworm was dropped instantly onto the muck. He lay on it, shivering, until the Longworm poked through it.

"I just dreamt I was a bird—" the Notsolongworm said, his voice shivering with his body, "—and woke up to find myself eating myself."

"You dolt," said the Longworm. "Do what I do. I dreamt I was a wildcat. I always wondered what bird tastes like." He paused, as though considering, and then said, "Satisfying."

Above them, the laburnum tree woke from a dream in which it had been felled, pulped and turned into a sketchpad. On its first page, a child had crayoned a picture of several trees together, coloured it in yellow, and labelled it *The Latter Wood*. While this was, to say the least, disconcerting for a tree, when the laburnum woke, it felt as though it had a new lease of life. To celebrate this, it—daringly—grew an extra millimetre that year.

MR HIM WOKE.

His arm rifled pain into his shoulder. He growled and rolled onto his side. His neck muscles clenched and sank nails of agony into his spine.

"Argggh," said Mr Him and rose to his knees. He didn't know how long he'd been knocked out by the blast, but his tongue was a landed fish that had swollen with rot.

The disabled toilet, gaping before him, was thoroughly broken, and Mr Him's body knew how it felt. On the floor, Sunshine lay beside him. She smelt of old urine but breathed. Mr Him slapped her. She didn't move, apart from her pale chin, which went sideways and red. He slapped her harder.

"Wake the fuck up," he shouted.

He staggered to his feet, pulled Sunshine to hers, and dragged her through the entrance to the toilet. Its back wall had been exploded open, revealing a cave beyond and, at the edge of his sight, the gloaming of the cave's opening. Cursing, wiping a jacket arm that was white (with dust) and not the tweedy green it had been, Mr Him stumbled into the toilet and, from there, into the cave, pulling the girl after him.

IF IT HADN'T BEEN for the sound of his swearing, she wouldn't have woken. Even in the sleep of unconsciousness, the teacher in her kicked, like a baby in the womb.

"How dare you?" Mrs Her croaked. "Stand up. Right now." Her tongue cracked across its skin and felt as though it had been snapped in two. She shifted, and half a toilet door slid from her prostrate form. Her hair, a tangle at the most combed of times, was now a cloth that had been used as a duster. Her beard had at least an additional day's growth to it. Flattening her hand to the floor and feeling loose pins and screws and splinters prick it, she pushed herself up. Unable to stop herself, Mrs Her coughed, hacked and spat on the floor, and stared first at the gruel and then at her front. She found herself quite disagreeable.

After this, she turned her head to stare between her fringe and the blasted jambs. There, in the distance, she saw the jacketed back of a man she found even less agreeable. She spat again, despite being a teacher and despite being in school, and followed Mr Him.

AIMEE WAS ASLEEP, finally, and dreaming.

She was in the dark, and shadows made a deeper pitch of shards at the edge of her vision. She wasn't herself. Whoever and wherever she was, she was moving. Gradually, a faded duskish mouth of grey appeared. There was a shadow shifting across it and weaving, like a hairy tongue. Aimee realised she was following another person. The silhouette stopped at the entrance to the cave and snuffled and ran its right arm across its nose. There was the sound of a slight slickage of mucus being wiped across tweed. The silhouette was dragging a girl, as her mum would drag Amy away from school.

Mr Him, she thought, as slow as treacle might think, if it were dreaming.

Her field of vision was still on the move, though it wasn't a field but, rather, a cave. In the nooks and niches and darkest places of the cavern, arachnids could be heard, the hairy crackle, here and there, of a giant spider leaning forward, the chord of thick saliva drawn fang-to-fang. Aimee tried to ignore this and managed to do so, possibly because she wasn't her and was, in the dreaming, somebody else entirely. She was taller, of that Aimee could be sure. And she had a beard.

Mrs Her, she thought.

Mr Him left the cavern, hunched as though against the sudden onset of wind. In the dream, Aimee followed. By the jagged lines of her strides, Mrs Her was very angry indeed. As she rose into the Latter Wood at the end of the cave, her vision blurred and Aimee woke up.

On a table.

Linen spread down from her chin.

The smell of herself filled the hut.

She had the aching, pressed cheek of being in the same position for a long time. The cramped fingers. The desiccated throat. The dried lines of mucus around her eyes, from where she'd been crying in her sleep. The chapped, flaked nose. The caked lips.

It was then she realised she was no longer asleep, no longer wearing her lilac dress, no longer pale-skinned.

"Where am I?" she said.

She was lying on a table in the Christian's hut. In the silver plates he'd offered to someone's ancestors, she saw herself. She didn't look like Aimee anymore. She looked like Amy.

IN HIS DREAM, A BLONDE-haired woman sat on the bed, pinning one of Piglet's hands. Yes, he thought, *hands*. She had the look of the Witch, but skinnier.

The beautiful woman methodically drew his pinned arm from the linen, as though drawing a tapeworm.

"Look," the woman said to somebody Piglet couldn't see. "Look at the fingers. Yellow. Fucking yellow. She's been eating that poisonous tree. That's why she won't wake up."

From the side of the bed came a shifting sound of awkwardness, but only silence from the mouth of the man who stood there. Piglet could tell it was a man without looking. The woman gave him such a look of contempt.

"Cat got your tongue? Aye, useless bastard. That's the best thing you've said today."

"Whatever."

The woman's eyes narrowed, concentrating their scorn, which seemed too much for the slits to hold and escaped into a curling of her lips.

This, thought Piglet, could be the Witch's skinny twin.

The woman's eyes wavered. "Aye, and on her teeth. Look. Fucking look."

The plumage of the dream was fading, feather by feather, into the hues of the forest and Piglet woke.

A girl was walking towards him, up the folded curve of mud. At first, wiping his trotters across his eyes, Piglet thought it was Aimee but, in the next second, knew it was as different from her as the woman in the dream was from the Witch. Which was to say, not much at all. The girl wasn't wearing Aimee's dress. The dress she wore was blue not lilac, had legs, and appeared to be cut from denim. Her stride, also, was not sprightly now but haphazard, like a ghost that had forgotten, thanks to the intervention of death, how its limbs were supposed to work. Aimee's skin tone, once pale as a princess's in a fairy tale, was now beige and had a touch of the gypsy.

Moreover, thought Piglet, mind as bleary as his eyes, Aimee was pretty.

"Piglet," said the girl.

At least she knows me, thought the little pig.

"She took Barnaby. The Witch did."

This didn't seem to be a question, and Piglet decided to stare at it and the girl until they both went away.

"We're going to get him back. Him and my baby. You don't need to worry, Piglet. The Witch won't hurt us. She can't. This world isn't real. And I'm not Aimee."

Piglet tried to voice a sentence, but it stuck in his mouth. He hacked and spat a thin line of saliva into a handy puddle. "Who are you?" he said.

"Amy," the girl said.

Piglet frowned, but the girl walked past him. Paying no attention to his facial expression, she rose to the crest of the hillock. Piglet's elbows and shoulders creaked as he went to join her. He felt old.

"What do you mean, this world isn't real? Am I still dreaming?"

The girl turned to stare at him. "You knew?" she said.

Piglet blinked. He opened his mouth, but the girl put a tanned finger to her lips and pointed down into the dale below them. At its far side, a human scrambled up the bluff, sending out small exclamations of dirt and cursing insects. He was dragging a little girl. He stopped, snuffled, wiped his nose with the tweed arm of his dust-hued jacket, braced as though a gale were building, and continued to the peak of the next rise before disappearing over it. Strangely, it wasn't windy in the least.

"Strange," said Piglet. "I was just dreaming about him… and him." A giant of a bearded man followed, crouching and hustling from tree to tree, from bush to bush.

"That's a her," said Amy. "Mrs Her. Nothing is what it looks like it appears to be, and fewer things are what they seem," she added in a whisper.

With that, she followed them. Shrugging what little he had in the way of shoulders, Piglet followed the girl.

Chapter 2

THEY WALKED NORTH and the Latter Wood, as woods do in this hemisphere, grew colder. Between the trees, when the land rose, could be seen the hills at the northern rim of the world. The horizon. The hills were as big as mountains but rolling, and under them, like a snowstorm turned on its head, could be seen the Under Hill. And in its darkness, hanging upside-down from the concave curve, was the Dark Tower Block where the Witch lived.

Amy preferred it when the land was hillier and the trees tighter or hanging with the yellow confetti of their pods, because the sight of the Witch's home, hanging illogically as it did from the inside of a hill, made her mind ache.

They didn't creep, but they made no noise. There was little noise in this part of the forest to make. It was as frozen as a realm could be, from top to bottom. The trees were encrusted in so much rime that every bough looked identical. The pods that hung in chandeliers couldn't so much as twinkle, so fixed with frost were they. Besides which, when they travel, a piglet and a young girl travel quietly without trying. The fully-grown teacher before them, shuffling along the path, made more sound than they did.

So did Mrs Her, but Mr Him didn't notice. He seemed intent on the horizon, his feet in a hurry to get past each other. He stumbled as he came close to a run. The path of the forest they followed bent and curved into a dale so that the Under Hill was no longer visible, and they—Mr Him, Sunshine, Mrs Her, Piglet and Amy—tripped over small streams that had become popsicles of green, trip-trapped and tripped over slippery wooden bridges and, eventually, walked along a road that seemed, in the twilight, so sallow it was almost yellow. The light level in the north of the Latter Wood was always night. The snow, though, shone.

The road had sprung up in the northern eaves of the Latter Wood like, Amy could imagine Uncle Chris saying, a line of piss, and it led to what seemed, from glances through the flora, to be snow-laden roofs. Even below the white and in the dusk, the tiles of the roofs were visible like buried bodies, red and vibrant as blood, and, as they came into view, the houses beneath them were built of mortar and brick as buttery as the colour of the road under their feet.

"The Chocolate Box Village," said Piglet to himself but a little too loudly, so it reached Amy.

"I know," she said. "I copied it from a box of chocolates."

It wasn't only chocolate. The roofs, closer up, were sculpted of jelly and oscillated in a wind Amy couldn't feel. The walls were made of marzipan. The well at the village's centre was fudge-cake bricked. The trees that avenued it were Black Forest gateau. From the well led a length of chain, at the end of which was something that was not, by all measures, confectionary: a lump of pelted flesh, fur that scarcely covered its skin, and skin that didn't cover the wounds that had been dug into it.

"Barnaby," said Amy, but Piglet grasped her hand. They held each other, fingers to trotter.

There was a click and a catch of flame on wick, and Mr Him hurried out into the village, bearing a bell that swung as though excited. It clanked as Mr Him licked his lips. In his free hand, he held Sunshine by the hair. He didn't so much smile as grimace with expectation as he rang the bell.

As one, the houses in the village sang, "Ding! Dong!"

The male teacher laughed—short, guttural breaths floating away in clouds of grey vapour. He rang again.

"Ding! Dong!" the houses in the village repeated and, like strippers from a score of birthday cakes, children burst from their doors.

They were singing.

"Ding, dong!"

Then the other side of the village: "Ding, dong!"

Then as one: "Wake up your stupid head, ding, dong."

The children were naked. Amy didn't like to look, and didn't like herself much once she had.

"The bear is dead," they sang. "Wake up your stupid head, the bastard bear is dead."

The bear, though, was not—not yet. Barnaby tried to rise, bloodied at the umbilical end of the chain, then collapsed back to the earth. There was a splatter of loose fur falling with him.

Mr Him rang the bell, and the children danced. Even from the distance of the bluff behind which she and Piglet hid, Amy could tell the children's eyes were as blank as the glazing in the village windows, smiles as contorted as the melted treacle down the side of the doors. In one of the many books she'd read, she remembered a breed of dogs called Pavlovs, who salivated when a bell was rung: dogs that did whatever a scientist wanted them to do. These were Mr Him's Pavlovs.

"Ding, dong, wake up your stupid head. Ding, dong, the bear is dead."

Piglet said, "They're baiting him."

Amy didn't need to be told. The children were kicking and punching the broken-furred bear, and then withdrawing as Barnaby slashed out with his claws. The bear was rapidly tiring. At their provocation, something other than his skin appeared to be tearing. The children's skin was already torn.

Mr Him was giggling.

Reddening, Amy rose with her blood. She couldn't see her bear suffer.

Piglet dragged at her arm, and she turned to push him away from her.

"Look," he said, pointing a trotter.

Amy wasn't alone. Mrs Her had also risen and was striding out across the first few tiffin cobbles of the village square. Her footsteps didn't appear to be stalking anymore.

For some reason, Amy remembered Mr Him saying, "The things you feel will one day lift houses off the ground. Whole houses clean off the ground."

"Ding!"

The bell faltered in Mr Him's hand. It clanked.

"Dang!"

There was a crack, like the creak of a house in deep midwinter when frost works into the rendering, but deeper and more integral. Jelly took to the air, then marzipan, then chocolate, then the tiffin cobbles.

One of the houses rose.

Mrs Her fell to her right knee, cracking a perfectly good tiffin.

Mr Him didn't so much speak as squeak, and he flung himself to the side, away from the bell. The airborne house spun once as though caught in a hurricane, and then shattered against the village square. The chocolate mortar was more substantial than it looked. Three children who had been staring up at it disappeared beneath its impact.

"What did you do to them?" Mrs Her shouted. "You were their teacher."

Without the bell, the children didn't dance.

Mr Him did, dodging away as Mrs Her brought another house to the sky. Blood fell in lines from her bottom lip. She tried to shout, but couldn't. From her books on anatomy, Amy thought: collapsed lung. And then she stopped thinking and ran. She bore down the slope with Piglet at her heels. She could hear his trotters.

As she neared, there was a crack that wasn't made by shortbread crumbling, but that came from the area of Mrs Her's spine. She collapsed as all the remaining houses were torn from their foundations of cake mix. A hurricane would've been proud.

Amy crouched at Barnaby's side, pulling and tugging and hefting at the iron collar at his throat.

"No," she said desperately. She looked at the sky.

Mr Him was doing the same. There was a score of houses flung high, but not for long. The village outskirts were too far away to reach in time. Mr Him's eyes fell on the well.

He loped towards it, pulling Sunshine with him. She screamed and began to struggle.

A house smashed down two feet behind Amy's knees. She and the bear were covered in a thin filigree of sugared dust.

Mr Him jumped, looking for his all his whiskers and pale skin like a rabbit about to enter its hole and escape the fox. The moment ended abruptly when Piglet hit him from the side. Mr Him let go of Sunshine and she rolled away to freedom, where a house landed on her.

"Barnaby," said Amy in a shout. "I'm sorry. I'm sorry it took me so long to come. I was scared."

He looked up at her, his eyes darker than before with pain and shock and the abnegation of what'd been done to him by children.

She looked away and ran to where the chain was attached to the well. Amy closed her eyes and remembered what the children had done to her bear; there was a whistling sound, like pretend wind through pursed lips, and the fudge brick that the metal was nailed to cracked, rose into the air, and flopped down the well. Amy wrapped the end of the chain around her forearm and tugged at Barnaby. "Quick," she said. "Into the well."

The children stood still, like plastic soldiers, falling one after another under the houses.

"I can't," he said, and she saw that he'd lost too much blood, on too many occasions.

Moved by a feeling she didn't understand, Amy gripped his pelt in a hug and felt something she'd only ever felt in her bed when she was cuddling her teddy bear. It was pure as sunlight in a mountain spring. With a sound like a leech being flattened, the wounds closed.

Barnaby's snout moved. It may have been a nod but, whatever it was, it was enough. They jumped at the well and, as the darkness of the falling baked masonry impacted about them, they entered the tight circle of its darkness.

PIGLET HUNG ONTO MR Him's shirt-tails. There was a rip, but not long enough to sever the material.

"You-you-you—" Mr Him said. He couldn't move. The piglet was incredibly strong.

"Little pig?" Piglet offered, though he knew you should never complete a stammerer's sentence. Looking up, Piglet said, "Oh, you cun—" but the collapsing house ended his word, his sentence, him, and Mr Him all at once.

THE BRICKS OF THE WELL hared by and passed into the light above Amy. The light dwindled, and all the quicker because she couldn't help but look down. They fell improbably fast. Not at an impossible speed, of course, but only possible if you were a light wave. Everything was a blur, and that included herself and the bear. They stretched out, spaghetti-ing—even their eyes.

Amy was sure she could, at one point, see her own irises. They plummeted straight down, then straight sideways, and then vertically once more, though Amy couldn't tell if this was down again. The well seemed to have no end until, abruptly, Barnaby came to a halt and Aimee slammed into his back. He shifted in a jolt.

"Wha—?" said Amy.

"I'm stuck," growled the bear. Imperceptibly, like a trick of the light, the well shaft had narrowed and Barnaby was wedged within it. Amy twisted her head around and craned her neck. The grey gloaming far above appeared to wink.

"We'll climb back up," said Amy. She didn't like the feel of where this hole was leading. There was a nasty smell rising from below her and it wasn't the bear, or at least, it wasn't just the bear.

"Okay," said Barnaby, stretching his paw up towards a protruding brick. In a nauseating, grinding moment, the teeth in the gears of time seemed to stick and then roll forwards, as the bear resumed his downward slide. Screaming, Amy followed him, the chain between them stretching out until it became taut. Her screams ceased only as they hit the water, which enveloped both bear and little girl. She spluttered and gagged and spat into the mirk. The liquid tasted of urine and faeces and the rot that would congeal between both if they were left together alone and for long enough. The smell would have been appalling if there'd been room in the girl's mind to be appalled. As it was, she was drowning and the screaming had restarted, if only inside her mind. In the dark, she got turned around and couldn't locate which way was down and, more importantly, which way was up. She bumped against Barnaby and couldn't get past him. She felt sure he was blocking the passage to air. Her lungs shivered in the convulsions of the dying. The fits were spreading. Her chest, her arms, her hands. She clawed at the bear's back, forgetting that he was her friend. Searching, searching for what she'd taken for granted. Air. Her lungs pancaked and burnt and separated into long grasping fingers. It was all she could do to keep her mouth closed. Her throat panicked and tried to get through her lips. She broke the surface.

She gasped and took in oxygen. The well was lighter than she remembered, and it pained her eyes. Below her, the miasma of water was greyed by the imprint of the light source above. The sun. It shouldn't be—not above her, and not lit. It was dusk and, with the directions she had travelled in the well, that way couldn't be up. In her experience, everything she saw was nonsense. She shook her head. In the liquid, she could see the bear desperately stretching. He was still stuck. In the water, as through a lens, his form was fattened. His eyes bulged until they were black as the eyes of a shark.

The chain was still in her palm, and she tightened her fingers and, pinioning her slight frame between the well's wet walls, pulled. Barnaby didn't move. Gritting her teeth on her bottom lip until it bled, she did this again, and Barnaby's snout came through the liquid. He snuffed and sniffed. With another effort, she brought forth his head. The bear, though, would budge no further.

"I'm stuck again," he said unnecessarily.

"Yes, you are," said Amy. She was breathing hard and dripping. "I'm wet," she added. Then, "It smells like pee and poo in here."

After a moment, Barnaby said, "We *are* in a toilet."

Amy stared at him and then, shifting, she gazed up the well. Above her was the sun. It was hard and unblinking. In between her and it there was a bulge of white china, and the impression of a rim of black plastic.

"We *are* in a toilet," said Amy.

"Climb up and flush it," said Barnaby. "I'll be able to get free. The wee is slippy."

Amy nodded. With an effort of cold and wet limbs and gagging, puling lungs, she crabbed, feet on one wall, back on the other, up the shaft. Two lines of bricks up, and one slipping downward, she eventually made the shining white bowl. The toilet, thankfully, had no U-bend. She drew herself from the toilet and out onto an encrusted, hard desert floor. Her mind swam and spun. For a moment, she felt as disorientated as she had been in the latrine below, before she realised that the toilet faced sideways not up, and that where the sky should've been, there was a jagged landscape of broken mountains and spikes of leaf-shorn pines. The ground she lay upon was concave and, she realised slowly, the ceiling of a giant cave. With a mental spasm, she said, "I'm in the Under Hill."

The sun she had seen was visible in the arch of sky between the hill's ceiling and floor. It was setting, though by this Amy thought she meant it was reddening, as it didn't really have anywhere to set and could only stay framed in a bell curve of space, going gradually black. It wasn't alone. Also as dark as black could be, and still some way off, stood the Witch's home. The Dark Tower Block. As the sun went crimson, the tower block's electric-sallow lights were going on, one-by-one.

Amy turned and puked on the cave's ceiling. Part of what forced it up was the smell on her skin and on her browned dungarees. Part was the disorientation of the landscape. What came up was mostly pale water with a little bile.

"Amy!" the toilet shouted.

"Barnaby," said the girl through beige lips, remembering. She crawled across to the sideways toilet and yanked at its chain.

THE BEAR STOOD BESIDE her, dribbling onto the brown lily pads of the caked desert floor. He sounded like the end of a shower or the sputter of her mother peeing into the toilet next to a bath Amy was taking. Behind them, the latrine was broken, ruptured by the bear's passing out of it.

"This is the Witch's kingdom. The Russian Dolls must've brought the children here through that toilet in the school and the well. It's good that night is coming," Barnaby said. "It'll be harder for the Witch's winged monkeys to see us."

"For God's sake. They aren't monkeys—they're bloody Gorillas," said Amy, surprising herself by how like her mother she sounded. It must be swallowing all that shit, thought Amy. Barnaby turned to look at the girl. Once, she would've been scared of him eating her. Now she thought she was too bitter to swallow, and not just because of the faeces that coated her skin. At some point, she'd forgotten how to care about anything but her baby.

"We're going there, you know," said Barnaby. His voice was low and small, eroded as the dunes around them.

Amy nodded and started to walk toward the Dark Tower Block. She could hear him following.

NIGHT TURNED TO DAY and day turned to night and back again, as though all the sun had to do was change its clothes. The cold then the sun beat down upon Amy and the bear, and the space between the toilet and the tower block seemed to take on a dimension that was not entirely that of distance. Sweat washed Amy's forehead and mingled with the odours in her armpits. There were times when she didn't know where she was, and others when she wished she didn't. They hurried from sand ridge to sand dune, to compacted bluffs of hard brown earth. From time to time, the cries of Gorillas filled the Under Hill, sounding for all This World like children tortured until they were mad. Then, Amy and the bear would crawl, or stop, cowering smudges of brown in a beige landscape. The Gorillas couldn't circle though. The ones they saw flew lopsidedly, with tattered or thoroughly torn wings, and could barely manage an oval of flight before screaming and retreating. They didn't seem able to face the bear again.

At other times, dehydrated and exhausted, Amy thought she would fall then she looked up and, seeing the spined, jagged ceiling, wondered which way falling would be. This brought her round, and quickly. She stumbled, often at the end of the chain that was still attached to the bear as though he were a dog on his leash. She stumbled as though in a daze and...

... AMY OPENED HER eyes. Her eyelids cleared, stretching several days of gunge between them. The yellows and whites in her sight coalesced and she realised she was looking at the ceiling and walls in her bedroom at 4 Anstil Place. "No," she said and squeezed her eyes shut and fell asleep again...

... "I'M WAKING UP," she said to the bear. Her lips were frazzled. She tried to scream and managed a whisper, "I'm waking up."

Barnaby was holding her.

"Don't hold me, don't hold my hand."

"You have to go now, but you'll come back to where I am. I'll make it for you. I'll reach the tower. I'll carry you."

Amy's voice cracked. "LET GO OF MY HAND."...

... HER FEET SCATTERED left and right as she went down the stairs. She reached the door and turned its handle, entering the porch. She reached its door and turned that handle. She was dressed only in the skin of her pyjamas and was barefoot. She walked out onto the path, then the pavement, then the road. No one, it seemed, heard her go.

"No," she said, to no one in particular. Perhaps to this world. "Can't wake up."

She was walking the other way from her Day School, through a tight green-fenced walkway and across another road.

A car's beep turned into a beeeeeeeeep, but she didn't hear it. Her hand closed around the paw of a teddy bear that wasn't there. She walked across grass. The thin green leaves of it plucked at the spaces between her toes and wiped moisture across her soles. The grass went away as she walked onto the squidgy black tarmac of a children's play area. As she approached the slide, she collapsed...

... SHE LOOKED SIDEWAYS, which was the natural way for her to look given that she was lying on her side. Hard-baked sand nibbled at her cheeks. The sun was a basketball of orange repeatedly bounced into her eyes.

"Leave, girl, you can't walk. You can hear me. Leave. Wake up in your world. I'm not at the tower yet. Wake up!"

She did...

... SHE WAS IN MALE arms. The groove of poorly formed biceps was unmistakable. Sometimes on the way home from the local, Uncle Chris would carry her from the car. Then, the sound was the same as the one she could hear now. Feet, heavier than they were used to being, on gravel. This time though, there was no turning of a key in the door, but a pressing on a doorbell that didn't work, followed by a knocking.

The door opened.

"Amy," said her mum.

"I found her in the park."

Her mum grabbed her from the stranger's arms.

The man continued, "She'd collapsed. Right by the slide, love."

"What the hell were you doing there? Stupid child!" said her mum. Shock made her sound younger than she was. The same age as the woman in the Polaroid.

"Is she alright?" said the stranger-man. His voice was an unrecognisable blur, not unlike his face. "She looks ill. Her lips are yellow."

"Aye," her mother sounded older. The words were shorter. Bent out of shape. "She's fine."

"Does she need to see a doctor love?"

"Mind your own," said her mum.

Amy could've told him to stop there. To stand very still. To avoid eye contact. To nod when necessary, but not too much. Amy could've been full of useful advice.

The man, however, said, "Look, do you want me to call a doctor? The kid looks really ill."

Her mum: "What's it to you, eh? What were you doing hanging around the park, anyways? Looking at little girls? What are you? A paedo?"

"Okay, love, okay—"

"Don't you fucking 'love' me. You fucking paedo."

He was backing away. Amy could almost hear him glancing at the other houses in the street.

"Okay, okay," he said, though the tone in his words said it wasn't.

Her mum slammed the door and threw Amy against the stairs. Through the fog of her body, pain reverberated like the echo of a yell. Her mum was standing over her, slapping her. Something was digging into her cheek. It may have been a step. It may have been her mum's nails. Mum was swearing, but the world was whining like a bomb about to go off.

Her mum was dragging her up the stairs.

SHE CAME ROUND IN front of the Dark Tower Block. It was dusk.

They arrived, in a short time, at a door with a gate in it and an intercom on that. Barnaby pressed the button labelled *In* in orange and taped on with sellotape that had long since gone beige in the middle and brown at its tattered edges. The gate and the door and the intercom were all graffitied with synonyms for 'whore', and one line that read *Needless to say I hate you*. There was a scrawl on the door, which said *If there are any problems with vandals please call 078837384992 and she'll give you good head, the dirty bitch.*

"Yes—" said a voice from the intercom. It was shot through with static, or with bile—Amy couldn't tell.

"I need to come in," said Barnaby.

"No."

"I have a little girl with me." Barnaby raised his chain to the door's window and, by extension, Amy.

A pause, in the background of which Amy thought she heard screaming. It couldn't possibly have been, of course; it went on for far too long.

Above the door, the Dark Tower Block loomed and beyond it the sun, under the hill. The sunset had almost set. The sky was turning necrotic, and bits of it had the look of wanting to fall off.

"Yes," said the intercom.

The door opened. Within its foyer, the Dark Tower Block was incongruously well lit.

UNDER THE BARE electric lights that went up the stairwell, the floor tiles of the Dark Tower Block were not black and white, but black and blue and shiny as shiners. There was blood in puddles around the blues, and the blacks seemed slightly swollen. The lights fizzled, but did so slowly.

Amy followed Barnaby. Her skin shivered in lumps and tried to migrate around to her back. All of the doors to the flats on the ground floor were open. There were too many of them for the floor plan, and each held the sound of fingers on keyboards, incessant as rabbits on their greens. In one, she saw a figure hunched over a screen. He was malnourished—more wraith than human—and whatever he watched was doing the screaming she'd heard earlier. Somehow, the sound had not yet stopped. Three bottles of unlabelled pop stood opened by his chair. The pop was a dark rusted yellow. Amy thought she saw children in the computer screens.

There was a click and the monitors switched off. The inhabitants of the flats began to scream in chorus. The one she could see turned. His eyes were big and square and vacant as the screen haloing them. His cheeks were bones, his fingers seemed to hang from his knuckles. He was naked. The door modestly swung shut, clipping his scream like a belt around the ear. All the other doors did the same.

"This doesn't look good," said Barnaby. He looked at Amy. There was a patch of desiccation in the wetness of his gaze. Whatever was the opposite of a glint, she thought.

The lights fizzled out, and the squares went all black.

Then all white, as the electricity came back on.

"Oh," said Barnaby.

A Russian Doll stood before them.

"Hello little girl, have you got a smile for your granny?"

There was a grinding creak as the Russian Doll bent down, as though ligaments gnashed within her knees. "Oh you smell nice, Little Fart. I bet you'd be good for the eating."

There was a moan, despairing and low. It didn't come from Amy's oesophagus though, but from the bear's.

"Oh dear, the bear knows he can't save you." The Doll wasn't looking at Barnaby, but at Amy. Her puffy flesh moved and shifted and wrinkled like a pie made from game that were still up for a fight. "The last time we met in a knockdown scrap, I knocked him out. The Witch told me to knock him out, you know. Then, you know what she said? She said, "Eat him." "Teddy bears taste yummy," she told me. But I prefer little girls. They're lip-smackingly good." The Doll illustrated her words. A slight line of spittle landed on Amy's chest. The gunge was thick and lime green and reminded her of a witch's finger. She couldn't move to wipe it off and it lay there, as cold as her mum's skin at night.

"Really," said the bear. "How do you know what bear flesh tastes like? It might taste better."

Barnaby held up his right arm, its pelt blistered by the sun. He put one of his claws in a wound. He ripped it open and staggered, his face mesmerised by the pain, to the edge of the foyer. A blue electric light hissed and fizzled next to his head. The Doll made a sniffing sound beneath its skin. It seemed to smell things the girl could not. Bear blood wet the floor tiles, coloured pink on the blacks and crimson on the blues. It sprayed as Barnaby punched the light's housing. The light fell into smithereens. The wiring hissed and sparked by the bear's ear.

"What is it doing?" said the Doll. In its abdomen, Amy could hear the question repeated. The Dolls inside were becoming curious. There was a ripping sound as one of them put its nose through the granny's solar plexus.

It sniffed.

Barnaby put his bleeding, pussing right arm into the electric wiring, and his bulk jerked. He was lifted onto the claws of his feet. There was a scorched aroma of charcoaling bear flesh misting into the foyer. Amy could hear Barnaby's fangs clenching, chattering. He couldn't let go. The Doll licked its teeth and more molars appeared through its cheek, nibbling in an ecstasy of hunger at its flesh. Saliva dribbled around the edges of the Doll's chin.

"Oh that smells so good. So very good."

It smelt to Amy like gammon frying.

The granny brushed past her. Amy retched but couldn't open her mouth. (A head that had emerged from the Russian Doll's torso snapped, trying to taste her, but missed.)

The Doll reached the bear and sank its teeth in. Half a doll had emerged from its belly and did the same to Barnaby's thigh. As contact was made, the Doll jerked and writhed against Barnaby's pelt as electricity passed from skin to teeth. That didn't stop the ripping sound of more of the mouths joining in.

Amy ran to the stairs. Amy fell. Her skin barked on the lip of a step. The concrete felt like a long tooth. Blood seeped onto the step, across it, then up the next, and along that. Abruptly, the cut began to drip upwards, falling up the stairs' shaft and disappearing into darkness beyond the electric lights. Amy's eyes followed it, her head tilting upwards. With her teeth, she ripped off a line of her dungarees. She spat it out before her, across the beginnings of the stairs. Soft as feather, the denim began to float upwards with the blood. She stretched out her hand and it twisted the same way, as though gravity had been reversed. Her mind hurt more than her shin.

Somewhere up above, she heard a child's cry.

Or is it down below? she wondered.

"Aidan," she said.

She couldn't step onto the stairs.

"Shut it, you little brat," the Witch shouted above her in the darkness. There was the slamming of a door, and Aidan shut up.

Amy ran around the base of the stairs. She stared at the space under the steps. With a stretch of legs like a gymnast, she strode out onto the underneath of the stairs. She stood there, bent foetal so she could fit. Above her—now—were the black and blue tiles. Upside-down, she ascended, walking round and round the central shaft on the underneath of the steps.

AMY, STANDING ON THE ceiling of the landing, had to jump to reach the button of the lift. It lit as she hit it but, instead of the rumble of the gear mechanism and shafts spinning into action, there was only a sound of laughter. It rumbled. Laughs surrounded her, behind the wall, not only of the lift doors but also that of the central shaft of the stairwell, as though Amy stood in the lung of a ho-ho-hoing giant. Her chest ached, though that may not have been her exhaustion but the sound of the bear being electrocuted below her... or above her.

"Well," she said. "I guess I'll have to climb." It hurt to talk—her lips were cracked from her passage across the Under Hill—so she stopped. Instead, she clambered onto the top of the window and, using its bars, shimmied up to the lip of what would have been its ledge if this world weren't upside-down. She didn't look out of the window, let alone look down, her mind felt vertiginous already. She couldn't risk seeing the fall.

Amy then leapt, catching the first black cane-like railing of the next flight of stairs, hoisting herself to stand under its step, and restarted her climb on the underside of the concrete staircase.

THE EYEHOLE IN THE penthouse door was more an eye than a hole. It winked at Amy, then closed. It was rimmed by eyelashes.

"Knock, knock," said the door.

Amy stared at it.

"You say, 'Who's there?'," said the door.

"What?" said Amy.

"You say, 'Who's there?'," said the door, sounding peevish.

"Who's there?" said Amy.

"A door," said the door.

"A door who?" said Amy, catching on with all the quickness of a child.

"Adore the witch," said the door, "or she'll fucking kill you."

The door opened.

Inside the penthouse suite lay the lounge of 4 Anstil Place. The dimensions, though, had warped. The TV set was bigger than the settee. The fireplace was smaller than one of the postcards on its mantel. Everything was upside-down and stuck to the ceiling. Looking in made Amy's mind swell.

"Come in lovey," said a voice from above.

Amy nodded to herself. The action of it felt older than her skull. She entered.

She glanced upwards. Between the artex fins of the ceiling stood the Witch. She was breastfeeding Aidan, despite his age. Her breast was blue and her nipple large and flaccid, looked as though it had been pressed to something cold. Aidan coughed, and she forced him back on, his legs struggling against her hips.

"What are you looking at, you little pervert?" the Witch said.

"Give him to me," said Amy. "He's my baby, not yours."

The Witch laughed as hard as the artexing.

"You're a little confused, aren't you mite? He's mine, not yours. You're not old enough to have children." The Witch took to the air. Her tight black dress exposing curves that turned into bulges, lifting at the hem.

"You did bad things to him," said Amy. "You're not his mum anymore. You're not my mum anymore."

"It's my baby and I'll do with it as I please. Just like I did with you, love." Her upper lip curled.

The Witch turned, becoming Amy's way up. She held Aidan up and out. His arm hung oddly, as though he'd been dropped. Her hand held him by the throat. His lips went as blue, as pendulous, as her wide hanging tit. Where her grip tightened, he went purple like a newborn's skin. The Witch's cackle had slid down into a moist smile.

"Let him go," said Amy.

The Witch reached up to Aidan's body with her free hand. Her talons caressed his skin.

"No," Amy said. She couldn't see her own face. If she had, she would've seen her eyes milking over. Not white, but like a chocolate milkshake. Going brown and blank and deep and thick. If she'd looked down, she would've seen her clothes begin to fray at their edges, to rise up, to make small, crooked fingers of the denim, whispering metal mouths of the buttons. There was a sound like the rumour of a storm.

The Witch giggled. "He's mine. No one can take him away from me."

Outside the lounge window, there was the roaring of a building wind. It had the look of a tornado being born. If it was screaming, Amy could understand.

The Witch's fingers stopped moving, her grip relaxed, and the little boy cried. The coffee table, on the ceiling, took off and shattered against the mantelpiece, sending cards clattering across the artex. The television fell off its stand and broke into fragments of moving pictures. They set to whirling.

The Witch was shouting, making herself heard above the tempest in Amy's ears. "Think about it, girl. Think about it, eh? Do you really think anything you do here does anything in the real world? Anything at all? Do you think any of this is really happening? Haven't you noticed you look the same as you always did? Haven't you noticed you're just as ugly as you always were? You're away with the bloody fairies, you little shit! How many times do you have to be told?"

A window exploded, the bits of it fell outwards and, in a swirl, the moving pictures of what was left of the TV set joined them. It looked, as it whirled past, like Corrie.

"You've been reading too many fucking books! I can't be killed. Only I or my minions do the killing here."

"Witch," shouted Amy, pointing upwards, in the direction the tower was falling. "Do you know the last thing to go through your brain when you die from falling on your head?" She didn't wait for an answer. "The rest of your body… and you have a lot of body. So *you* will kill you."

The Dark Tower Block shifted and made a cracking sound. There was a wrench, and the floor felt free.

The Witch reached out to her. "You will stop this nonsense right now! I and my line will never die and will never end! Who do you think you are, Alice in Bloody Wonderland?"

CRACK.

CRACKLE.

The electricity went out as the Dark Tower Block detached itself from its power grid. Barnaby and what was left of the Doll fell to the chequered floor. What was left of the Doll was her skin, like popped balloons in the aftermath of a children's party. Dozens of smaller figures, draped with her organs and dunked in her blood, turned away from the bear and started up the stairs. In an eager rush of limbs and grinding maws, they ascended, taking the stairs from underneath and swarming toward the Witch's penthouse.

Barnaby stepped from a black to a blue tile to follow them, but paused. Through the lattice-worked security doors to the foyer, he saw the world begin to move, not away, but downwards.

He knew what the girl had done.

Barnaby smiled and looked up after her and said, "Well done Amy."

He ran and, not bothering to stop for the large square disabled button on the door's right, he shattered through the glass. Arms raised above his head as though a samurai without a sword, Barnaby leapt from the concrete step to the barren desert earth that was receding away from the tower as it dropped into the Under Hill. With a crunch of sand and a roll, he made it.

"THIS IS MY HOUSE, young lady, and while you are under my roof you will do as I say."

The roof is under us, thought Amy.

There was the CR... of a crack, then silence, as there was nothing left to rend. The Dark Tower Block, hanging upside-down in the Under Hill, had fallen off its foundations. Outside, through the windows, the rest of the world was going down. Then, as the tower started in on the next horizon, the world began to come down on them.

The Witch turned to look. Hand falling open as her mouth did, she let go of Aidan, who was near enough now for Amy to grab him. As before with the bear, she hugged him with her love and her arms. There was a sound under all of the rest, like a slug with diarrhoea, and colour returned to his cheeks.

Outside the door, a horde of footsteps and screams could be heard, if only Amy had been listening.

The little girl held the boy and looked down. His cries stifled and he looked at her, eyes as round as a world or two.

"I brought down the tower," she said to him. He didn't respond.

Unseen by Amy, the Witch continued to stare out of the window as the Dark Tower Block hit the ground.

There was a flash of white light, as pure as fire, then a darkness that looked an awful lot like a dreamless sleep, or so Amy imagined. The last thing she knew was hugging…

… hugging…

… hugging him.

THE CRACKING SOUND flooded out across the Latter Wood. Above it, a crevasse appeared through the centre of the Witch's Moon, which gradually, before the eyes of birds and small creatures and trees, became a half moon.

"Hear that?" said the Longworm, who'd not been watching on account of having no eyes.

"Aye," said the Notsolongworm. "The Witch is dead." He stretched and yawned. "Do you think that means this world will fade away?"

"Fade away! Why?"

"The girl is finished here. She won't come back."

The Longworm turned, incredulity showing up in the curl of every section of his body. "You young idiot! Don't you think other children will need to come here? This world doesn't revolve around you, and it didn't revolve around her!"

The Notsolongworm struck the earth with his tail. "Stop calling me an idiot, you stupid old sod. You don't know anything—I could get more wisdom from squeezing a slug!"

The Longworm settled back. It wasn't visible, but he was smiling. He liked it when the young were cheeky to him, even if they weren't supposed to have cheeks at all.

... HUGGING... AMY woke, her arms around Barney. The bear's head was wet. He'd been crying, or she had been in her sleep. She shivered in the way of skin telling the body good news. The Witch was dead. Goosebumps rang out like church bells. Ding. Dong. Amy smiled and gripped the bear.

"Thank you, thank you," she said low, into his ear. "You're always there for me."

He felt weary to her, as tired as she felt, but he lived. Deep in his innards was the warmth of a heartbeat. Sequestered in some bower or below a holly bush or in the roots of a tree, he would be hunkered, recovering. How many times had he sacrificed himself for her? Never before had there been such an old, battered bear. Amy felt like him, exhausted to the core. She closed her eyes and slept, a smile shafting sunnily across her mouth. Aidan was safe. She had saved him.

HER DREAMS WERE EMPTY and black, like arms pulling a face into a bosom, a maternal breast, a heart that pulsed with love.

Healing spread, passage by passage, through her veins and arteries. This deep in slumber, she didn't dream that she could ever awaken again. But wake she did…

… TO THE SOUND OF Aidan's door opening. Then she could hear Aidan's door closing. It moved across the ill-fitted, cheap carpet in hitches, like an asthmatic's death rattle. They were in Aidan's room. 'They' were Mum and Uncle Chris. Amy was standing on the landing without realising she'd risen. Barney wasn't in her arms. Amy walked to Aidan's door and fell, softly, to her knees. They wouldn't hear her. They were talking.

Aidan cried out.

"Put a bloody pillow over him. Don't want to wake the bloody neighbours." Mum's voice was as fast as excited blood.

"Aye," said Chris. "Aye, aye, aye, aye."

Aidan's cry increased and then ended.

Amy reached towards the door and touched it with her fingertips, but she could no more open it as she could save her baby in the real world.

"You fucking bastard, you fucking bastard," Uncle Chris was saying, in rhythm.

Amy got up then and walked down the stairs. She walked through the lounge, then the kitchen and, after taking the key from its drawer, the patio doors. She strode down the garden path to the laburnum tree that overhung the fence. As she walked, she softly sang Somewhere Over The Rainbow. In the streetlights, the pods were yellowy orange and fluorescent as two-penny sweets.

Amy climbed onto a bin bag and then the bin and over the fence, whispering, "Birds fly over the rainbow, why then—oh why—can't I?"

She reached and took clumps of the seeds and ate. They tasted of cloying, of being trapped.

Fingerfuls became fistfuls, but they, sappy and mulched, would not gulp down her throat. She retched up over the roots, and her snot and tears joined the dark splatters on its bough. Amy tried to eat again, but the pods wouldn't go down. Something in her throat was closed to her fingers.

She rose and, still bent, climbed back into her garden, walked back up to the patio doors, locked them, put the keys in the kitchen bin, and returned to her room.

In the bed lay Barney. She picked him up and, with a malicious twist of her wrist, threw him at the bookshelf. What was left of Winnie the Pooh scattered. The adults in the house were too busy to notice.

Barney lay in the dark, his head unseen.

"I hate you." Amy said. "I should've left you in the bin."

A pause, then, "Look at me, Aimee."

It was hard, through the tears, but she tried.

"You saved him in That Place. But these are two different Places and you have to choose, Aimee. You can only have one world. The world with me or the world with Barnaby. You're too old to have two anymore. It's time to grow up, Aimee."

"I don't want to grow up. I'm tired of having to grow up all the time."

"I love you, Aimee, and I always will. But you're nearly a big girl. Choose… This Place or The Other?"

"No," Amy gripped her duvet and squeezed, but no wind came. She couldn't bring this house down.

"You know what to do. I'm proud of you. You're my little Aimee."

Around the agony in her head, she managed not only to nod, but also to stand.

I KNEW THEN WHAT SHE was going to do, even before she came back for me, before she scooped my soft, useless body into her arms and pressed me to the boy. I knew this was the end, and in my head I said goodbye to Amy. It sounded very much like this:

Goodbye.

HER MUM AND CHRIS had gone to bed. Their sleeping heads and shoulders and hands were upturned amongst the beige linen like scattered white shells on a beach. In her right fist, Amy gripped the front door key. This will stay down, she thought. She put it to her lips, then her tongue. It was as cold as a small dead fish. She swallowed it. Downstairs, in the kitchen, the gas hobs were on but had not yet been lit. She held her mum's lighter in her left hand.

Before swallowing the key, she'd taken Aidan from his bed, cuddled him, kissed him, wrote a message in crayon and strung it around his neck. He'd been bleeding slightly and that was why he hadn't woken, she remembered thinking. Why he didn't cry, at least. He knows what happens when you cry out, she'd thought. He played dead. She took him down the stairs, through the door, and placed him, wrapped in his Spider-Man duvet, on the doorstep next door. He wouldn't be there long. Her home smelt of gas.

Amy walked along the space between her mum's bed and the single mirror. The Russian doll was an egg of shadow in its place on the dresser. Amy prodded Uncle Chris.

"Man, what?" he said.

"Daddy, can I sleep with you?"

"Aye," he said it without thinking, almost without being awake.

She got into bed. She didn't cuddle Uncle Chris and she didn't cuddle Barney, because he sat on the doorstep next door with Aidan, pelt as cold in the night as a potato before it's cooked.

Amy had read, as she had about many things, about Hiroshima. She knew about the silhouettes burnt onto walls and wondered how Uncle Chris would look. She traced the outline of his nose. On the wallpaper, in the shadows, in her dreams, it was straighter—and stronger—than Chris's.

"You never came for me," she said, but not to him.

Fully unconscious now, Chris didn't reply.

"My name's Aimee," she said. The smell of gas was making her feel dizzy. She lit the lighter. Everything became light.

IT SHOULDN'T BE DAY There, but then for her, perhaps, it always would be. Motes drifted along and through the slants of sunlight that came down, angling through the canopy of the Latter Wood. They drifted thickly, glutinous enough to be laburnum pods, though they weren't. Wearing her lilac dress, Aimee spun amongst them, as slow as their progress and as ethereal, as though—between the sunbeams—she didn't exist at all.

She danced, and the sun touched her bare, translucent shoulders.

Sometimes, though he didn't take to dancing, or to merriment for that matter, a bear named Barnaby would come and watch her. If you didn't mind getting close to a bear's maw, you could see the twitch of a smile across his fangs. You can imagine, if you want, that the bear would sometimes join in.

The bear does—imagine, that is. He never actually dances. He would say to the contrary (and often did), but he loved to watch that little girl dance.

Imagine them together, in some corner of the Latter Wood. You might as well, because they're there, together, at least for a while.

Mrs Riley of number 6 woke with a BANG.

"George," she shouted. They were both up, out of bed before realising they'd been asleep.

"Earthquake," her husband shouted back.

"Fire," she screamed in return.

Somewhere, a child joined in.

Then their dog Jack, with his barking.

There'd always been strange noises from number 4, but nothing like this. This was harder to ignore.

The next moments passed as if Mrs Riley hadn't woken. She ran out of the bedroom. Downstairs. The little boy on the front steps. The brown, battered teddy bear next to him. The boy, quick as maternal instinct, was in her arms. Equally quickly, she picked up the teddy and pressed it to his grip.

George was banging on their door. No response. The explosion hadn't blown the house up, but the roof was caved in; the upper storey had collapsed like a disapproving frown. Someone shouted, "999". The street was gathering. Everyone moved to its end. Men took charge. Number 4's downstairs window exploded like a smoker's cough.

Blue lights and crimson fire engines.

Mrs Riley looked down at the little boy. He had red marks around his throat and down his chest, both of which were exposed. Hanging around the pinkened skin was a piece of paper on a line of string. On the sheet, in crayon and in a child's hand, were written the words ***Do Not Touch***.

The boy was cuddling the teddy bear and twitched, as though dreaming. Mrs Riley didn't know how he could sleep through this.

THE HALF MOON WAS rising through the arbour of the Latter Wood's canopy. The Witch's Moon wouldn't rise, at least for now, and the wood was darker than it'd been for a long time. The laburnum pods responded to the moon with a slight shaking, as though stretching off the long hard day that'd gone before. Aidan stared up between the curled fingers of wood at snatches of white, distant, cross-hatched moon. He squinted. There was a movement in the shadowed undergrowth, but Aidan didn't dare to look. He did his best to scrunch up his hands and his resolve, and not to darken the azure robes he wore. It was the bear. He was scared of the bear.

"Come on," said Barnaby, reaching out with a paw.

Aidan wouldn't yet take it, and it would be several weeks before he would, but he followed the bear through the wood.

"It's time to go to school," said Barnaby.

Part 4

Chapter 1

Aidan stared down the bed at his daughter Amy.

"Night, baby," he said, but she didn't hear him. She was already asleep, having listened to Harry Potter and The Philosopher's Stone until she drifted off. Aidan had read her favourite chapter: The Boy Who Lived.

Aidan smiled and ran his hand down the bristles on his chin. His daughter's bedroom was warm and cosy, and the soft smile on her face spoke of a happiness like the one his own childhood had held, for as long as he could remember. He didn't close the door when he went to his room and his wife, but left a shaft of the landing's light on the white cupboard.

Years later, Aidan was still alive to see little Amy, when she grew up, hand Barney on to his grandson, but died before Barney was passed from that generation to the next, or to the generation that followed.

Teddy bears, if they're cared for, can last for decades, especially the ones with something of the Other about them, and Barney's smile never lost so much as a stitch. Despite this, and despite the contentment of the children he cuddled, the teddy would—from time to time—feel sad to the touch. It was at these times that Barney would stare at the shadow-smudged face of a sleeping child and try to remember his favourite charge. To imagine the strong, beautiful woman Amy would've become if only she'd had the chance to grow. She'd been so long ago though, and both of the faces she used to wear were mussing, like Aimee's blonde hair, and fading into the vagueness of dusk under trees.

Having little choice in the positioning of his head, Barney would continue to stare at his current ward. And having little choice but to smile, his grin would become wistful as he wished and wished he could let go of the child's abdomen, and clasp his paws together, and fall into the Glade where a little girl danced, to do what he had never done before and dance with her. He couldn't though, because now he was an everyday teddy bear, and the children he cuddled were safe, and he never needed to be Barnaby again.

Acknowledgements

I would like to thank the Monday Night Group of central Manchester for their feedback and for teaching me to be mean to my prose. Aimee and the Bear would have been a trilogy without you.

I would also like to thank my beautiful wife, my family and my friends for having the forbearance to read my earlier work and for their comments. Finally, thank you to my publishers, Hic Dragones, for their hard work, excellent editing and expertise in Kwik Save's own brand alcoholic products.

About the Author

As a child, Toby went to the same school as Batman (Christian Bale) and Benny Hill. Not all at the same time, which is a shame as the chase sequences would have been amazing. Going to this salt-of-the-earth establishment made Toby think it normal to announce, at the age of twelve, "Mother, I have decided I shall become an author." The school was single-sex, needless to say, which probably saved Toby from a large number of rejections. Choirmaster Gareth Malone, presenter of The Choir, also attended, but Toby has asked that this is not mentioned.

During his teenage years, various hobbies led Toby to fist-fight a Russian soldier and learn to shoot guns with a Navy Seal. These activities taught him he could be punched in the face repeatedly, and that a gun's recoil would cause him to miss a target at twenty feet. Which was a surprise, as Toby thought his other teenage pass-time would strengthen his wrists. (I mean, of course, his writing.)

In his drive to become a writer, Toby briefly considered becoming a journalist. This lasted until a local radio station asked him to conduct a street poll on how often men change their underwear. The first respondent, who was lying on a bench at the time of the interview, advised, "Never." He had a rather large beard.

As an adult, Toby has been a toy-seller, an Avon Lady, Double-Glazing Salesman of the Week, a mortgage broker, a suspicious barman, a school governor and a bingo caller. Now he is a writer, which is a pity as, with an aging population, we could do with fewer writers and more bingo callers.

Toby currently lives in Manchester, where the weather is generally downward or, when windy, downward and slightly to the side.

This is Toby's first published novel.